Praise for *Born for Trouble*

"It doesn't get much better than one of the best crime writers in the business serving up brand-new stories featuring his most iconic characters. Lansdale isn't just a brilliant storyteller with heart, he's also funny as hell, with tales of mummified dachshunds, homicidal bookmobiles, and a psychopathic hunt club. This collection is an absolute blast and a gift to all of us devoted fans."
—Ace Atkins, author of *The Heathens*

"If you already know Joe Lansdale, you don't need me to tell you to read *Born for Trouble*. If you don't, you're in for a hell of a ride. Pulpy, blackly humorous, compulsively readable, and somehow both wildly surreal and down-to-earth. Lansdale is a national fucking treasure."
—Christa Faust, author of *Money Shot*

"If you've met these dudes before, you won't be surprised to hear that these latest stories are a treat; if you're a Hap-and-Leonard virgin, well, I'll overlook the fact that you've spent your recent years living in a cave and congratulate you on the adventure upon which you're embarking."
—Lawrence Bloch, author of the Matthew Scudder series

"You could call *Born for Trouble* a collection of stories. But that's like calling *Paradise Lost* by Milton a poem. *Born for Trouble* is a road map through 20th-century crime fiction, and your guides are two of the greatest, most intriguing characters ever created, Hap and Leonard."
—S.A. Cosby, author of *Razorblade Tears* and *Blacktop Wasteland*

Praise for Joe R. Lansdale

"A folklorist's eye for telling detail and a front-porch raconteur's sense of pace."
—*New York Times Book Review*

"A terrifically gifted storyteller."
—*Washington Post Book Review*

"Like gold standard writers Elmore Leonard and the late Donald Westlake, Joe R. Lansdale is one of the more versatile writers in America."
—*Los Angeles Times*

"A zest for storytelling and gimlet eye for detail."
—*Entertainment Weekly*

"Lansdale is an immense talent."
—*Booklist*

"Lansdale is a storyteller in the Texas tradition of outrageousness . . . but amped up to about 100,000 watts."
—*Houston Chronicle*

"Lansdale's been hailed, at varying points in his career, as the new Flannery O'Connor, William Faulkner-gone-madder, and the last surviving splatterpunk . . . sanctified in the blood of the walking Western dead and righteously readable."
—*Austin Chronicle*

Selected works by Joe R. Lansdale

Hap and Leonard

Savage Season (1990)
Mucho Mojo (1994)
The Two-Bear Mambo (1995)
Bad Chili (1997)
Rumble Tumble (1998)
Veil's Visit: A Taste of Hap and Leonard (with Andrew Vachss, 1999)
Captains Outrageous (2001)
Vanilla Ride (2009)
Hyenas (2011)
Devil Red (2011)
Dead Aim (2013)
Hap and Leonard (2016)
Honky Tonk Samurai (2016)
Coco Butternut (2017)
Hap and Leonard: Blood and Lemonade (2017)
Rusty Puppy (2017)
The Big Book of Hap and Leonard (2018)
Jack Rabbit Smile (2018)
The Elephant of Surprise (2019)
Of Mice and Minestrone (2020)

Other novels

Act of Love (1981)
Dead in the West (1986)
The Magic Wagon (1986)
The Nightrunners (1987)
The Drive-In (1988)
Cold in July (1989)
Tarzan: the Lost Adventure (1995) (with Edgar Rice Burroughs)
The Boar (1998)
Freezer Burn (1999)
Waltz of Shadows (1999)
The Big Blow (2000)
The Bottoms (2000)
A Fine Dark Line (2002)
Sunset and Sawdust (2004)
Lost Echoes (2007)
Leather Maiden (2008)
Flaming Zeppelins (2010)
All the Earth, Thrown to Sky (2011)
Edge of Dark Water (2012)
The Thicket (2013)
Paradise Sky (2015)
Fender Lizards (2015)
Bubba and the Cosmic Blood-Suckers (2017)
Terror Is Our Business (2018) (with Kasey Lansdale)
More Better Deals (2020)
Moon Lake (2021)

BORN FOR TROUBLE

THE FURTHER ADVENTURES OF HAP AND LEONARD

 STORIES

JOE R. LANSDALE

EDGAR AWARD–WINNING AUTHOR OF MOON LAKE

Cover design by John Coulthart
Interior design by Serah Boey & Elizabeth Story
Author photo by Karen Lansdale

Tachyon Publications LLC
1459 18th Street #139
San Francisco, CA 94107
415.285.5615
www.tachyonpublications.com
tachyon@tachyonpublications.com

Series Editor: Jacob Weisman
Editor: Rick Klaw

Print ISBN: 978-1-61696-370-5
Digital ISBN: 978-1-61696-371-2

Printed in the United States by Versa Press, Inc.

First Edition: 2022
9 8 7 6 5 4 3 2 1

"Coco Butternut" © 2017 by Joe R. Lansdale. First published by Subterranean Press, Burton. | "Hoodoo Harry" © 2016 by Joe R. Lansdale. First published by the Mysterious Bookshop, New York. | "Sad Onions" © 2019 by Joe R. Lansdale. First published in Odd Partners, edited by Anne Perry (Random House). | "The Briar Patch Boogie" © 2016 by Joe R. Lansdale. First published by Gere Donovan Press. | "Cold Cotton" © 2017 by Joe R. Lansdale. First published by Crossroad Press.

For Rick Klaw, intrepid editor and friend.

And in memory of Michael K. Williams,
who brought the character of Leonard to life on the
Hap and Leonard *TV series. I couldn't have asked for*
a better actor to play the part. Talented, smart,
a good human being. You are missed.
— Joe R. Lansdale

CONTENTS

INTRODUCTION
"THE BOYS"

I HAVE BEEN WRITING ABOUT the "Boys," as I call them, for many years, and my children have grown up with them almost as if they are living, breathing uncles. My wife thinks of them as close brothers of mine who can be both humorous and annoying, who arrive on our doorstep with checks in their hands, both for novels and stories and the TV series, even comic adaptations, to help us pay bills and be quite comfortable. So, we don't fuss much at their occasional bad manners and destruction of the furniture. Not to mention all those vanilla cookie bags and Dr. Pepper cans lying around.

Thank you, Boys, you have done well by us.

Writing about them has given me great pleasure, and thankfully they have given pleasure to others. I get numerous emails, letters, notes, even phone calls, to tell me how much the characters have meant to them. How they have given them relief in difficult times, helped them navigate sickness and death, as much as such a thing is possible, and that information alone makes it worth the creation and writing of Hap and Leonard.

I write for me. I never try and figure out what others will like when I'm writing, but when I finish with a story or novel, whatever form of writing I'm undertaking, I always hope there will be those who feel as I do. That the story I've written was worth the effort and that perhaps, just perhaps, it'll spark flame to some kindling in your thoughts, soul, or at least kill a few hours.

I also include in the Hap and Leonard stories bits of social commentary, ribald humor, and the feelings and look of the East Texas environment. Contrary to what some might think, East Texas is not all redneck ignorance and racism and gun violence, but those things certainly exist. The reason it is so prevalent in my fiction is not that a better and positive side of East Texas doesn't exist; it is that the negative elements are what I wish to comment on, and stories that frequently are about crime or criminal elements will certainly have some bad characters in them. If I wrote about the ocean, there would be fish, and if I wrote about the sky, there would at least be occasional clouds.

That said, the Hap and Leonard stories truly do run the gamut. *Blood and Lemonade* and *Of Mice and Minestrone* both tell about when Hap and Leonard were growing up, and for the most part tend to not be 100 percent crime stories. They are what you might call How We

Lived Then stories. They are a kind of autopsy of what ticks inside the characters, Hap primarily, although I have written a few very short stories from Leonard's POV that will in time be gathered together in one volume that I might cleverly call *Leonard*.

This volume is different. It has elements closer to the novels, but with less social background than some, and more excitement. When I wasn't writing Hap and Leonard stories, was busy on a novel, I would sometimes find myself missing them in the way you might miss a family member who had gone on a long vacation and had been completely out of touch.

I would dream about Hap, hear his voice, and abruptly I would have to put away whatever I was writing—tuck it into a computer file to be more accurate—and take a break to let Hap and Leonard speak to me. Most of these are stories of that ilk. Hap showed up. He talked. I took notes.

There are times when I need to take a vacation from Hap and Leonard, or I am happy to see them pack their suitcases and hit the trail. I sometimes need a rest from those guys, but I am always glad when they come back.

This collection contains some previous visits. They are collected here for the first time together in one volume. I hope they will serve as more than a placeholder until a novel arrives. I think they are good stories, and varied.

A note. This really should go without saying, but some readers say, "Well, wouldn't they be old by now? Unable to do what they do?"

In reality they would be slightly older than me. And I am no spring chicken. Though I'm spry. But here's the thing—as real as they seem to me, they have a different relationship with time than the rest of us.

I let them age, but I have never done it on a year-by-year basis. Like Travis McGee, Philip Marlowe, James Bond, and numerous other fictional characters, they move at a different pace and have multiple adventures that no living person might have in a lifetime, or two.

I consider a year when I do not write about them to be a year in which they remain, time-wise, in amber. When I return to them, or they return to me, the clock starts again, though I don't worry if it's the year it should be after their last adventure. If I wait eight years between novels, or what have you, they are only slightly older than when I ceased writing about them eight years before. Their current adventure will take place in the current year, which means they do not maintain a realistic chronology. I may even decide to write about them when they are younger, or middle-aged. I get to choose.

Some folks are really bugged by this. I'm not sure why, but they are. It pops up in a lot of discussions. At the same time, this approach is one that has been around forever; story heroes are not necessarily subject to the ticking of the clock.

As long as I enjoy writing about them, I will age them slowly, though there may come a day when I age them out. I don't plan too far ahead when it comes to books and stories.

So, folks, bring some vanilla cookies and Dr. Pepper for Leonard, some iced tea and animal crackers for Hap, and let's have a party.

Of course, don't mind me if after the cookies and such, I toddle off to bed early. That bunch, fun as they can be, can wear me out. And unlike them, I do age.

But I must admit, to a great extent, the Boys, with all their boisterousness and frequent juvenile humor, keep me young. I like that.

Joe R. Lansdale
Big Bear Manor
Nacogdoches, Texas
2021

COCO BUTTERNUT

*"Heaven goes by favor. If it
went by merit, you would stay out
and your dog would go in."*
—Mark Twain

"ALL I WANT YOU TO DO is make the exchange. Give them the bag, and they'll give you Coco Butternut."

We were all in the office of Brett Sawyer's Investigations, me and Leonard and Brett, my daughter Chance, and this little, chubby guy, Jimmy Farmer who wore a very bad toupée. He wanted us to make an exchange for him. Give some blackmailer a bag full of money in exchange for a dog called Coco Butternut that had belonged to Farmer's mother, as did the pet cemetery, a mortuary, and a cemetery for humans called Oak Rest.

Our German shepherd, Buffy, was also present, lying on the couch, about as interested as a dog can be in conversations that don't involve the words "treat" or "outside."

What was odd about all this was Coco Butternut was

1

as dead as a stone and mummified.

"Let me see here," Leonard said. "You got a pickled dog stolen from you, and you want us to give some money to a guy that dug him up—"

"Her," Jimmy said. He had a condescending way of talking and a face that somehow made you want to punch it. He had all the personality of the Ebola virus. I hadn't liked him on sight, and I wasn't sure why.

"Okay," Leonard said. "Her. You want us to give a bag of money to a dead dog-napper and he gives us the mutt, and that's it?"

"That's all," Farmer said. "Only one of you can do it. He said to send one person to make the exchange. He said I could do it, but I'm not comfortable with that, and I told him so."

"You two talked person to person?" Brett said.

"No, we . . . does this girl work here?"

"That's my daughter, Chance," I said. He had been eyeing her since he first came in, as if she might have designs on his wallet.

"She can be discreet?" he said.

"She certainly can," Chance said. Chance had her thick black hair tied back in a ponytail, and she was dressed the same as Brett, tee-shirt and blue jeans and tennis shoes. She looked like a fifties teenybopper. Even in her twenties she could have easily passed for eighteen or nineteen. She was so sweet she broke my heart.

Farmer paused a moment, taking time to consider how discreet Chance could be, I suppose.

"Okay," he said. "This thief, we didn't talk face to face. First he sent me a note that said he had the dog.

"I went to the pet cemetery to look. There was a hole where she was buried, an empty grave. No question the body was gone.

"There was a sealed plastic bag in the empty grave. Inside of it was a burner phone. There was a note with a number on it. I called the number. That's how we spoke, and that's when he told me what he wanted. I threw the phone away like he asked."

"You know the man's voice?" Leonard asked.

"No. It may even have not been a man."

"You keep saying he," I said.

"Look, it was one of those synthesizer things. You can't tell who you're talking to. Sounds more male than female on those things. I couldn't tell the sex or age really. Voice said they had my mother's dog, and he wanted money."

"They?" Brett asked.

"What the voice said."

"Why was the dog pickled?" Leonard said.

"Embalmed and wrapped like a mummy," Farmer said. "Not pickled."

"Same thing," Leonard said. "Except for the duct tape."

"No tape. Cloth. Mother had it done five years ago. She died shortly thereafter. The wrapping is stuck to the dog with some kind of adhesive. They embalmed her, and then wrapped her. It's not duct tape."

"Can I ask why?" I said.

"We own a pet mortuary and cemetery. Most dogs are

cremated, but we offer a variety of services. Embalming and mummification for example. Coco Butternut was a show dog. A dachshund. She had won a number of dog show awards. Nothing big, but Mother adored her. She had all her dogs embalmed. Coco Butternut was the first one to be wrapped, mummified."

"I know we can become very attached to our pets," Brett said. "But it isn't your dog, and well, it's dead. You sure you want to pay for a mummified dog corpse?"

"I never really cared for the dog," Farmer said. "It bit me a few times. Nasty animal. But Mother was sentimental about it, and I'm sentimental about her. The dog meant a lot to her."

I didn't actually find Farmer all that sentimental, but you never really know someone at first blush, and truth is, you may not ever know someone even when you think you do.

"When you say a lot," Leonard said, "the next question is how much is this sentiment going to cost you?"

"I'd rather not say. Just deliver the bag and bring home the dog."

"I got one more question," Leonard said. "Who names a dog Coco Butternut?"

"Mother," Farmer said.

"Not to step on your mother's grave, but why the hell would she name a dog that," Leonard said. "She just go by Coco, or Butter, or Nut?"

"Dog had a chocolate body, but butternut-colored paws. That's how the name came about."

4

"Could have just called her Spot or Socks or some such," Leonard said. "Hell, Trixie. I had a dog named Trixie. That's a good name."

Farmer was paying us good money to deliver the bag, and the good money was considerably more than what we normally made for a few hours' work. He really wanted that dog back.

Plan was I would make the drop and exchange, and Leonard would find a place to hide in case things went south. We weren't hired to take the body snatcher down, and in fact, Farmer insisted we didn't. Said things could go wrong if we tried to do that. Thing was make the exchange and keep it smooth and simple.

Leonard went over to Farmer's house, picked up the money and was bringing it to us. I was looking out the office window as he drove up. It was a nice spring day and bright and the young woman downstairs that owned the bicycle shop was wearing shorts and her legs were long and brown and Brett wasn't looking at me right then and Chance was sorting out the lunch she had picked up from a Japanese restaurant. Buffy was watching me, but she didn't care what I was doing.

I kept a steady vigil as the fine-looking shop owner leaned over a bike she was repairing. Those shorts certainly could ride high.

It wasn't that I wasn't fine with my woman. I'm a one-woman man. But I still like to look. I think it's good for my heart or something, maybe even the liver.

Leonard parked and came across the lot, nodding at the blonde as he did. He looked up and saw me at the window and smiled. He came up the stairs and inside and placed the satchel on the desk. It had a clasp lock on it with a ring and through the ring was a tiny padlock.

Leonard said, "Brett, I think Hap was looking at that blonde's butt out there."

"Daddy," Chance said.

"I was merely looking out the window," I said.

"I've noticed you do that a lot when she's out there," Brett said. "Don't con me, Hap Collins."

"Okay, the con is over," I said. "So I can look at will?"

"I didn't say that," Brett said. "I prefer you think you're being sneaky. It shows you have some pride."

"That's one way of looking at it," Leonard said. "Now, you all thinking what I'm thinking?"

"How much money is in that bag," I said.

"That's right," Leonard said.

"We don't need to know," Brett said. "And besides, it's locked."

"Hap's going into this with a bag of money, someone bringing a dead dog to him. I think it might be wise to see how much is in the bag. I don't like that Farmer guy, anyway."

Brett came over and looked down at the satchel. "Like I said, we don't need to know. But, my lockpick kit is in the drawer."

Chance opened the drawer and removed the kit, handed it to Brett. She took out her tools and worked on the lock for a moment or two. It clicked open.

"He gave me a key to give to the kidnapper," Leonard said. "But I just wanted to see you work that lock."

Brett grinned at Leonard. "You rascal."

"And then some," Leonard said.

Brett opened the satchel. There were a lot of bills in it, stacks bound by paper binders. She took it out and thumbed through it.

"Jesus," she said. "There's something like a hundred thousand dollars here."

"For a dead dog?" Leonard said.

"This guy must be rich," Chance said.

"He is. Should have seen his house. You could park my apartment, your house, and this building in it. Well, there might not be room for the couch."

"Ha," I said.

"Yeah," Leonard said, "that putting dead bodies in the ground pays mighty good."

Brett said, "Now we know," closed the satchel and put the lock back on it.

We decided first to have a recon mission before we made the actual drop. The team, as I like to think of us, drove out to the drop spot. That means me and Leonard, Brett and Chance. Chance decided she wanted to get in on things, and we decided to let her, as long as it wasn't dangerous. It was pretty much a family business, so why not.

Drop was to take place at a graveyard, which when you think about it is kind of ironic. Dog was dug up from a graveyard, and was to be returned in one.

This one was an old graveyard for black citizens. It was called the Colored Graveyard by some, and there was a historical marker that called it a Negro Graveyard. It stopped being used mid-twentieth century, and though it was kept up, it was a piss-poor job. Someone hacked the weeds around the graves now and then with what appeared to be a stick. The drop was to happen at a grave for K. Hollis Colby. It was one of the few tombstones that was still intact. It was the only large tombstone and it was one of the few where you could see the name clearly on it. The dates of birth and death were not so clear. Looking at it I thought no matter who you are or where you are or when you're from, time passes away, and so do you and the memory of you. Maybe someone keeps it alive for a few generations, but most of us aren't remembered after the last shovelful of dirt is thrown in the hole.

"So this kidnapper's supposed to bring Coco Butterbutt here," Leonard said.

"Butternut," I said.

"I know. I just don't like that guy, and by proxy I think his dog is an asshole. Who names a fucking dog Coco Butternut?"

"His mother," I said.

"The dog's mother?"

"Now you're being a jerk. Farmer's mother."

"What kind of mother does that? Gives a dog a name like that."

Chance was coming across the graveyard to meet us. She had a device in her hand.

When she came up, she said, "Kind of sad here, isn't it?"

"Oh, I don't know," Leonard said. "They're dead. I'm kind of over it."

"Leonard," Chance said, "you are a turd."

"Just a little bit," he said, and tipped his fedora back. He had taken to wearing it all the time. It wasn't a hat that irritated me, like some he wore. That goddamn deer-stalker I took care of, and I don't think he even missed it, which means he merely had it to mess with me. He walked around in that thing, strutting like a peacock, drawing attention to himself because he knew that drew attention to me, and he knew it embarrassed me to be seen with him in that damn thing. The fedora. That was cool.

"Brett said you have to find some place to put this it can't be seen. It picks up voices good. You plant it, and we'll be back across the way, and we can hear everything."

"Where you'll be," Leonard said, "something goes down, by the time you or Brett get here with a big ole pistol or a long stick, Hap'll be dead and bleeding on ole Colby here."

"Don't be so morbid," Chance said. "He'll be all right. He's got you closer by."

"Girl, you are what we call a goddamn optimist,"

Leonard said. "You ain't been around your dad enough to know trouble follows his ass around."

"Maybe it's you trouble follows," Chance said. "You two are always together."

"Might be something to that," Leonard said.

There was a thin pine sapling that had grown up in the graveyard, and it wasn't far from the grave where we were supposed to make the exchange.

"Put it there," I said.

Chance went over to the sapling and Leonard walked over to help her. I stood where I was, thinking something about this whole thing smelled like the ass end of a dead elephant. Outside of what we were being asked to do, something else wasn't right.

"We got it," Chance said.

"I think I actually got it," Leonard said.

"I held it while you fastened it down," she said.

"Yeah, but I turned it on," Leonard said.

"Children," I said. "Back to the car."

Driving us back to the office, Brett said, "We'll get there before dark so Leonard can hide in the woods. He's got a mic, and I got one. We can both hear what's going down and Leonard will be close if something turns sideways."

"I can hear it too," Chance said.

"Of course you can," Leonard said.

"Uncle Leonard," Chance said. "I am going to hit you

in the eye."

Leonard laughed. "You are my kind of kid."

"I'm not a kid."

"Of course you aren't," Leonard said. "You are in your twenties, and therefore you are grown and know all there is to know."

Chance was in the front seat beside Brett. She leaned through the crack in the seats and popped a knuckle into the top of Leonard's thigh.

"Damn, Hap, I was hoping she wasn't like you," he said, rubbing his leg.

"Me too," I said.

"What we could do," Leonard said, "is we could keep the money and shoot the guy in the head and give Farmer back his dog and no one would be the wiser."

"You talk some shit," Brett said, "but you wouldn't do anything like that."

"Maybe it's about time I did. I'm starting to look for retirement money."

"Retirement's a long ways off," Chance said.

"That's what Hap told me when I was thirty-five. Don't worry. We got plenty of time, he said. How'd that work out, Hap?"

"Not so well," I said.

We got there three hours early. Come too close to time, the man making the drop might see us and figure we were planning on nailing him. We weren't planning that at all. We just had the microphones for insurance. Our plan was to make the drop and take Coco Butternut home to Farmer, who was waiting nervously. Then we would cash the check he gave us.

I parked a pickup I had borrowed inside the graveyard, as that would be how I was to haul the coffin away. Farmer said it was a full-sized coffin and wouldn't fit in a trunk or backseat.

Leonard hid in the tree line beyond the graveyard, and lay flat. I insisted he not bring a gun. I was sick of them. Instead he brought a baseball bat. I brought a Yawara stick: a little stick nubbed on both ends, used by Jujitsu folks to strike and lock with. I was fair with it. Nobody was going to give me a job making an instruction video, but I could fuck you up with it, if I needed to. I had it in my back pocket under my coat.

The days were mildly warm, but as winter moved in, some of the nights were a little brisk. I tugged my jacket tight and zipped it up. It was not only a chilly night, but a dark night, and maybe our kidnapper planned on that. I saw him or her coming in a large truck along the road toward the graveyard.

The truck wound down the road and the headlights flashed through the thin run of trees along the edge of the graveyard, and then the truck roared down the dirt drive that led into it, the tires large as those of a semi. If the driver was being sneaky about it, I couldn't tell it. I noticed the license plate had been removed from the front of the truck, and I guessed the back was the same. He'd probably slip them back on when he was out of our sight and continue on his merry way. The headlights were in my eyes, but there was enough residual light from them I could see the truck had been spotted with paint. Most likely a kind of paint you could hose off. It was too dark to know what color paint the spots were, and it didn't matter; it wouldn't be there long enough to make any difference should I want to identify it. The underneath paint was white, though, of that I was certain. Like me, the driver had showed up early, but me and my crew had shown up earlier.

I stood framed in the headlights for a moment and then the driver backed the truck and turned it into the graveyard and bounced across a couple of headstones, knocking them over, snapping them underneath the truck tires like peanut hulls. Rest in peace. The bed of the truck was covered with a camper, and it looked cheap, and my guess was that was more camouflage, and once the job was done, the driver would get rid of that too.

The driver's door opened and someone got out of the truck, and it was high enough from cab to dirt, they had to drop to the ground instead of step.

Then the driver came around in front of the truck with an odd waddle and stood there for a moment. I was certain it was a guy, and I could see he had a gun strapped in a holster on his hip. It was a big gun. He wore a black hood over his head. It had eye holes cut in it.

After a moment of staring at me, he opened the camper

at the back with a tiny bit of a struggle, dropped down the tailgate and lifted the top of the gate, the part that had a little window in it.

He gestured for me to come to him. I left the satchel on the grave and went over. He took a small light out of his coat pocket and flashed it inside the truck. I could see a coffin in there. It was rusty looking and it was full size, far bigger than what you'd expect as the last resting spot for a weenie dog.

The man motioned for me to grab the handle of the coffin, and I did. I pulled, and when the end got close to the tailgate, he took the handle on that side. Lifted it out, and we set it on the ground.

He held out his hand, implying I should give him the money.

"I need to see what's in the coffin before I do," I said.

This was something I thought might get me shot for a moment. I wished now I had let Leonard bring a rifle, but then again, another reason I didn't want him to have one is he's not that good a shot. Not bad, but he might just as easily shoot me if things went asunder. Right then I thought we should have switched jobs. I can hit a dime on edge at considerable distance with nothing but a glint of moonlight shining on the dime. It's an inborn knack for someone who really didn't like guns at all.

We stood that way for what seemed long enough for the season to pass, and then he nodded his hooded head, and motioned for me to open the coffin. I could see where it had been pried open before, so all I had to do was lift the lid.

Inside there was a small cloth-wrapped thing that might have been the body of a real dog or a wooden cutout covered in cloth. The cloth had turned brown and was rotting in spots. There was a musty odor, but no real stink of death. The dog was long past that.

"I need to cut the cloth and see what's beneath it," I said.

A nod from the hooded man.

I took out my pocket knife and bent over and cut loose some of the cloth. The hooded man helped by shining the flashlight into the coffin. It looked like there were bits of dog under the cloth. Gray, loose skin, and in some places the withered muscles were visible. I decided it was a dog. Was it the right dog? I couldn't tell. I had done my part. I hadn't been hired as a forensic expert, which was a good thing.

As I backed off he put his hand on the lid to close the coffin. He had very small hands compared to the rest of him. He closed the lid, placed one hand on his gun grip, and the other he used to make a kind of gimme motion.

I walked back to the grave, picked up the satchel and brought it over. He placed it on the tailgate, opened it for a look, made a satisfied grunt, and closed the satchel and looked at me.

I hadn't moved.

He pushed the tailgate up and the upper portion down,

walked swiftly to the driver's side carrying the satchel, pulled himself into the cab and closed the door.

I gave the truck a good onceover. Yep, spray paint spots, and I still figured it was watercolor. The truck rumbled and the lights came on, and then it moved away, swiftly, down the dirt and gravel graveyard drive on out to the asphalt road. There was a flash of taillights through the trees, and that was it, he was gone.

Leonard, Brett and Chase all had microphones, so they heard me, and in a moment Leonard came walking out of the woods swinging his ball bat slightly above the ground. I thought he looked disappointed. He hadn't had the opportunity to hit anyone.

A few moments later I saw headlights through the woods, and knew that was Brett and Chance coming around to meet us.

They stopped the Prius, got out and came over.

Brett looked at the coffin.

"So that's all there was to it?"

"Yep," I said. "That was it."

"Silly fool paying for a dead dog, and we're talking one hundred thousand dollars, not a few hundred."

"I think it's sweet," Chance said. "It's not the dead dog, though I can understand that, it's about his mother."

"Yeah, Farmer and his dear old mother," Leonard said.

I went and pulled the pickup around, and me and

Leonard loaded the coffin up, and we drove out of there with Brett and Chance following us.

As we rode along in the pickup, I said, "I keep thinking who would know the dog was worth that much to him, and then, why all the mystery, why hire us to do it? He could have done what we did."

"Said he was scared," Leonard said. "So I got a feeling he might know who had the dog, and whoever it was wasn't in love with him. Knew he came to get it, they might take the money and shoot him in the head and that would be the end of it. But if one of us came, the kidnapper might not feel the need to kill anyone he didn't know. Just make the exchange and drive away."

"Could be," I said.

"What I'm getting is we're being made monkeys for something we don't understand, and I don't like that. This stinks more than a dead dog, brother."

"Dog didn't stink that much, actually."

"Well, it stinks to me. I don't believe that Farmer fucker at all."

"You are a skeptical man," I said.

"Find a place to pull over. I want to take a look at that dog myself."

"Already have. Musty. Loose fur. Mummified under the wrap."

"Pull over."

We were still out in the country, so I pulled over by the side of the road near a stand of trees next to a little, trickling creek.

We got out of the truck and the Prius pulled up behind us and killed the lights. Brett and Chance got out.

"Car trouble?" Brett said as she and Chance came over.

"No," I said. "Leonard wants to look himself. He thinks Farmer's story stinks."

"Really none of our business how true his story is," Brett said. "We've done what we were paid to do. I don't think swapping money for a dead dog is illegal."

"Unless you consider that whole extortion thing," I said.

"When you're right, you're right," Brett said.

Leonard had the tailgate on the pickup down and was tugging at the coffin, paying us no mind. I went over and took hold of the other handle and we set it down behind the pickup. Leonard opened it up. He had a flashlight in his pocket, and he was shining it around on the dog.

I said, "Okay. There is one odd thing. The dog is lying on a bottom that's higher than the real bottom. I didn't notice that before."

"I noticed it right off," Leonard said.

"I have your word for that," I said.

"Looks obvious to me," Chance said.

"Remember, I am your dad," I said.

"Yes, Daddy," Chance said.

By this time Leonard had lifted the dog out and placed it on the ground. There was a small hole in one corner of the false bottom and Leonard's finger fit in there. He lifted the false bottom out, and on the true bottom of the coffin lay a corpse.

I couldn't distinguish age, but enough of the flesh and features had survived that I could tell that it was most likely a woman, way the hips were set, way the wide edges of the bones cut through the rotting flesh.

Chase said, "Yuck."

"Damn," Brett said.

Leonard stepped back, pushed the fedora up on his head and looked at me. "What kind of dog is that, Hap?"

Leonard and I took the Prius. Brett and Chance took the pickup and drove the body to the police station. Me and Leonard went to Farmer's house. We might get our nuts in a vice over that with the police, even if the police chief was a good friend.

Farmer's home was inside a gate and there was a tall rock wall around it and great oak and hickory trees that might have been around when Davy Crockett died at the Alamo bordered on either side of a long, white, winding drive. We stopped at the gate and pushed the button on the device outside, but the buzzer we heard went unanswered.

I walked up to the gate and looked through. It was a big house at the end of that long, white drive. It loomed like a mountain and was as dark as a murderer's dreams.

"He was expecting us to deliver," I said. "So why doesn't he answer?"

"Might not like the answer to that question," Leonard said. "Grab a flashlight."

I went back to the car, got a flashlight out of the glove box and gloves for both of us. They don't call it a glove box for nothing.

Leonard walked along the fence until he found a thick vine that wound down off the wall. He took hold of it, and pulled himself up and got over the wall, nimble as a squirrel. I followed, doing the same, less nimbly.

We walked along the drive toward the house. A walk like that you damn near needed provisions. The shadows from the trees were as thick as chunks of chocolate cake. A chill wind was blowing hard, lifting dead leaves, tumbling them over us and across the drive in an explosion of crackles and pops. More leaves snapped underfoot like locust husks.

When we came close to the house we could still see no light, not even in the side rooms. There was a brace of dried winter trees and evergreen shrubbery all about. At the back of the house we found a door pried open, as if with a crowbar.

We pulled our burglar gloves on and nudged the door open further and slipped inside. It was a corridor, and we went down it into a room large enough to keep a pet pachyderm. I moved the flashlight around enough to see that the furnishings were expensive and the paintings on the wall seemed to be as well. The frames were all impressive. I got my frames at Walmart, so I might not be an expert.

I found a light switch and hit it and the lights came on. We wandered out of the main room and down another hallway and poked our heads in rooms along the way, switching lights on, but nothing jumped out at us. We turned lights off as we left the rooms. The hallway was very long and the walls on either side were covered in dog photos in nice frames: all weenie dogs. There were award ribbons too, lots of Best In Show stuff, and there was a large photo of Coco Butternut. I knew this due to my superior sleuthing skills and because underneath the photo which was encased in a gold frame was a metal plate that read: COCO BUTTERNUT, MY SWEETIE.

Last room on the left, Leonard turned on the light at the edge of the door and we went inside. More nice furniture, a fireplace you could have roasted a whole hog in. Farmer lay on the floor. He was not napping or watching a bug crawl across the ceiling, which was one of my pastimes. He lay on the floor next to the couch and there was blood all over his head and all over the floor and his head was a lot flatter than when we had last seen him. He hadn't just been smashed in the head, he had been worked over good. One of his arms was at an odd angle. His toupée lay in a puddle of blood, like a dead kitten.

"Now we call the cops," Leonard said.

We didn't need to, because no sooner had we walked back to the main room than we saw flashing lights out the front window at the top of the drive. We stood where we were until someone got the gate open, and then three cop cars came rolling down the drive to park in front of the house.

I turned on a light that gave the front porch illumination, that porch being a giant concrete slab surrounded by shrubs, except at the steps which led down to a concrete walk. Leonard and I walked out there and stood with our hands loose in case the cops thought we were burglars or might be reaching for something.

Chief Marvin Hanson, our friend, got out of the head cop car and came over. "You guys," he said. "What assholes."

"What did we do?" Leonard said.

"Brett and Chance gave us the scoop, showed us the body, and we came here to talk to Farmer, and who do I find, but two salt and pepper assholes."

"That asshole stuff," Leonard said. "That hurts."

"You won't get to talk to Farmer," I said.

"He not home?"

"Oh, he's home, but someone in a very bad mood got here before we did and rearranged his head."

"Yeah," Leonard said, "he's all over the place in there."

"Shit," Marvin said.

So Marvin and some of the cops took a peekaboo while me and Leonard sat on the steps and shot the shit with one of the officers who had been assigned to make sure we didn't turn to smoke and disappear. The officer's last name was Carroll and last time we had spent any time with him was when Leonard was beating the hell out of a dog abuser and Carroll had been called to make sure Leonard didn't kill the guy. Leonard and Carroll got along well and they were laughing about this and that and pretty much cutting me out of the conversation, though I tried several ways by which I might enter into the discussion, only to find myself ignored or given short shrift.

I was still looking for my opening when Marvin came out on the porch and sent Carroll inside to do this or that. Marvin said, "Thing is, we get here and there's a dead body, and we got you guys, and this after making a trade at a cemetery for a dead woman in a coffin."

"We thought we were trading for a dead dog," I said.

"But you didn't call the cops when this blackmail was going on, now did you?"

"We did not," I said.

"Bad us," Leonard said. "You guys really would have cared about a guy trading money for a pooch corpse? That would have been like a priority?"

"Maybe not too much," Marvin said, and sat down on the steps by us. He shooed the other cops away.

"So how bad a trouble are we in?" I said.

"I don't think you did it," Marvin said, "if I take Brett and Chance at their word, and I do, but I'm not sure how a judge and a courtroom would take all this."

"He was our client," I said. "We came to find out why he had lied to us about getting a dog's body back, and there was a woman's with it. We wanted answers."

"You should have come to me," Marvin said. "I'm the law. We get paid to get answers."

"Okay. Here's a thought. Is there some kind of privilege for private investigators and their clients?" Leonard said.

"Only in the movies, boys. Only in the movies."

They took us downtown but didn't throw us in a holding cell. We sat in Marvin's office with Brett and Chance. I had that feeling I had in grade school when the teacher made you write something or another on the blackboard multiple times.

"Here's what we're going to do," Marvin said. "I'm letting everyone go, and I'm saying you told Brett and Chance to tell me that you were going to Farmer's to do a welfare check, cause the guy in the cemetery looked dangerous, and you thought he might be a threat, and you thought you should get there and see he was okay. He wasn't."

"Could be the guy in the graveyard did it," I said. "We were farting around with loading up the body, stopping along the way to look in the coffin, and Leonard gave me bad directions, so it took us an extra ten minutes."

"I gave you bad directions?" Leonard said. "Bullshit, you can't follow a straight line if a string was tied to your dick and to where you wanted to go. Oh, sorry, Chance. No offense meant."

"None taken, but now I got that image in my head."

"Sorry again," Leonard said.

"He's not sophisticated like me," I said. "You'll have to forgive him."

Marvin said, "What I'm going to do is let you two go home, and then you're going to need to stay out of it. This could still come back to you, you know. No use adding fuel to the fire. Stay away from this."

We left out of there and drove our respective rides back to the office where Leonard put on a pot of coffee and got a bag of vanilla wafers out of the desk drawer.

As he did, he said, "These help me think."

"Sure they do," I said.

Brett and Chance drove up slightly after we arrived and came upstairs and into the office.

Brett said, "That was not too smart, boys."

"Yep," Leonard said. "Our usual."

"You know, guy in the cemetery would have to have been in a real rush to get there and do the job before you went over," Brett said. "I mean, he had to figure you might take the coffin right to him. He wouldn't know you were going to spend time looking inside or getting lost, so that would be some chance he was taking."

"Good point," I said.

"Means he probably had him a partner," Leonard said. "That means they get the money and while we're fucking around with Coco Butternuts and a corpse to be named later, he's got this other guy over there playing T-ball with Farmer's head?"

"Butternut," I said.

"What," Leonard said.

"It's Butternut, not Butternuts."

"Whatever."

There were no more revelations in the offing that night, so we all went home. Later, upstairs Brett lay in my arms, her sweet breath close to my face, her hand on my naked thigh.

"You know that gets me excited?" I said.

"I'd be disappointed if it didn't," she said.

"That's why you let Buffy stay downstairs, huh?"

"She likes it downstairs now, since Chance is there. You know, we could do it if we did it quietly. I don't want Chance or Buffy to hear."

"Perhaps we could do it in slow motion," I said.

"I like slow motion," she said.

"Somewhere in the midst of it, though, we can move a little faster, if that's all right with you."

"Sure, but not too soon."

"Sounds like a plan," I said.

And it was.

I'd like to say with our great powers of deductive reasoning we figured out who did what and why by the next morning, but we didn't.

When I came downstairs Leonard had used his key to come in, and he was fixing breakfast and Chance was in her footy pajamas with dinosaurs on them, sitting at the table, sucking at a large cup of coffee. Buffy was sitting at Chance's elbow, waiting for her to drop something.

"I fed Buffy already," Leonard said.

"Thanks, bro."

"Leonard makes good coffee," Chance said.

"It's a Keurig," I said. "Anyone makes good coffee with that. You turn it on, the water heats, you stick a pod in and wait."

"Gave it my loving touch," Leonard said. "Waved my magic black hand over the pot. Gives it a kind of richness."

"I'm going to have to agree," Chance said.

Strands of her dark hair were loose from her hair tie and some of it clung to the side of her face. It made her look cute and young and made me feel even more father-ly, more protective. I had found out about her late in life, but I hoped I could be as good a father as I could from each day forth, but considering who I was and what I sometimes did, I had my doubts.

Leonard had gone all out with the cooking, scrambled eggs, bacon and cinnamon rolls. I ate a small amount of eggs and one piece of bacon and a cinnamon roll. As I got older, weight and I fought it out on a daily basis. I won for a while, and then it would come back and sneak up on me, climb into my belly and swell it. I worked out, but it didn't seem to matter, least not the way it used to. Fat was tenacious in middle age. I guess middle age is a silly term when you're fifty.

Brett came down in a bit. She was wearing sweat pants

and a sweat shirt and her hair was tied back and her eyes were half closed. Time had stopped for her, and her aging was done in inches while mine was done in yards.

"I'll have a cinnamon roll and that's it," she said, and sat down.

I knew what that meant. I stood up from the table and got her a cinnamon roll and poured her a cup of coffee and sat it in front of her. When she had a couple sips of coffee, and had dunked her roll into the big cup, she said, "I think what we got to do is go to Farmer's business and see how things were there."

"He paid us to deliver money and pick up a coffin, and we did that," Leonard said. "Since he's dead, I don't see any more money forthcoming."

"That's never stopped us before," Brett said.

"You can't let it go either, can you?" I said.

"Nope," she said. "I don't like unsolved mysteries. I want to know who Jack the Ripper was and if Bigfoot lives in the woods. It's how I am."

"I'm curious," Chance said. "I know it's not my right to be curious about your work, but I am."

"Sure it is," Brett said, and reached out and patted Chance on the arm. "You're family, and we're a family business."

"I'm actually a reporter, and I need to go to work," she said. She stood up from the table and gave Brett a hug, went around and gave Leonard one, and then me. "I'm still curious though."

"We'll keep you in the loop," Brett said.

Chance went to get showered and dressed. When she left the room, Leonard said, "I think that DNA test was flawed, brother. She can't have come from you."

Me and Brett drove over to the mortuary and cemetery owned by Farmer. Leonard went to the cop shop to see if he could pry any new news out of his new friend Officer Carroll.

The cemetery and mortuary was off the main highway and down a dirt road. The road would be dusty in the summer, but for now, during the cool and dry times, it was solid and smooth. We wound our way between trees and pastures and came to the mortuary and cemetery. There was a section for humans, and one for animals. As we drove by, I glanced over the rock fence around the cemetery. Both sections appeared to be pretty full.

The metal bar gate was wide open, and we drove through it and stopped in the circular drive close to the curbing near the main building, which was a goodly size and at first glance looked nice, but at second looked worn around the edges; I knew how the building felt.

I had combed my hair and put on dark jeans and had tucked my shirt in and had on a nice jacket. Brett thought it might be the thing to do, going there. She thought they might see us as more professional. She had on a black business suit with a white shirt, and a business-looking tie made of silk that she wore loose around the collar. The black boots she had on added to her height.

Inside it was a little too cool and it didn't look all that clean either. There was a lady behind a long desk. She was well dressed and a little plump, but it was a firm-looking plump. Fact was, she looked healthy enough to turn over a truck and make it beg for gasoline.

We stood in front of the desk and she smiled at us. Brett said, "We were working for Mr. Farmer. Private investigators. We are doing some follow-up, and would like to ask a few questions, if that's okay?"

The woman studied Brett, then she studied me, and then she leaned back in the desk chair and smiled a smaller smile than before.

"He didn't really operate this place, or had anything to do with it," she said. "He inherited money. Got a chunk of it every month and didn't so much as come in to see if the plumbing worked. It does, but not as well as it should."

"You sound a little unhappy with him," I said.

"I guess I shouldn't speak ill of the dead, but I couldn't speak about him at all until he was dead. Living, he had too much control here."

"Does that mean ownership has changed?" Brett asked. "I mean, the boss is dead so life goes on."

"Like I said, he was no boss. Just collected money. But he was the owner."

"Who owns it now?"

"I guess I do."

"Guess?" I said.

"The will is still being examined, but it looks that way. Jimmy quit having anything to do with this place five years ago, when his wife took off."

"Where did she go?"

"No one knows. She supposedly ran off with the dog mortician."

"How do you mortician a dog?" Brett asked.

"Not with mortician putty. We cremate them and we stuff them with chemicals after we pull out their insides, and sometimes we mummify them. That's extra. Got to be honest. The chemicals don't keep the fur from falling out, so some like the idea of mummification."

"Who in the world would be checking on a dog after it's in the ground?"

"It's the idea of it that the bereaved like. Frankly, it's nothing to me."

"You don't sound like a dog lover," I said.

"I'm not. But I can have them burned up or wrapped up for a nice fee."

"Question?" Brett said.

"Ask it," she said.

"First, to whom am I speaking?"

"Jackie Bridges," she said. "I guess I should throw in that I'm Jimmy's ex-wife."

"Ah, that's how you got in the will," I said.

"Nope. His mother did that. She never liked the second wife. I didn't either, but I wasn't married to her. I don't think Jimmy liked her too much. She looked good but wore badly."

"How's that?" I said.

"She was a bitch on wheels. Jimmy kept me on here after the divorce, and she didn't like it, but he wouldn't change it. Okay, not true. He couldn't change it. It was part of his mother's will that I could work here until I didn't want to or I died. The second wife was given a piece of it too, as his mother didn't want to alienate Jimmy. She loved him even if he didn't care that much for her."

"Why didn't he?" Brett asked.

"He wanted the entire thing to go to him. He went to a shrink of some kind and got told he had potty-training issues, like not being able to shit right is going to cause you to make stupid choices. They got a lot of stuff for that problem in the drugstore. I don't think Jimmy minded me working here because that meant he didn't have to deal with someone new who didn't know the business, but the wife didn't work here, not a day, and still got a cut, and I won't lie to you, that chapped my ass. His mother, bless her soul, had it in her will that if she died I got half of the business and got to stay on. That was a big bite out of things for him. Meant his wife's share came out of his half, instead of what ought to be my half."

"So this places makes big money?" I asked.

"Nope. But she has a lot of other businesses and property rentals, so they make big money, and this is a nice foundation. Me and Jimmy and Betty Sue, that's the wife, all got a cut of that. Still do. This place does better than you think, but not as well as I would like. I haven't exactly been on the ball the last five years due to the fact Jimmy wouldn't allow me to make certain changes to upgrade. I had some power, like I said, but there were certain things I couldn't do without his permission, and he wasn't giving it. He didn't want any more cuts to his money, and I couldn't convince him we could make more money by upgrading here and there. Way people are about their pets, hell, we could convince them to dress them in suits and sweaters that we provide. There's all manner of possibilities. One woman wanted us to have her dog put in capsules that she could take every morning until the dog was gone. Nice idea, but it's not sanitary and there are laws against it."

"One more question," Brett said. "Is it possible we could see where the body of Coco Butternut was buried?"

Jackie had a paper with all the graves listed on it, the names of the pets labeled. She gave it to me and I folded it up and put it in my shirt pocket.

"Just for the record, what's your view on cats?" I said.

"Don't like them either. Neither did Jimmy. His mother was the animal nut. I only like to eat them. Not cats and dogs, but animals like cows and such. Them I like with a side salad. Though, I don't know, you fix a dog or cat right, I might eat them too."

We went out and around the side of the building, having been given permission to look about.

"She doesn't like cats and dogs," Brett said, "so she's on

my shit list. But at least she's an asshole on top of it all."

"Her husband was probably a worse asshole," I said.

"Could be. But I don't like her. I think she was checking me out. You see the way she looked at me?"

"You have scrambled egg on your shirt."

"Oh. Right. I do."

Around back we looked out over the field of markers and stones.

"That's a lot of cats and dogs," I said.

Walking through the rows of animal graves we came to one that was nothing more than a hole and there was a large marker there made of granite. It read: COCO BUT-TERNUT, CHAMPION AND FRIEND. There were no dates on it.

"Odd," Brett said. "Someone broke into the dog cemetery and dug up the coffin and carried it out and no one noticed."

"It is off the main road," I said.

Brett nodded. "Yep, but it would have taken awhile."

"Looking at the grave, I think they used a backhoe."

"So he drove up on a backhoe?"

"Seems unlikely, but not impossible."

Brett nodded again. I could see she was working some ideas around in her head.

A young man walked up. I hadn't even noticed him. "Can I help you?" he asked.

He was tall and thin as a shovel handle and had a wad of blond hair on his head that looked to have been styled into a bird's nest, something for a condor to sleep in. I had never seen hair bunched up like that and so blond it was nearly white. He had a nice face though. At first he looked young, in his thirties, but the more I looked at him the older he looked. Forty or so, I reckoned.

We explained what we were about, and when we finished he nodded.

"Of course. Look about all you want."

"So, obviously," I said, "you work here."

"I'm Jackie's son."

"So you're Jimmy's son too, I take it," Brett said.

"I'm Scanner. Mom named me after part of a science fiction book title. She was married before Farmer, but her husband, my father, James Sundrey, died when I was about ten."

"Sorry," I said.

"No sweat. He was a son-of-a-bitch too, just like Farmer. Can't say I miss him. He was about as fatherly as an earthworm."

"I take it earthworms are poor parents," I said.

"That's my take," he said.

"So what's your job here?" Brett asked.

"Whatever is needed. I have my own business. I make prosthetics and sell them."

"Your own company?" I asked.

"Online, but I make good stuff. Have some patents. I'm catching on. I'm anxious to get out of the pet smoking and wrapping business."

"There's another branch to the cemetery, though," I said. "People."

Scanner pointed. "It's over there, but I don't care that

much for smoking or burying people either. What I want to do is end up going to Hollywood, make special effects for movies. I can really do some cool things with prosthetics, you know foam, make-up."

"Good luck with that," I said.

"Thanks," he said. "I guess I'll go now. I have to attend to a few things. Hey, you got something on your shirt there."

"Scrambled eggs," I said.

"Ah."

"Question," Brett asked. "When you do deep burials, and it looks like Coco here got a nice one, how do you dig the holes?"

"Backhoe," Scanner said. "We keep it in the shed."

And he pointed to the back of the cemetery where there was a long, high-roofed building made of aluminum.

A lot of things were clicking as we drove away, and we discussed them.

"Okay," Brett said. "The ex-wife didn't like him, and her son didn't like him, and there's a backhoe in the shed, and yet, it doesn't quite come together."

"If she knew there was a body under Coco Butternut, she didn't mention it."

"Because she knows she's not supposed to know. She's in on it, I bet you an enchilada dinner on it."

"What kind of enchiladas?"

"Focus, Hap."

"You brought up enchiladas."

"I also brought up I think she's involved in all this."

"Guy that drove that truck was a big dude, not a woman and not as skinny as Scanner."

"Still think she's involved. Maybe we should come back tonight and look in the shed?"

"So they have a backhoe?" I said. "Scanner said as much, and a business like this would have one."

"Yes, but maybe they have a big truck as well, like the one that brought the coffin. As for the big guy, maybe they got a third partner. It could easily be that way."

"If they're the ones did this," I said.

"I don't have the proof yet," Brett said, "but I think we can bumble along until we do based on that assumption."

"I'm a good bumbler."

"You and Leonard both," she said. "It makes me proud."

Me and Leonard made an appointment with Marvin while Brett went to the office to hold down a chair in case a new client came in, one that wasn't dead and was paying. What we were doing was now gratis, but damn if we wanted some skunk to use us as a way to get money and kill Farmer.

Day before Leonard had visited with Officer Carroll and asked him a few questions, things that could help us nail the murderer. I called Marvin and let him know we hadn't been good, and that we were snooping, just what he'd asked us not to do. But when I told him what Brett and I had learned at the mortuary, about the financial arrangements and the will, it stirred his interest.

"I kind of hate you guys," he said. "You never do what I ask."

"We're like teenagers," I said.

"Assholes," he said.

Marvin was seated with his feet on his desk and there was a steaming cup of coffee on the desk as well. He had a file in his hand.

"Officer Carroll seems to be talking out of school," Marvin said.

"He might have been led to think I had your permission," Leonard said.

"He might have been led that way, might he?"

"Yep," Leonard said.

"Alright, to hell with it. Maybe you boys are actually onto something."

We seated ourselves in chairs in front of the desk and Leonard perched his fedora on his knee.

"Can we have some coffee?" I said.

"Go to the break room and get it," Marvin said.

"Don't you have minions?" I asked.

"For police work."

"Get mine too," Leonard said. "And if they have any cookies, vanilla in particular, bring some of those."

"We don't have any cookies," Marvin said.

"If I ran this place vanilla wafers would be a constant."

"If you ran this place there'd be a lot of fat cops," Marvin said.

"I'm not fat," Leonard said.

"You're a freak of nature," Marvin said.

"Actually," I said, "he's showing his age some. He recently had to drop ten pounds."

"So did Hap, and he could drop ten more."

Marvin eyed me. "I was thinking twenty."

"You're probably right," Leonard said. "He doesn't work out as much as he should."

"I have other things to do," I said.

"He's lazy," Leonard said.

"Well," I said. "That too."

"Okay," Leonard said. "About that coffee, Hap. Stir my sugar in good. You know how to fix it."

"Fuck you," I said, and got up to get the coffee.

When I came back, Marvin had pulled his feet off the desk and tucked them underneath it. He had the file open in front of him.

"I'm assuming that file has to do with the death of Jackie Farmer's first husband," I said.

Marvin smiled. "You arrived at the same place I did. Here she is with two husbands, and they are both dead and with their deaths, money is to be made. The first there was a fat insurance policy, and with Farmer she made money as a business partner as well as a wife, and when they split, she made money just as a business partner. But Farmer's mother liked Jackie, and it seems that gave Jackie a home court advantage. Then Farmer got a new wife and that led to new complications, until the new wife disappeared. Way I think Jackie had it figured was she was in a good position to get it all, due to Farmer's mother making her a big dog at the mortuary. With Farmer and his new wife gone, she would own the mortuary, the cemetery, the whole business. And there's the insurance on Farmer too. The mother put in her will should Farmer die, a sizable amount of the insurance money she had on him would go to Jackie. That's a really large incentive for murder, you ask me."

"What Jackie told us," I said. "She didn't try and hide it. Though she left out that whole advantage for her due to murder."

"I had to look around for a file on her first husband's death, and that took some work, and it's interesting in what's not in it," Marvin said.

"Like the dog that didn't bark in the nighttime," I said.

"Like that," he said. "The first husband started feeling bad and ended up in the hospital, and the doctors couldn't figure the problem. I think if we dig him up we'll find out what the problem was. I'm guessing poison. I think this Jackie is an operator. She didn't kill Farmer while the money was easy, even after the divorce, but at some point my guess is she thought it was a good idea."

"And Farmer's wife?"

"That might be a bit more complex. Farmer didn't like her much, and there had actually been three or four calls to the police by the missing wife, saying he was abusing her. And there was the whole business about her fucking around with someone, and then suddenly she's gone and so is the guy. Old Police Chief thought it was kind of suspicious, but he couldn't prove anything and Farmer just went on being Farmer."

"And Jackie went on being Jackie," I said.

"Right," Marvin said. "My guess is she somehow knew what Farmer did, kept it in her back pocket. Why not? She wanted to be rid of the wife too, and then one day she gets the bright idea she can get some money for the body, and then get rid of Farmer too. The time was right with the mother dead and her knowing where the body was and the will lined up to make her golden. She could sit around with her feet up and a fan blowing up her dress for the next ten years and not have to hit a lick at a snake."

"What about her son?" Leonard said.

"Checked on him," Marvin said. "Has a jacket. Had a few little notes added to it on a regular basis." Marvin shifted to pick up another folder, opened it. "All of it petty stuff. Peeping Tom, stealing women's clothes at the laundry mat. Stuff like that. He got caught on that one and they found selfies of him wearing stolen panties on his head. His history of panty hats was right there. He's one of those dreamers thinks he's going to be something he's too lazy to be, a special effects artist or some such."

"He told me and Brett just that thing," I said. "But wearing panties on your head is a long way from murder."

"Course," Leonard said, "we don't know the dead woman in Coca-Cola Butterasses coffin is Farmer's wife."

"We should know that in a few hours," Marvin said. "I got some guys in Tyler owe me a favor, so they're making DNA tests. Can do that stuff quick these days, they take a mind to, and there aren't a bunch of cases lined up in front of it. That's where the favor comes in. But I think we know who it is."

"And probably there's a dead boyfriend somewhere too," Leonard said. "You know, the wife is underneath Coconut Butterballs, then there's a good chance that boyfriend of hers is lying under another dog out there. Farmer killed them, the ex-wife threatened to expose the murdered wife, got some money in the deal, then got Farmer whacked. It's a tight idea, you think about it."

"I know I like it," Marvin said, "but thing is, even with one body on hand from the graveyard, we got to have a bit more reason to dig the other body up."

"Why would they care if you dug it up?" I said. "They got what they wanted, the money and Farmer dead. Farmer most likely put him there, so why would they bother not letting you check the graves out? It just puts more guilt on him, I'd think."

"Well, something is bothering them," Marvin said. "We asked and they said we would need a warrant."

"That paints things a different color," Leonard said. "Ah, I got it. The other body, maybe Jackie helped dispose of it. Maybe she helped in the murder of the wife too."

"Yeah, but still all things point to Farmer, not her," I said.

"Jackie may have played her hand too far, blackmailing him and killing him on the same night," Marvin said. "But what I'm thinking is she's thinking there's something in that other coffin that points back to her. My guess it might even be something she can explain away, but if she can get rid of the body, dig it up, cremate it and put the boyfriend's ashes in the flower bed, she's laid out smooth as silk. I think Farmer had a good idea who stole the body. He may not have known she knew he did what he did, but at that point, someone blackmailing him with his wife's corpse, he had to have an idea."

"Why he sent us," I said. "Had it figured right. They wanted to kill him. He thought he'd be all right if he stayed home, that paying her off would save his neck, but it didn't."

"Which brings me to a thought. You see, as Police Chief I have certain restrictions. You know, my hands are tied on some things. But I'm thinking if someone who didn't have those restrictions was able to find some evidence, maybe not too illegally, but you know, real soon, and it was something a Chief of Police could use, and those people, two guys say, were to present it to me in a fashion where I could find out about it in a good way, and I could use it in court, wouldn't that be nice?"

"So, you're talking about us?" Leonard said.

"Maybe," Marvin said. "You know, there might be something at her house, inside, or somewhere. Something like a big, white truck, which would be a nice place to start, though not quite good enough to finish, but what if they had four hundred thousand dollars under the bed in Farmer's satchel."

"That might be hoping too much to find," Leonard said. "Even for those two guys you're talking about."

"I think Jackie is too smart to just poke that satchel under the bed," I said.

"True," Marvin said, "but you never know, and you know what, they might have hidden it at the mortuary, but you see, I got this warrant I got to get, and the best I can do is get it tomorrow, and I'm not entirely sure the judge is going to give it to me, not in time, anyway. He's kind of stickler. But I'm thinking I get enough to pull them in, and get that Scanner fellow in interrogation, I can dangle a fine set of panties in front of him and he'll spill the beans."

"You'd dangle panties in front of him?" Leonard said.

"No," Marvin said, "I think he's the weak link in all this and he'll spill with little more than a cup of coffee and me giving him a stern look, but I thought that part about the panties sounded good, so I said it."

Chance, being part-time at the newspaper, had a day off from work, so we gave her the job of going out to the cemetery road and parking close to where it emptied into a highway. There was a parking lot there that went with a grocery store of some size. She could sit there in her car and see the road clearly.

There was a back way out of the cemetery, but it was

a long way, and it stood to reason they would use the shorter route. If they did, if Scanner or Jackie left the place, went home, went anywhere, we would know because Chance would use her cell to let us know. She had on a baseball cap and a loose shirt and shorts and sandals and had her lunch with her in Brett's Star Wars lunch box. I think Chance liked playing detective. The idea of it anyway, but after lunch, if she was still sitting there and waiting without news, she might be less interested.

It didn't take much research to figure out where Jackie and Scanner lived. Scanner still lived with his mom, which was no surprise, and he had a place in the backyard. We knew that because we drove over there in Leonard's pickup and walked along the walk and went straight up on the porch. We had on khaki clothes and caps that could have fit any city worker doing any kind of city job, jobs that might require someone to go from house to house, or do work inside, say on a gas line or a phone line or electrical problems, plumbing perhaps. We could make a lie go in any direction we needed to.

At the front door Leonard took out the lockpicking kit and messed around for a while, and when he clicked the lock, he discovered there was a dead bolt as well and a chain. He locked the door back with his tools.

If they had the front door locked like that, it meant they locked it up inside and went out another way. We strolled casually around the side of the house, next to some ill-kept shrubs, and finally we were at a chain link fence with a gate in it. The backyard was high in weeds, but there was a walk along the side of the house and it came to where we stood at the gate. The gate had a padlock on it.

There was an old travel trailer in the yard with grass grown up around it. Behind that was a large shed and the pines in the yard on either side of it had dropped rust-colored needles on the roof making a thick carpet. We could see a padlock on the shed door from where we stood. The sunlight dappled through the pine limbs and leaves and gave the place a camouflage look.

"Like their privacy," Leonard said.

"Lot of people do," I said.

Leonard worked the padlock easy with his tools, and we went inside the yard, closing the gate behind us. "Bet you the kid lives in that travel trailer, and that's his workshop out back for the things he sells online," Leonard said. "Also betcha he doesn't sell much online. I think that's just his story so he doesn't seem like the loser he really is. Grown man living with his mother like that, they always got excuses, usually about how they're taking care of Mom, but it always seems to be the other way around."

"You used to live with us," I said.

"You shut up."

We pulled on gloves and started at the back door of the house. Leonard cracked the lock quickly, and went inside. It was marginally neat, about the way mine and Brett's place looks before we clean up for company. The air had a cinnamon smell. There wasn't much of any great interest, some photos on the wall of her and Scanner. One of them he had a mask of some sort pushed back off his face and it nestled on top of his head. I couldn't make out what it was supposed to be, but my guess was he had made out of foam or plastic. His face beneath the pushed back mask was young and happy. My heart hurt for him. Once he thought he'd have more to life than a trailer in the backyard, maybe have a Hollywood career making masks and such for horror movies.

In that same photo Jackie had her arm around him and was smiling. She looked pretty good. Thinner then, healthier, less angry. Maybe she had just poisoned her first husband and was happy about it. Around her neck was a necklace with a dangling pendant. It was fairly large and silver with a green stone in the center.

We made our way through all the rooms. Leonard stopped to use the bathroom, and then we slipped out back and locked the door again. We went out to the travel trailer. It had a padlock on the door. Leonard used the lockpick and in a moment he clicked it open.

"I'm getting good at this," he said.

Inside, the place looked to be more a nest than a home. Clothes were strewn about and the sink was full of dirty dishes and the place smelled like old food and mildewed clothes and too much jacking off.

"Yeah, Scanner lives here," I said.

"Guys like Scanner always got a story about how they're going to become something or another, but they aren't going to get there, and they know it," Leonard said, flashing the light around.

"What about us?" I said. "We aren't exactly living high on the hog."

"It's a higher hog than we used to live on, rose field work and such."

"Yep. We're growing up."

We went through the travel trailer which took us about two minutes. We searched for another ten or so, found some nudie magazines under Scanner's mattress. "I wouldn't touch those too much," Leonard said.

I put them back under the mattress. There was a little TV mounted at the foot of Scanner's bed and a stack of DVDs, all popular movies with lots of explosions and car chases.

We gave the place a bit more of a look, but all we found were some shit-stained underwear on the floor and a drawer full of clean women's panties.

"Scanner's head gear," Leonard said.

We went out and snapped the padlock into place.

"Nothing exciting here."

Out back we got in the shed easy. That lock might as well have been a piece of thread tied across the door.

There was dust in the place and it was moving about in the flashlight beam. There were tables with oddities on them, pieces of this and that. There were superhero masks and chunks of foam, artificial limbs.

"Okay, he really does make prosthetic limbs and such," I said. "And they look like they're pretty good quality."

"I know you, Hap Collins. You're thinking if he'd just

had the right encouragement he might not have become a sad asshole who lives with his mother."

"Well. . . ."

"Let me tell you something, he decided on his own to be a sad asshole who lives with his mother. Sometimes there are just assholes, Hap."

I shrugged. "Maybe."

There was a window at the back of the shed and it looked out on a little road that ran up to a fence that bordered the back yard. There was a truck camper on the ground out there. I recognized it. It was the one that had been on the back of the spotted-up truck that night.

I heard a sound at the back of the shed, but when I changed my place and looked where I thought it had come from, I saw nothing. Cat probably. I was getting jumpy.

"Look here," I said.

Leonard looked out the window at the camper.

"That's the same camper cover that was on the truck that night," I said.

"Lot of those out there," Leonard said. "And they all look alike."

"That's it," I said.

We looked around and found more of the same, and then in a closet we found a set of legs and arms and a torso. Not real ones, but prosthetic ones. There was a foam head with eye holes and a black hood was pulled over it.

"No wonder our man at the graveyard walked funny," I said.

"Scanner was wearing this shit." Leonard said.

"Why he looked big and his hands looked small. He had this on to disguise himself, made him look more formidable. With the hood on, gloves and clothes, it being night, I couldn't tell. I just thought he walked a little funny."

Leonard pulled one of the legs out and used his hands to bend it at the knee. It bent easy.

"Feel it," he said.

I took it. It was light as a feather. If Scanner had the whole thing on it would have been a little cumbersome, but I could tell it was easy enough to move around in it if you practiced.

"Okay," I said, "how do we get it so Marvin can come in here and check things out?"

"I was thinking we set the travel trailer on fire and call Marvin and the fire department."

"So they put it out?" I said. "Stuff we need is in the shed."

"Leave it to me."

Leonard took out a burner cell. We got so we carried one each on us or in our car or pickup.

A moment later the call was made.

"Hey, Marvin. This is Leonard. . . . Of course that Leonard. Listen, there may be a trailer on fire out back of a house on Prichard Lane, 303, and it might need to be put out, but you know, the shed behind it, you might come with the fire department, just in case you might need to snap the lock and look inside to see if anyone's in there. Fire might spread."

Leonard listened, then closed the phone.

"Okay. He's coming in twenty, so let's find a way to set a fire in the trailer."

Outside of the shed Leonard put the padlock back in place, and then he picked the lock on the trailer again. Inside, Leonard pulled the curtains over close to the electric cook stove and placed the end of one of them over one of the burners. He filled a frying pan with cooking oil and put it on top of another burner and heated up the grease. I understood then. I got some frozen French fries out of a bag in the refrigerator and poured them in the grease, and we let that heat until the potatoes were popping, then Leonard placed the hot pan on the curtain over the other burner and turned that burner on. In a moment the curtain caught and the flames ran up the curtain and along the wall. I poured the oil and potatoes from the frying pan onto the stove and the hot burners caught the grease and then the top of the stove was on fire. We went out of there and locked the door. It wasn't that we thought Scanner would think he forgot and left potatoes on the stove, but it would sure look that way to the fire department at first glance.

"What if it doesn't catch good?" I said.

"Say some driver drove by, saw smoke and called it in but didn't want to leave their name. That driver wouldn't know how bad the fire was, only that smoke was seen. Hell, it might be out by the time the fire department gets here, but they got to go on and take a look, don't they?"

"They do, indeed."

Away from the house we walked along the street and glanced back. No smoke was drifting from the backyard. The fire might be out, but it was the excuse Marvin needed. He'd have the fire department break in there and then he'd say he thought he smelled smoke coming from the shed to, and they'd break in there too, or that's how I figured he'd do it.

In the pickup I took off the work cap and Leonard did too, slipping his fedora in place. I called Marvin on my burner.

When he answered he said he was already en route. I said, "I was you, I'd look close in the shed out back. Fact is, I'd look in a closet there where you'll find the disguise of the guy that brought us the dog and we gave the money. There might be a camper shell out back like the one the blackmailer was using."

I explained a little more to him, and then I picked up my personal cell and called Chance.

"They still there?" I asked.

"They didn't come out this end."

"You can go home now."

"Good," she said. "I'm out of coffee."

We thought if Marvin found the prosthetics and I said that Scanner was wearing that rig when we gave him Farmer's money, it would be good enough and over with.

But it wasn't like that, and of course, thinking back on it, there was no reason it should be.

Marvin came over late afternoon, and sat at the table finishing off coffee with me and Leonard, Chase and Brett.

"We can't go to the DA with what we got. We know the little bastard was in on it, probably his mother too, but we can't prove it. The rig he had, all you can say is you think he was wearing it. You didn't think that until you saw it in the storage building, and I can't say you were there, as they would get your asses in trouble for breaking and entering, and I kind of encouraged that. I mean the fire is suspicious as it is, but it did get us in the shed and we did find the prosthetics, so it's something. But, not enough. We didn't even take the stuff or them into custody. We got a free look, and that helped, but that's the end to it. Have to give me more, if you're up for it, and frankly I don't know what more is, but if you say I asked you for more, I'll deny it."

"Like the way you didn't ask us in the first place," Leonard said.

"Just like that," Marvin said. "Here's the thing, this isn't really your problem, and you could let it go. It's really my job to figure this out."

"Don't have sympathy for Farmer," Leonard said, "but I don't like us being saps in all this."

"I don't like we were handing Scanner money and in the meantime, Farmer was getting his brains knocked out, and right now, I'm figuring Jackie did that herself," Brett said. "If it was Scanner at the graveyard, then Jackie was most likely the muscle. She looked stout enough to swing a tire iron or a bat and make it count."

"You got a bother about it all, then you got to come up with more proof," Marvin said. "And let me tell you, that setting fire to Scanner's trailer was an iffy idea. That could have gone way wrong."

"But it didn't," Leonard said.

"Still, try and play it a little safer, okay? We had Jackie and Scanner come in and fill out some papers, you know, and the general consensus was that juveniles broke into the trailer and set the fire."

"That isn't far off," Brett said.

"Ha, ha," I said.

"Wow," Chance said. "Meeting people in a graveyard to swap money for a corpse. Murder. Arson. Bad language from my father and uncle, a stakeout. I certainly have been living a sheltered life. I like this one better."

After Marvin left, we mumbled about this and that for a bit, but didn't come up with anything constructive, but after we poured ourselves more coffee, Chance said, "I got an idea. It might not be a good one, but do you want to hear it?"

"Right now even a bad idea might sound good," Leonard said.

"In our case, they usually do," I said.

Leonard said, "Wait a sec," got up and pulled out the

stash of vanilla cookies we keep for him in the cabinet and put them on the table. He opened the bag and stacked a half-dozen cookies in front of him and started dipping one in his coffee. "All right, I'm ready," he said.

"Okay," Chance said. "From what's been said, it appears Jackie is worried about someone digging up that other body in the graveyard. She told the law they had to get a warrant. Right so far?" We agreed she was.

"She may not be hiding anything. That might just be good business, trying to keep the graves intact. She wouldn't want her customers to think that whoever, animal or human buried there, will be excavated at the drop of a hat, so she makes a stand. But if she doesn't want them digging graves up for another reason, could that reason be she knows there's something in the other grave, the one with the boyfriend in it, that might somehow tie her to the murders?"

"Like what?" I asked.

"That's where my plan falters a bit," Chance said. "I don't know. But that could be it, couldn't it? And if we got to the grave before she did, that would be good, because if there's something there, she'll try and get to it before a court order goes through. She might fight it off a few days with a good lawyer, but she's got to know in the long run the law is going to win out on this one. Those graves are going to be investigated. She may have dug up the one she needs to check already, but you know what I'm thinking is she'll wait until late tonight so as not to be so conspicuous. She's stirred up by today's events, and by the law's request to dig up some graves, so she knows that fire wasn't merely an accident. She's bound to suspect the law did it so they could snoop. She knows they want in that graveyard bad, and she's got to figure that court order is coming soon, so that means she's got to get to it and hide whatever evidence she believes might be in the coffin. She would most likely want to go there late at night to make her move, dig the grave up when fewer people might notice. What we need to do is beat her at her own game."

"Well," Brett said, "it's some kind of plan."

We didn't go there when it was fresh dark, but we tried not to wait too long. When the sun was solid set and the stars were high and bright, we drove out there.

Brett was the only one of us that could drive a backhoe, as she had worked for the street department when she was young for a summer, and claimed she could make that machine purr, shit and call other machines bad names. I was her partner in the venture.

Leonard and Chance went in Leonard's truck, parked at the same place where Chance had waited to keep a look out before. Since the lot was empty, they parked close to the building there to look as if the truck might belong to the owner.

They had a good view of the turn off to the cemetery as long as Jackie or Scanner came from that direction. It seemed the most logical path for them to take. It was the most direct route.

Driving past the cemetery, me and Brett scoped it out. There were lights in the front building and behind that was the dog graveyard, and beyond that was a long building where the backhoe should be, and there was a tall booger light on a pole.

We parked down a ways and walked back. I had a crowbar in my hand and a flashlight in my coat pocket. Brett had a flashlight in her hand, one of those big heavy cop things, but had yet to turn it on. We could see clearly enough. It was a bright starry night and the moon was near full. The air was cool and crisp as a starched collar and the air smelled like pines and it tingled in the nose and throat. As always, doing something like this, I was nervous and excited at the same time. In the sky bats were flying, chasing insects. You could see the bats well enough, and if you looked hard you could see the insects flying in the celestial light with the bats swooping down on them.

When we got to the cemetery the gate was locked. It was one of those tall, iron bar things with the bars pointed at the top, and there was a big lock where the gates closed and hasped together. I got out my lockpicking kit and couldn't do shit with it. Brett took the kit and went to work. It took a while, but she got it. We swung the gate open slightly with a haunted house creak and slipped inside and pulled it closed with the same creaking sound. It locked when it snapped together.

The wall around the cemetery was made of worn stone and mortar. It wasn't real high, but it was damn sure solid. It had most likely been built by the WPA during the Great Depression. Where we were had certainly contained something other than a cemetery back then. I think I had heard somewhere about there had once been a school in this location, but it was torn down in the sixties and eventually the acreage became the cemetery.

We eased along the drive, past the front building and the outside light that was on a large telephone pole, and then we started across the graveyard toward the long, high, storage building.

It wasn't that long a trek, but out there in the bright celestial light it seemed a long ways. I felt as if I were on a hike to Antarctica. You could see us easy from the road, and in fact maybe from the moon.

"If the keys aren't with the backhoe," Brett said, "we get a shovel and I can watch you dig."

"Hoping for keys," I said.

The shed had a padlock on the great doors that were chained together. Brett made quick work of it with the lockpicking kit, and then I pushed the doors open and we went inside. Brett took her light out of her pocket where she had tucked it, and turned it on, flashed it around the shed. It was really more a warehouse than a shed. The roof was tall and the room was wide. On the walls we could see all manner of gardening tools hanging, but the thing that interested us was what was in the center of the building, resting on a concrete floor like a dinosaur. A yellow backhoe, and an orange bulldozer, both of good size. They had cabins surrounded by glass. I guess if you're going to scrape ground and dig holes, you needed the right equipment. More interesting was a big white truck, and even without its spots, I felt certain that was the truck I had pulled the coffin out of. I went over and looked at it and was even more convinced.

"You know we are breaking so many laws right now," I said.

"Yep," Brett said. "I have become as gangster as you."

We looked around a bit and I took some photos on my phone. They might not be legal photos in a court of law, but they would certainly show Marvin that mother or son owned a big white truck and the camper in their backyard would conveniently snap together over it.

Brett climbed up on the backhoe, slid back the glass door and looked inside.

She called down to me. "Key's here."

"And you're sure you can drive it?"

"I said I could." She was already settling herself onto the seat.

"I know, but that's been a long time ago."

"It's like giving a blow job, you just don't forget something like that."

"Ouch," I said.

"By the time you and I got together I had perfected the art."

"Ouch again."

"It's not like I was doing it for pay."

"Ouch even again."

"I'm not making this any better am I?"

"Not much."

Brett turned the key and the backhoe growled to life.

"Climb on up," she said.

The backhoe had a lot of controls. Brett buckled her seat belt. That made me nervous. I didn't have a seatbelt. Why did a backhoe have a seatbelt?

Brett released the parking brake and shifted the transmission into forward. The bucket was already up. She drove us through the open doors and the backhoe rumbled us out into the cemetery.

It seemed obvious to us that if there was another body out there under a dog, it would most likely be next to the grave of Coco Butternut. If Farmer had to get rid of the boyfriend too, it seemed natural and simple that he would do them side by side and be done with it.

Brett stopped the backhoe, said, "Which grave are we digging up, one on the right or left of Coco Butternut?"

"It's a crap shoot," I said. "Go for either."

Brett chose the one on the left and started working the scoop. She had a delicate touch. I knew that already, but it was interesting to see it applied to a backhoe. She dug down a few scoops, and we were already there. I could see a coffin.

I climbed down with my crowbar and jumped into the

grave and stuck the bar under the coffin lid and pried. It came open easy. There was a dry, musty smell. I could see right away that the dog inside was resting on the bottom of the coffin. I climbed out of the hole and stood there, shaking my head at Brett.

She went back to work. Two scoops and she scraped the top of the coffin in the other grave. I got down in that grave and did what I had done before. The dog lay high in the coffin and I used the tip of the crowbar to move the false bottom back. There was a human corpse underneath.

I looked up at Brett and nodded.

No sooner had I done that than I heard a roaring and looked toward the sound and saw the bulldozer come out of the warehouse at the end of the cemetery.

"Shit," I said.

Brett leaned out the side of the open backhoe, said, "You better come up."

I clamored back inside the backhoe.

"Looks like our watchdogs failed," Brett said.

"Whoever it is, they came in another way," I said. "Leonard and Chase wouldn't have missed them."

"I don't intend to fight a bulldozer," Brett said.

I figured the bulldozer driver had come in to do what we thought they might. Dig up the grave, but we had beat them to it, and then they had fooled us by coming earlier than we expected. That's how it goes. You can't assume shit.

Brett whipped the backhoe around and we started

heading for the closed and locked gate. Bulldozers run faster than I thought they might, and it was closing on us. As we came closer to the gate, Brett said, "Hitch up your nuts. We're going through."

"The gate? Really?"

"Easier than the wall."

She gave the backhoe all the juice she could, and away we went. She used the bucket like a knight's lance. It hit the gate and there was a noise like someone skinning a cat, and then the gate buckled a little, but held. We were pushing so hard at it the tires began to smoke. I looked back.

The bulldozer was coming fast, whirling onto the drive, and inside its glass cabin I could see Jackie. She had a look on her face that I can only describe as goddamn unpleasant.

The back of the backhoe lifted up and the front tires smoked like a bonfire. Brett changed gears, and the rear end settled. She went at it again. The gate groaned like someone who had just had their knee capped, and then it snapped open. Brett gunned it through, but the bulldozer was as tight on our ass as a hemorrhoid. It hit our rear end and pushed us through and off the drive and onto a patch of grass beside the main road.

Brett turned the backhoe deftly. We bumbled across the patch of grass and then we were shooting onto the road, the dozer banging against the back of the backhoe as we did.

Another move by Brett, and we swung wide and to the

right. The dozer was surprisingly dexterous in its moves, but not as swift as the backhoe, and with that maneuver we got away from the dozer, at least by a few paces.

We raced away, but the dozer was back on track and coming fast. There was a crack in our windshield where it had hit the gate and cold wind came through the crack to add to our misery. I looked back.

Behind us, the dozer dropped its blade so that it skimmed over the road. I knew what that meant. Jackie was going to try and scoop us from the bottom and flip us. Seemed like a good plan that I didn't want any part of. I felt a turd loosen inside of me and thought it might be surfacing soon.

Down the road toward us came a pickup. It was Leonard and Chase. I didn't know why they were coming, but they were. Leonard's truck was bent up in front and I could see there was a third person in the cab with them.

Chance was driving the pickup. Leonard was sitting on the passenger side, and then they were so close I could see who was in the middle. Scanner. It wasn't so much that I could make out his features in detail, but I could see him well enough to know it was him. They were heading right for us at what one could politely call an accelerated rate of speed, and we were on their side of the road. So, there we were, the backhoe flying along as fast as it could go, the bulldozer right on top of us, and Leonard's pickup heading straight for us. It was like me and Brett were about to be made into a sandwich between them, and then—

I hurt a little.

I could smell gasoline.

I woke up in a dry ditch and I could see the stars through the boughs of a pine that draped over me. I couldn't remember how I got there or why I was there, and I don't know if I even knew who I was for a moment without checking my driver's license. That's when I realized I was lying in a ditch. I didn't normally lie in a ditch. Why was I in a ditch?

And then I thought about Brett, and that got me moving, slowly, and then I thought about Chance and Leonard, Jackie and that goddamn bulldozer, and by then I had rolled over and was pushing up with my hands and climbing up out of that ditch. It wasn't a deep ditch, but I felt so damn weak it might as well have been me scaling Mt. Everest.

Chance was driving right at us, and then she veered, and when she did, Brett tried to take the backhoe to the right, but the bulldozer climbed up our butt, and the backhoe did a crazy slide and there was the sound of metal against metal and the sound of our machine blowing a tire; it was like some kind of weird music for the damned, and away the backhoe went, spinning.

When it came to a stop, the dozer hit the machine in the rear, crunching it a little, since it was pushed up against that brick wall that ran for a long ways at the edge of the cemetery. We really hadn't gotten that far.

I remembered the dozer blade being lifted and being smashed down on the back of the backhoe like a giant fist, and then I remember the glass cab shattering and me flying. My moment as Superman, but the landing was my moment as a mortal. Next thing I knew was I was waking up in that ditch. As I climbed out and stood on the road, I moved my parts to make sure they were all there, and they seemed to be. Nothing fell off. I could feel blood seeping at the knees of my pants and my hands were scraped and so was my face.

The dozer had the backhoe pushed across the road and up against the long stone fence, and it was pushing it and crushing it, and I could see Brett still in it, slumped over in the shattered cab.

I tried to dart toward the dozer, found I wasn't darting too well. In fact I was limping like I had one foot in a bucket of solidified concrete. I saw the crowbar I had been holding lying in the road and picked it up.

I glanced right and saw Leonard's pickup was turned over in the same ditch I had been lying in, only a little farther up the road. Gasoline was leaking out of the busted gas tank, and my heart sank. Then I saw Chance slip out of an open window, and behind her came Leonard. They were staggering about like drunks, but they were all right. That's all I needed to know. I didn't give a flying damn about Scanner. I came up the back of the dozer and scrambled up it as it eased back for another run at the backhoe. My pain seemed to go away. I was on top of the dozer and I could see Jackie. She had her back to me and she was shifting gears and the dozer was lurching forward.

I swung the crowbar, hit the back glass and the crowbar bounced back and nearly came out of my hands. I swung it again, and saw Jackie turning her face toward me. A warrior's face. She gunned the dozer backwards and I nearly lost my footing, but I bent low and held on. The dozer's movement paused, I came up and swung the bar again. The glass fell like chunks of shiny ice. I went through the hole to get at Jackie, ripping my shirt and cutting my arms a little on the broken glass. Jackie was up and out of her seat now, and she was like a wildcat. She grabbed me by the throat and rammed me backwards.

We went through the gap in the glass and I felt my arm being ripped by the glass, and then we were tumbling over the back of the dozer and falling to the street.

Jackie jumped astride me and started swing her fists, knocking my head from side to side like a piñata. I had lost the crowbar during all that, but Jackie found it. She stopped hitting me long enough to reach over and grab it and then she lifted it above her head with both hands and was going to drive the sharp end into me. I drew both legs back quickly and put my heels inside her thighs, close to her waist, and kicked with all my might. She went back and the crowbar came down and hit me without design. It hurt, but not as bad as it would have. I grabbed the bar, and then me and her were on our feet.

She was a strong woman and I was an injured weak man. We both had hold of the bar now, and I was trying to wrest it from her, or at least keep her from whacking me with it, when a fist flashed out and hit Jackie in the side of the head, hurtling her head over heels without the crowbar. I was left holding it.

Brett was there. Her face was scratched and she was bleeding from the mouth and nose.

"Fuck with my man, and you'll have the undertaker wiping your ass," she said, and kind of collapsed against me. I held her. She was breathing heavily, but she seemed all right.

"It's okay," I said.

"Of course it is," Brett said.

I looked at Jackie. She was out cold.

Leonard limped over with Chance.

"That was some punch," Chance said. She was all out of breath and hopped up on adrenaline. She was vibrating.

"I brought that with me from hell," Brett said, righting herself.

"Scanner?" I said.

"Good thing they own a cemetery," Leonard said.

"It's going to make his burial cheaper."

"How did you know we needed you?" Brett said.

"Didn't," Leonard said. "We saw Scanner drive by and we started following him and he made us and started driving fast, and we thought, well, shit, he knows we're here, so Chance drove faster. Scanner lost control of his car and put it between two trees. I don't know how he did it, but he spun out and flew off the edge of the bar ditch and landed ass backwards in it, his car about three feet off the ground. It was like a goddamn circus trick."

"It was kind of funny," Chance said. "Well, I hate he got killed later, I think. But it was kind of funny right then, that car in a tree."

"You been hanging around Leonard too long," I said.

"I pulled him out of the car and asked him a few questions that he didn't want to answer," Leonard said, "then I interrogated him with my knuckles and he started to talk. His mother had come the back way, she always went that way, he said. A road we didn't even know about. Jackie was going to do what we thought, brother. Dig up the body. She thought she lost a necklace in the coffin. Hadn't thought about it in years, just knew it came up missing, and then when Marvin wanted to dig up the coffin, she got to thinking she had been wearing it the night she saw Farmer bury the coffins. She went out there and dug them up to see what was in them, saw the bodies, realized it was good for her, them being dead, and later she had Farmer's crime in her back pocket. And then she thought maybe that's where her necklace had gone. Had come off in one of the coffins when she was prying the lids open to look inside. Thought it had come loose off her neck and fell in one of them. It didn't turn up in the wife's coffin, so she figured it had to be the boyfriend's."

"It's like I thought," Chance said. "Well, mostly."

"Yep," I said. "Thing is, I looked in that coffin pretty good. I didn't see a necklace."

"It's probably under a couch somewhere," Brett said, "and she should not have bothered. She was golden and didn't know it."

I looked at Jackie sprawled on the road like a collapsed puppet. She hadn't so much as twitched a muscle. "That was one hard lick," I said.

"She wakes up, I'll give her a fresh one," Brett said.

Marvin came over later that night after we had all been arrested, and then released, except for Jackie. I don't know there was enough evidence to nail her even then, but with the death of Scanner—he ended up with Leonard's truck radio pushed into his chest when the truck flipped—Jackie had had enough. She wanted to come clean. She told Marvin everything, filled in the gaps. Marvin told us we were going to have to pay a fine for digging up the cemetery, commandeering a backhoe that didn't belong to us and breaking into a closed cemetery, but considering Jackie's confession, he figured we'd come out all right. We might have to pick up trash along the highway for a few days in orange jumpsuits and pay a fine, but that was the worst of it.

"I'd get to wear a jumpsuit?" Chance said.

"Darling," Brett said. "Don't be too proud."

Here's some of the stuff Marvin told us. It isn't all that new, some was obvious, some we guessed, but he had the facts from Jackie now.

Farmer buried his wife and her lover after killing them. Jackie was working late one night at the mortuary, looked outside and saw Farmer using the backhoe, digging up graves. She started to go out and ask him what was up, but hesitated. She watched from behind a shrub on the back walkway out of the mortuary, and watched him dig the holes, climb off the backhoe and pull the coffins out of the holes. They were cheap coffins, too big for dogs, really, but they were bought in mass and were cheap. They were light metal. She watched Farmer pry them open, take out the mummified dogs.

She watched him pull some bags out of the back of the truck, let them smack on the ground. He pushed them into the coffins and fitted in the false bottoms he had prepared, put the dogs on top of those, closed the lids, and pushed the coffins back in the holes, covered them up with the backhoe. Tomorrow he could claim he was doing a bit of cleaning work around the graves, and that's why they looked freshly dug.

A few days later when Jackie knew Farmer was out of town, one night actually, she dug up the graves and found what was in them. She covered them back up. It was to her advantage to have the wife dead, and now she had a secret that Farmer was unaware of. She literally knew where the bodies were buried, and as we also suspected, she waited until the time was ripe to play that card.

It hadn't quite worked out the way she thought.

Jackie also admitted she killed Farmer. Still had a key to the house from when they were married. He never changed the locks. She waited on him in a closet with a baseball bat, and surprised him. It took her one lick to knock him down, and then she finished him with more than was necessary. There was a lot of rage in that lady.

Scanner had been in on it, of course, but Jackie claimed he didn't know she was going to whack Farmer, only knew about the money part of it.

It didn't really matter. Scanner, innocent of murder or not, was as dead as those who were under those dogs.

Some time has passed. The cemetery is closed down now. No new customers will grace its grounds, human or otherwise. I drove by there the other day for no reason at all other than I wanted to.

I parked at the front of the cemetery and walked through the gate, which was still open and wrecked from us ramming through it. I walked over to Coco Butternut's grave. The dog had been reburied there by the county. Farmer's wife and the wife's boyfriend had been hauled away by relatives who finally knew where their kin ended up.

I looked down at Coco Butternut's grave. Thanks to that mutt we had caught a killer.

"Good dog," I said and went back to the car and drove away.

HOODOO HARRY

ONE

THE SUN WAS FALLING BEHIND THE TREES as we came over the hill in Leonard's pickup, pulling a boat trailer loaded down with our small boat. We had been fishing and had caught a few. Our usual method was we terrorized the poor fish and threw them back at the end of the day, which for the fish, if you considered the alternative, wasn't so bad.

On this day however we caught about a half dozen good-sized perch and a couple of bass, and we thought we'd clean them and dip them in a thick batter and fry them in a deep Dutch oven full of popping grease.

I've cut back on my fried foods for years now, but once in a while a bit of fried fish or fried chicken sets me right for quite a few months and I thought this would be one of those times. But our intended fish fry was cut short before the fish so much as got cleaned for frying.

As we came over the hill, the trees crowding in on us from both sides, we saw there was a blue bus coming down the road, straddling the middle line. Leonard made with an evasive maneuver, but by this point the trees on the right side were gone, and there was a shallow creek visible, one that fed into the private lake where we had been fishing. There was no other place to go.

The bus seemed to come for us as we veered, and I saw right before impact that there was a black kid at the wheel, his eyes wild, working the steering wheel with everything he had, but it wasn't enough. He was out of control. The bus hit us with a loud smack and I remember suddenly feeling the odd sensation of the tires leaving the ground and the truck turning over in mid-air. I heard the trailer snap loose and saw the boat sailing along in front of us, and then it was out of sight and we were in the creek, the roof of the truck on the bottom of the creek bed, water coming in through the damaged windows.

I heard a slow groaning of metal and realized the bus was on top of the truck and the roof of the truck was slowly crunching down into the creek bed and the floor of the truck was coming down to meet us. Another few seconds and me and Leonard would be pressed like sandwich meat.

I tried to get out of my seat belt, but nothing doing. I might as well have been fastened to that seat with duct tape. I held my breath as the water rushed in through the shattered windows, but the belt still wouldn't come loose. A little, cardboard, pine-tree-shaped air freshener floated in front of my face, a shadowed shape against the dying sunlight leaking in at the edges of the side truck windows. A moment later the belt struggle was too much and I passed out, feeling as if I were drowning. Last thing I remember before going out was Leonard had hold of my arm—

That was it.

When I came to, I was lying on the ground on my side by the edge of the creek. I was dizzy and felt like I'd been swallowed by a snake and shit down a hole. My throat was raw, and I knew I had most likely puked a batch of creek water.

I turned my head and could see the bus, which I realized now was a bookmobile. ROLLING LITERATURE was painted in large white letters on the side. It was sitting with its tires on top of Leonard's truck, the windshield blown out. I could still hear the groaning sound as the weight of it slowly squashed the truck and shoved it deeper into the creek bed. Leonard was holding an open pocketknife in his hand, the one he had used to cut my belt loose. He looked exhausted.

"Good thing you come around," Leonard said. "Mouth to mouth wasn't going to happen, pal. Come to that, I was going to be walking home alone."

"The kid?"

Leonard shook his head. "What's left of him oozed out through the bus's windshield. Glass worked on him like a cheese grater."

"Shit," I said, sitting up.

"I was you, wouldn't go look. You don't need that in your head. Bet he ain't more than twelve years old."

Books were floating out of the shattered windows of the bookmobile and were pushed along gradually by the current like dead fish. The water was either red with sunlight or with blood. Night settled in and the red in the creek turned black as ink and the bus looked like a small island out there in the shallow water.

TWO

Few days later, Leonard and I attended the funeral of the dead kid. We were fine after the accident, but a little stiff, and Leonard had a bit of a hitch in his git-along. That leg had been giving him trouble for years.

The funeral was attended by a half a dozen people we didn't know. The kid was named James Clifton. He didn't have any real family and had been brought up, or more accurately jerked up, in a variety of foster homes. He lived in a small community called Nesbit. Nesbit was named after the black man who founded the place back in the early 1800s. At one time Nesbit had been home to over a thousand black people, surviving after the Civil War in their own communities, selling pulp wood to the white folks out and beyond.

Over time the bulk of the community faded, mostly

due to an attack on it in the late 1800s by Civil War vets and those that wished they had been Confederates. The mob decided to kill everyone in the place over the death of a little white girl. She had been savaged and cut up in a manner that didn't designate any known tool or weapon, but it was immediately assumed that "a nigger done it."

After the raid, only a couple hundred residents survived, and most of them hid out in the nearby deep woods and bottom lands for months. When they returned, the community was a shadow of its former self, with all the houses burned down, the businesses destroyed. Over time it built back up to some degree, but it was never the same. A thousand people may not sound like a lot to begin with, but in those days, it had been a sizable population for an independent black community. After the massacre, its independence was over. The surviving residents went to work for white folks. These days people still lived there, but they didn't even have internet access. A cell phone, forget it. Nesbit was like the ash from a once bright fire.

As a side note, it was later determined the little girl had been savaged by a pack of wild dogs. No apology was made. And in fact there was a sign placed outside of the community on a giant sycamore that said: DEAD NIGGERS ARE GOOD NIGGERS, AND IF THIS SIGN COMES DOWN, THERE WILL BE MORE.

Rumor was it didn't come down until 1925 when it became so weathered it could no longer be read. When it was removed no one was killed, but within weeks a new sign with the same words on it went up. In 1965, it was finally removed and never replaced.

Nesbit was now only a post office and a general store, not too unlike the one of old that had been set afire. There were a few other little businesses along the street, a garage and tire shop, a small sawmill and lumberyard, a thrift store.

Our buddy, LaBorde Chief of Police Marvin Hanson, had filled us in on most of this, and had ended it with, "Thing is, except for the county, maybe a Texas Ranger that wants to bother, there's no law in Nesbit, not even a constable. Well, no official law. Gardner Moost at the general store pretty much takes care of what can legally be done, and some that isn't legal. His wife runs the post office, which means she mostly sits there and reads books. As for Gardner, no one bothers him much if no one gets killed around the place."

"But the kid got killed," I said.

"Not in Nesbit. And not in LaBorde. Sheriff's office will poke around a bit, might find something, but they don't have a good record for that part of the county. There's people in that office that are descendants of the Confederates who burned the place down, killed all those people. Some of them are still fighting the Civil War, least in their minds."

"What about the bookmobile?" Leonard asked.

"Eighties bus. Small school bus refurbished to be a bookmobile. It made the route of a number of black communities for years, then disappeared fifteen years ago."

"Wait a minute," Leonard said. "Jump back on that disappeared part."

"That's the curious part. There was a black lady named Harriet Hoodalay who drove it. Everyone called her Harry. One day she and the bookmobile disappeared. I don't remember all the details, but I remember the story. Anyway, her disappearing like that, like a haint, she came to be called Hoodoo Harry. Nobody calls her anything now. Subject doesn't come up anymore. Pretty much forgotten. And until you guys got run over by the bookmobile, it was forgotten as well."

"That damn sure does fall into the range of peculiar," Leonard said.

"Where's the bookmobile now?" I said.

"Police Department impound. Accident may not have happened in our jurisdiction, but we're the ones that have the storage. We're also the ones that are going to give it a once-over and give the info to the county. Odd thing about the bookmobile is except for the window blown out, tires flattened, a few bangs and scrapes, it's in great condition, like it was the day it disappeared."

"What about my truck, the boat?" Leonard said. "Y'all took them in, too."

"Hope you got insurance," Marvin said. "You can collect what's left of them at the junkyard."

Leonard sighed.

"Question is," I said, "how did that kid get the bus? I mean, hell, he couldn't drive. He was all over the place."

"He drove well enough to take it from where it's been

all these years, just not well enough to keep it in his lane," Marvin said. "You boys are lucky you're alive."

"Yeah," I said, "but poor James wasn't that lucky."

"Since it was us he run over," Leonard said, "can we take a peek at that bus?"

"Not legally," Hanson said.

"How about illegally, but we don't call it illegal?" Leonard said.

Hanson pondered on that. After what seemed long enough for all life on Earth to die off, he said, "Tell you what, if you'll wear gloves and footies, and don't touch any-thing—and I'm especially talking to you, Hap—we might can do that. Come to the impound around midnight."

"I don't touch things," I said.

Leonard and Marvin stared at me.

"Sometimes," I said.

THREE

Before it was time to go over to the impound, we did a bit of research, taking advantage of other friendships at the cop shop, the local newspaper and the paper over in Camp Rapture. In some cases they gave us connections to people who had a bit of information they didn't have. What we got when we put it all together still wasn't much.

We discovered that James had been born in Nesbit. His father ran off when he was born, and his mother died of heart disease. Then his grandparents took him in, but when he was ten the grandfather died, and just six months before he ran over Leonard's truck with the blue bus and got himself killed, James's grandmother died. Since then, he'd been couch surfing with his relatives and friends of his relatives. Child Protective Services had missed a beat. No one knew where he'd been staying the last week. He had been out of sight and out of mind, and was now resting in a pauper's grave in Nesbit cemetery. But before he was sent there, his body was examined and it was discovered he had been tortured with burns and cuts and pokes from sharp instruments. He was also malnourished.

Online we read some old newspaper accounts about the disappearance of the bookmobile. It originated out of LaBorde, but its driver, the aforementioned Hoodoo Harry, kept it where she lived. One morning folks woke up to find she was gone, and so was the bookmobile. And no one knew where either one of them were. Or at least no one admitted it. She was supposed to go off on a vacation to visit her sister that day, catch a bus, but if she left she must have left in the bookmobile, as her car remained at home. She never arrived at her sister's.

I went over to Leonard's apartment around 10 p.m. and we had a cup of coffee to stretch our night out more comfortably, and then about ten minutes before midnight, we drove from Leonard's apartment to the city compound, which was more or less just down the street. When we got there, Hanson's car was parked in its place, and out back was the compound fence and there was light poking out of the windows of a large garage tucked at the back of the property. The lot within the fence was filled with cars and trucks and even a couple of boats on blocks.

I pulled out my cell and gave Hanson a call. A few minutes later he came out of the garage and took his time strolling toward the fence.

"It's okay," Leonard called out to Hanson. "Take your time. We're going to set up camp in a bit anyway. We brought supplies."

As Hanson arrived at the gate in the fence, he said, "You're lucky I'm letting you do this. I'm putting my ass on the line."

"Bullshit," Leonard said. "You're the police chief."

"But I'm not Police God."

"In our book you are," I said, "and oh so precious."

Hanson let us in without whacking either of us on the head with a rubber hose, and we all walked over to the garage. Inside it was so brightly lit you could almost see germs crawling on the floor. A man and a woman in evidence protection gear were wandering about.

There was a motorcycle and a few cars inside, but at the back of the place was the bookmobile, mine and Leonard's Moby Dick. The window had been replaced and the side door was open, and water still leaking out of it. There was a small smear of oil visible to the side of it where it had run out of the bottom of the bus. They had either repaired or replaced the tires to make it easier to maneuver and examine.

A short man, who might have been thirty or fifty, wearing a protective gown, gloves and footies, was standing near the bookmobile. He had a gray face shaped like the blade of a well-used axe, and a build like a stack of mud. The mud flowed when he moved, but he moved very little, just enough to reveal his natural shimmy as we introduced ourselves without shaking hands.

When we told him our names, he said, "Stump. Get suited out."

In a back room full of fresh and folded evidence suits, we dressed along with Hanson.

"Stump isn't much for lengthy conversation, is he?" I asked.

"No," Hanson said. "Bricks in his presence have died of boredom."

"Aren't bricks already dead?" Leonard asked.

"I was reaching," Hanson said.

"You got any news on the kid, or the bookmobile's sudden appearance?" I asked.

"Nope," Hanson said. "You know more than I know."

He said that because while we dressed we informed him the bits and pieces we had discovered, not revealing that in some cases they were people in his department speaking out of school.

When we were dressed we went back to the bookmobile.

Stump was standing pretty much where we had left him. I think he had moved a few inches to the right. Maybe he had peed in the old spot.

"What can you tell us?" Hanson said.

"I can tell you don't screw up my evidence, which is the whole damn bus. They got to do this, Captain?"

"No," Hanson said, "but believe it or not, they have solved a few things in their time. They don't have as much to do as we do, and they are dogged."

"Yeah, well, I guess that's some kind of reason," Stump said.

We went up the metal steps of the bookmobile and eased our way inside. I stood by the steering wheel and looked back through the bus. Though water still leaked from the bottom of the bus, the inside had been dried out after evidence was collected. There were lights strung in there. The books were all gone, and the shelves had warped a bit. In the back there was a curved metal hull that had been put in, perhaps to house a larger fuel tank. A small door was off to the right of where I was looking. The toilet.

It was so clean, I said, "Looks like you've already collected evidence."

Stump, who was behind us, standing on the top step into the bookmobile, said, "I have. But I don't want you adding any evidence that isn't evidence. Get me?"

"Yep," Leonard said. "We got you."

"That hull at the back," Leonard said, touching on what I had noticed first off, "what's it for?"

"Usually they put that kind of thing in to have a large gas tank, all the traveling they do out in the country. That was probably put in the minute it became a bookmobile."

"I've never heard of that," Hanson said.

"You an expert on bookmobiles?" Stump said.

"Point taken," Hanson said.

"Actually, I only seen a few buses and such with that," Stump said. "Sometimes it isn't a gas tank, but a crapper tank. That way the toilet doesn't need to be emptied out as often. Toilet works, by the way. Everything worked on this thing before it went off the road and took a swim. It has a bit of an oil leak that could be due to the wreck, but I don't think so. From looking it over I think that's been an ongoing problem, but other than the window and the original tires gone flat, it's in remarkably good shape."

I walked toward the back, looking left and right as I went.

"You two ace detectives find anything, please let me know," Stump said. "I wouldn't want to not learn a thing or two from the experts."

"You don't know our lives," Leonard said. "We could actually be smart."

Stump made a grunting sound. "I got a pretty good idea about your lives, and I'm thinking it isn't pretty."

"So you been over every inch?" I said.

"I might have missed a centimeter under the shitter, but yeah," Stump said. "You see, it's my job."

I ran my gloved hand over the top of the backend section, the place where the tank would be contained. "What if it isn't a tank in here?"

"What else would it be?" Stump said.

"Always ask questions," I said, "that is the path to wisdom."

"Fucking Confucius?" Stump said

"Hap Collins," I said.

"Look, I was about to take the bolts out of that thing. I was even going to lift off the top and look inside. Thought that up all by myself before you got here."

"Now," Leonard said, "don't start selling yourself for more than you are."

Stump grunted again and left the bookmobile.

"He seems to like you guys," Hanson said.

A moment later, the man and the woman we had seen wandering the garage entered with battery-powered tools, pushed past us, went to the back, removed the bolts and lifted the top off the covering. They carried it away with them without even looking inside. Curiosity would not kill those cool cats.

When they left the bus with the metal top, Stump reappeared and waddled down the aisle toward the now-open container. He had a flashlight in his hand. He turned it on and looked inside, turned his head from left to right, said, "Huh."

We went over and looked. Stacked from left to right, six in a row, were oil-covered, time-withered little bodies, and one larger one.

"How about that?" Stump said.

"We told you that you ought to look," Leonard said.

"And I told you I was about to," Stump said.

"You say that now," Leonard said.

"I hate both you bastards," Stump said.

"You now belong to a sizable club," Hanson said.

FOUR

You can bet that threw a wrench into things. Where before there was the problem of the long-missing bookmobile and its return due to a twelve-year-old boy driving it for reasons unknown, not to mention his death by accident, now we had six oil-covered bodies to identify, tucked up in the back of the bookmobile.

Who put those bodies there? Where had the bookmobile been for all those years, and why did it look brandnew? And while we're making a list, where was Hoodoo Harry? Was hers the larger oil-soaked body?

Well, I'd like to tell you it all came together, mysteries solved, but it didn't. In fact, a few weeks passed by. They examined the corpses and sent off DNA samples from the bodies, five of which turned out to be kids, but that was all they knew. No DNA matches. The sixth one was a female adult, but if it was Hoodoo Harry, no one had yet tracked down a relative to make the determination. But the search was in progress.

Complication on complication multiplied by more complications.

Me and Leonard felt pretty smart for a few weeks about the bookmobile container, but truth was, we weren't expecting bodies at all. And further truth was, Stump and his forensic crew were minutes from discovering what was there. So had we not shown up, they'd have found the bodies anyway.

As the weeks went by, I began to feel agitated, and had trouble sleeping at night. One night, lying in bed with Brett, I was tossing and turning, and she flipped on the nightstand light, rolled over and lifted herself on one elbow and looked at me.

"What the hell, Hap? You been acting like a jumping bean for a week. Moan and groan all night."

"I moan and groan?" I said, sitting up in bed, looking at the beautiful Brett, her flame-red hair tied back in a ponytail.

"Yep."

"I'm bothering you?"

"Only when I'm trying to sleep. Or lie still. And you go to the toilet all night. What's up with that?"

"Poo-poo."

"Six, seven times a night?"

"Well, I go in there and read."

"Why can't you sleep?"

"I don't know."

"It's the kid, isn't it?"

"Guess it is. Think about him a lot. I close my eyes, I see his eyes, looking out of the windshield of that book-mobile."

Brett fluffed her pillow and folded it against the headboard and put her back against it.

"You been looking into it?" she asked.

"No. Hanson said it was his case to investigate."

"That's never stopped you and Leonard before."

"It hasn't, but I guess we didn't know where to go with this."

Brett pursed her lips, said, "You know what? Just look up the old route of the bookmobile, and follow it."

"Marvin's done that."

"But he isn't you, Hap."

"No. He isn't. He's smarter and a good investigator."

"Yeah, well, you do have that going against you. But is he more dogged than you and Leonard?"

"Hanson used the same word. But I think he's the one that's dogged."

"More dogged than you and your bro?"

"I'm not sure how you measure things on a dogged scale. I'm not sure I know what a dogged scale is. I'm not sure there is one."

"I'll tell you right now, you are more dogged. You and Leonard need to get back on the trail and figure things out so I can get a good night's sleep. And here's another idea. How about you look up Cason Statler's friend, the one who runs the newspaper morgue in Camp Rapture. Have him check into things for you. He can find more in a day than the law can find in a month. That guy, isn't his name Mars, something like that?"

"Mercury."

"He has the mind for looking into conspiracies, or whatever is going on here. No one knows odd information and can evaluate it better than that guy. Or so you've told me. Get him to do some kind of . . . I don't know, chart about the route of the bookmobile, then look into missing persons in that area, on the route. Might be something in that."

"You're smart," I said.

"I know that," she said.

"Since you're awake, want to fool around?"

"No. And if you ever expect to again, you better quit tossing, moaning and groaning and talking to yourself."

"I talk to myself, too?"

"Yep."

Brett turned out the light. "Now, close your little Hap eyes and shut your little Hap mouth, and go the fuck to sleep."

FIVE

Cason Statler is a Pulitzer Prize-winning writer that works at the Camp Rapture newspaper. We've known him for awhile. Handsome and quirky, quick of wit, he can also hold his own in a fistfight. He's a guy with a bunch of odd friends. Including us. He's a big dog over at the paper. His friend, Mercury, works downstairs in the news morgue, sometimes known as the first level of Hell. Mercury is a kind of a genius. Cason told him about us, explained our problem and left us to it.

Down there they have all the back issues of the paper, as well as all manner of stuff, stacked up this way and that. You have to wind your way through it all to find Mercury. Down there he was king. Of course, he was the only one that worked down there, so the job position was easily filled.

Mercury was blond and pale, but looked strong. His job was to put all the old newspapers on the computer, then send the originals off to somewhere where they were collected by someone for some reason unknown. In his spare time, Mercury conducted investigations of his own. Some of them were nutty. Crop circles. Flying saucers. The Kennedy assassination, involving everyone but Bigfoot, though in time he might work him in as well. But he was smart and helpful, if you could point his nose in the right direction. He loved a good mystery, and he had a way of calculating odd situations into a recognizable patterns.

After we wound our way through the stacks and came up on Mercury, he said, "Welcome to the center of the earth."

The overhead light was thin back there, but there was a bright lamp on his desk, and there was another on a table that was pushed up against it. Both lamps had metal shades over the bulbs, but those had been tilted so as to let more of the light leak out.

On the table were books, assorted newspapers, clippings, an old microfilm machine, and on a chair was a small TV and an old-fashioned VCR. The VCR cord was fastened to the back of the TV and plugged into a plastic power strip on the floor. The wire from his computer was plugged into the bar as well.

"How are you men?" he said.

"We're fine," Leonard said. "Cason says you can help us."

"That depends. He told me what you're looking for, and I've pulled out a few things, got some stuff on the computer I can show you."

Mercury inched over to it, seated himself in front of it, touched a button. The computer lit up like a Christmas display. "There's not a lot here, but what's here is of interest. Here is the path of the bookmobile."

We took a gander at the place he was pointing, a map with a moving arrow.

"You can see that it covered quite a bit of ground, but most of it, the places where Harriet stopped, were right near Nesbit. Made a few stops in areas where there were neighborhoods, if you can call a half-dozen houses neighborhoods. Folks wanted books, they either had to be in town at the post office at the right time, or they had to be at one of these stop areas. Six altogether. Last two stops were well out in the country. Wasn't like it was a money-making business, driving the bookmobile. Harry came once a week, three times a month, then there was a week off. When she wasn't making this run through Nesbit and the surrounding area, she was on other routes. She drove four days a week, three weeks a month."

Mercury showed us a few more routes around LaBorde, a spot or two out in the country that were destinations.

"Those are routes on days when she worked outside of the Nesbit area. Way I'd think about it is Harry was from Nesbit, so that would be the hub of everything for her. Also, there have been missing persons cases around Nesbit in the last few years, couple of kids, and Harriet Hoodalay."

"Quite a coincidence," Leonard said.

Mercury considered for a moment.

"Place small as Nesbit, you want to connect anyone to the missing kids, you could make the case for everyone there, the community being so small, being so few people. And the missing kids came from the area. Also possible none of what happened in and around Nesbit is related, but that's where you can make the case that there might be too much coincidence. The law of averages come into play. Someone in or around Nesbit is most likely responsible for the kids, but are they responsible for Harriet and the bookmobile? Still likely."

"Harry and the bookmobile could have come up missing on one of the other routes," I said.

"Merely saying the most likely scenario is it happened near her home, near Nesbit, and probably someone who knew her, and the two missing kids are related to it all, because that's who a bookmobile is specifically designed for. Anyone can check out a book, but it's bored kids, kids that don't have library access, that they are trying to appeal to. Thing is, now even poor kids have computers and the internet, and with all the lights and bells and whistles, books get lost to a time when we had more patience and less to distract us."

"We found more than two kids in the bookmobile," Leonard said.

"Can't help you there, but if you nose around a bit, you might find more missing than have been reported. I'm going to strongly guess they are all from the same area, and what you're dealing with is a child predator, someone who likes to stick close to the place he knows. Way it usually works in these cases. And one reason you may not know about the other kids is they may not have been reported. Neglect is just the thing that puts them in a bad spot, causes them to fall between the cracks. Not the only thing, but a major factor."

"Think it could have been Harry?" Leonard asked.

"Could be, but then we got to ask, where has she been all this time? After she disappeared there were no more child abduction cases reported, so that leans toward her possibly being responsible, but she doesn't fit the profile, and nothing was known about the bookmobile until it nearly ran you over. The kid inside, that leans toward him being a victim as well, or a potential victim. An escapee. But I go back to what I said before. Just because we have a report of two children doesn't mean that's all there is. You found six bodies, and one not a child, that could be folks who haven't been reported, and the adult could just be Harry."

Mercury paused, tapped the keys. A new image came up. It was of a middle-aged black woman.

"Harriet Hoodalay," he said. "What I found from looking through older microfilm. You know about her supposedly taking a bus trip to see her sister, I assume. Her not arriving?"

"Do you know who first reported her missing?"

"Gardner Moost."

"General store guy?" Leonard said.

"Correct," Mercury said. "Said he got that information from her husband, Tom Hoodalay. Tom didn't report her missing when her vacation ended and she didn't come back. Gardner asked why she hadn't come home and Tom told Moost he figured Harriet had run off from him."

"What's Harriet's sister say?"

"She never arrived, but she did buy a bus ticket. No one was doing a head count when it came time to get on the bus, and the bus line closed down its hub here years ago. Whoever worked there back then has scattered to the wind."

"Maybe Harriet found out something about her husband," I said. "Like how Tom was using her connection to children to do something he wasn't supposed to. She decided to get away from him, go see her sister. He was afraid she'd spill the beans to the law, so he killed her."

"Possible, but unknown," Mercury said. "But Nesbit, that's where you begin."

SIX

We drove over to Nesbit in my car.

It was a nice drive and a nice day. Not too warm for the time of year. We cruised along the highway for several miles, and into an area where the trees grew thick and the houses were far apart.

Nesbit was off the highway, down a roughly paved road. As we came into the community we saw the post office on one side, general store on the other. Tire and mechanic shop, and so on, were all nearby. We were through the place before we knew it, and I had to turn around and drive us back. First place we stopped was the general store.

It was like stepping back in time. The place was chock-full of cool items, things that I forgot existed, like mule plowing equipment. Not a lot of it, but even some was surprising. There were long shelves of canned goods, prepared by locals, sold on consignment, and there were the sort of things you expected. High shelves with bolts of cloth. Tools. There was a series of bins in the middle of the store, stuffed with fresh vegetables and, according to a sign, locally raised.

There was a counter with a lot of old candies and soft drinks I had forgotten about. There was a break in the piles of goods on that counter, and there was an old-fashioned cash register with a black man behind it, sitting on a stool. He was a big fellow, and though he was sitting, I could tell he would tower over both me and Leonard. He had shoulders as wide as a bank vault. He had a red tone to his skin, what in the old days they used to refer to as a redbone Negro, when they were being polite. He had reddish freckles scattered on his cheeks. His hands, which were clutched around a hunting magazine, were about the size of catcher's mitts. He looked to be in his sixties, had a fringe of white hair around his head, just over his ears and nowhere else.

At the counter we greeted him. He put down his magazine and eyed us carefully.

"I help you fellas?" he said.

"Maybe," I said. "We work for a private detective agency out of LaBorde. We're trying to find out about James Clifton. I'm Hap Collins, and this is my associate, Leonard Pine."

"Gardner Moost," he said. "Yeah. Sad story. But what can be done for him now?"

"What we're trying to figure out," Leonard said, "is how he came by a bookmobile that had been missing for years, and what was he doing driving it?"

"Don't know what I can tell you. Poor boy was hard luck. Lost most of his family. Good kid, though. Had him a little part-time job at the tire shop. You know, picking up things a couple hours after school. Old tires, this and that. He was sleeping at different homes. He slept in the back here a few times. I was thinking of letting him stay full-time. Maybe give him a little work on the weekends. Tire shop didn't use him all week. As for the rest, I don't know. I don't think I saw him around the week he ended up gone. I doubt he was going to school. Was supposed to be, but I'd see him walking down the road, not really seeming to be going anywhere. An hour later, you'd see him walk back. I guess I saw him last on a Monday. Then the rest of the week he wasn't about.

Didn't think much of it. Reason I know he was missing is because he finished up at the tire shop, he'd come over, buy him a pop and a candy bar. Every day. Next thing I know he's dead, and I hear he was in that old bookmobile. Beyond that, I don't know a thing about him or the missing bookmobile."

"Did you know Harriet Hoodalay?" I said.

That gave Moost pause.

"Yes. I did know Harry. Lovely woman."

"Do you know her husband?" I said. I knew he did, from what Mercury had told us, but I wanted to see where he'd go with it.

He nodded. "Yeah."

"We ask," said Leonard, "because Harriet used to drive the bookmobile, then she disappeared. Supposed to be going up North to see her sister but never made it."

"I never believed that story," Moost said.

"Oh," I said, "and why is that?"

"I think she might have meant to see her sister, but I don't think the bus took a wrong turn at Amarillo and let her out in a pasture, or some such. I think her husband killed her. Tom's a mean sonofabitch. Me and him don't get along. He shops somewhere other than here. I banned him from the store when Harry came up missing those years back."

"You say he's mean," Leonard said. "But how mean?"

"He beat on her from time to time."

"So you and her were close?" I said.

"Look, if you two are going to be snooping about,

might as well tell you. Me and Harry, we had a thing. Went on for a while. She told me Tom was brutal. I saw the bruises. She was going to take a bus and see her sister, all right, but the plan was me and her would get together later. She'd get a divorce and we'd marry. But she didn't get a divorce, and she didn't come back. At first, at least a little, I thought she had changed her mind, didn't want what I thought she wanted. But deep down, always figured her husband did her in. Told the cops that, some sheriff's deputy, but they didn't find anything to prove it. They dropped it. I told Tom last time he was in here, years ago, not to come back, just because I didn't like him. Later, I married. Still married. Happily. But me and Harry, we had our moment."

"Slightly off the subject," I said, "but the bookmobile. Did she like that work? Ever have any problems?"

"She mentioned a bit of this and that. Kids stealing a book, acting up. But nothing special. She did seem tense days before she was supposed to catch that bus."

"Tense?" Leonard said.

"Maybe her husband was worrying her. He didn't know she wasn't coming back, but I think right before she left, she might have told him. Couldn't hold it in. Figure they got in a fight, he killed her, and she's buried somewhere out in the woods behind their house."

I didn't say we thought she might have ended up in a compartment in the bookmobile.

"Anything special you remember about the bookmobile from that time?" Leonard said.

"That's been awhile."

"Anything?" Leonard said.

"Just that Turner, over there at the tire and mechanic shop, was going to fix the bookmobile up. Needed new tires, some general maintenance. Always leaked oil. No matter what they did to it, it leaked oil."

"So her route was closed out for her vacation?" I said.

"They had another driver, and I think Harry was supposed to drive the bookmobile over to him, but then the bookmobile disappeared, and that was it. People out of LaBorde who had been paying for it decided they weren't going to try and replace it, so that was all she wrote."

"Who was this new driver?" Leonard asked.

"Will Turner, works over at the tire shop."

SEVEN

Will Turner was a skinny man that I judged to be in his early forties, dark of skin, almost as dark as Leonard. He had a pleasant face and skinned knuckles, probably from dealing with tools and tires day in and day out, though it was hard for me to imagine a lot of business in Nesbit.

"Yeah," Will Turner said. "I took the job, but then the bookmobile got stolen, and that was the end of it. So I just work here for Donnie James. I been working here since I was a kid, started just like James did, doing odd jobs."

"What kind of kid was James?" I asked.

"Quiet. Never said much, so you never knew much about him. Did his work, couple hours a day. Except for that, he was kind of wandering about, sleeping and eating where he could. I don't really know much about him."

We were standing inside the doorway of the tire and mechanic shop. It was one of those doors that was wide and made of the same aluminum as the building. End of the day you pulled it closed and padlocked it. It was a small building, and it was stuffed with tires, and there was an upper deck supported by a series of two by eights, and one in particular looked as if it was about to retire from the job. It looked as if insects had been at it. There was a long aluminum building out back of the garage. We could see it through the open back section of the shop. Having the doors open on both ends was a good choice, because a nice breeze was blowing.

"That post there," I said, "it looks as if it's about to give up the ghost."

Will looked toward it. "Yep. I have to go up there and get a tire, mostly for older foreign cars, I'm always a little nervous. Take it slow and easy. Been on Donnie for a year to get it fixed. He can be cheap."

"If you don't mind me asking," I said, "you get a lot of business here in Nesbit?"

Will laughed. "Nope. Still, we got a reputation, and folks bring their cars in from miles around. We mostly make money on mechanic work, but we sell a few tires too. But a lot of business? No."

"Moost was telling us you been working here a long time," Leonard said.

"I have. That's a fact."

"Let me ask you something about Harriet Hoodalay and the bookmobile. She was supposed to pass that job to you, right?"

"That's right. I was only a kid then, twenty-three, working part-time here, and I needed extra money. Driving the bookmobile wasn't much, but hey, it was something to add to the pot."

"Did Harriet drop the bookmobile off with you?" I said.

"Was supposed to, that night. She didn't show, though. Thought she might have got tied up with something and I'd find out about it the next day. Figured she could have left it for me here at the garage. We discussed that as an option and I was figuring maybe she got confused on what we had finally decided. Next day I found out she and the bookmobile had gone missing. And I was out some easy money."

"Did you know Harriet well?" Leonard said.

"Not really. Nice lady, far as I could tell. Saw her around. Knew she drove the bookmobile. She brought it here to be worked on time or two. We talked a little. You know, small talk. Nothing special. I think she liked the job, liked kids. Never had any of her own."

"Okay," I said, "we'd like to talk to your boss, Mr. James."

Will looked at his watch. "Back about two. On lunch break. Takes longer breaks these days."

"What's the building out back?"

"Oh, boss has a tractor, some equipment for this and that. He goes around and does farm work from time to time. Breaking up gardens, sometimes large fields. Side work."

"Where would Donnie be having lunch? Home?"

"Naw. He's not married and he's a terrible cook. He can't put a peanut butter and jelly sandwich together without it tasting like tar paper. There's a little place down the road. Ethel's. Not much to it, open for lunch and dinner. Used to be open for breakfast, but stopped doing that last year. Alright food. Ethel and her husband Bernard run it."

"Thanks, Will," I said, and me and Leonard went out.

EIGHT

Ethel's was indeed small. A little, yellow frame house. What would have normally been the living room had been turned into a dining area. A few tables and chairs were scattered about. A counter had been put in, as well as an opening into the kitchen: a cutout in the wall where the food could be passed to the waitress, who I assumed was Ethel. She was petite, had a look on her face of perpetual worry, as if she feared forgetting a French fry order. Through the gap in the wall we could see a big black man, possibly Bernard, standing in front of an old-fashioned grill, flipping burgers. He looked big enough to turn over the grill.

Waitress said, "Pick a seat."

That was easy, the place was packed, except for one small table in the corner, and we took that. The table wobbled when I put my hands on it.

"Shall we eat?" Leonard said.

"Yep. Let's hope the food is better than the furniture."

"It's packed here," he said. "That's a good sign."

"Choices are limited."

I looked around trying to spot someone I thought might be Donnie. That was easy. A man with TIRE AND MECHANIC SHOP written across the back of a khaki work shirt was moving toward the cash register, his ticket in hand.

I got up, went over, said, "Are you Donnie James?"

He nodded.

I gave him the synopsis version of what me and Leonard were doing, convinced him to sit down with us, but not before I agreed to pay his check.

"I got to get back to work, fellas," he said. "Make this quick. I don't think I know a thing that could help. Thanks for lunch, by the way. I hope you find out who did what to those children. Saw in the paper about all those kids, and the woman in the bookmobile. Terrible. Coated in oil. Why would anyone do that?"

"Preserve the bodies a little," I said. "I think whoever did it liked looking at them. Oil probably killed some of the stink."

"I guess so," Donnie said.

"How well did you know Harriet?" Leonard asked.

"Not too well. Except for driving the bookmobile, Tom kept her on a pretty tight leash. I was you, he's the one I'd talk to. I figure he's got her in a fifty-gallon drum under his front porch. Tom's a jerk. Always thought men were trying to take Harry from him. One time, right here, they got into it at suppertime over something. He called her a bitch. She got up and went outside and stood by their pickup until he paid up and went out. I was sitting over there by the window. I saw him grab her arm and push her into the truck. He's a bully, even at his age, retired and always on his front porch or he's out back in the yard lifting weights. Old as he is, I seen him get into it at the post office with a young man over something. I don't know what. I'm sure it was Tom started things. But he whipped that young man like he was a heavy bag. Hit him at will, and finally dropped him. Gardner Moost stood up to him, though, about how he treated Harry. I mean, hell, everyone here knows everyone else's business. Gardner's owner of the general store."

"We've met," Leonard said.

"Then you've seen Gardner. Tom's afraid of him, and with good reason. When he was younger, Gardner cleaned out a few bars down Houston way, or so I've heard. But Tom is no slouch either. Got a bum knee, but I think Gardner could take him. Someone like you two, he'd run you together so hard he'd make one of you."

"We talked to Moost," Leonard said. "He told us about

Tom, how he banned him. Another thing. James Clifton. What kind of kid was he?"

"Didn't say much. Did some little clean-up jobs for me. Knew he had it rough, so I was trying to help him out. That's about all I got. Who works for who, here? You the boss, white man?"

"I want to be, but he won't let me," I said.

"And he won't let me," Leonard said.

"Brett Sawyer is our boss."

"Who's he?"

"She," I said.

"Ah," he said. "Well, good luck finding out what happened to Harry. She was good people. Like me, she cared about children. That's why I fixed that bookmobile on my own time, even donated tires. It was mostly children got something out of that bookmobile. Me, I was never much of a reader. Always figured by not being one I missed out on things. Might be doing something other than a tire shop if I'd gotten a real education. Then again, folks need tires and they need cars fixed."

"No disagreement there," Leonard said.

"I got to go. Good luck."

Donnie got up and went out.

Leonard said, "Tom Hoodalay seems to get a lot of bad marks."

"Maybe we ought to check Tom's report card personally," I said.

"Not until I get a burger. I'm so hungry I could eat the ass out of a menstruating mule."

NINE

The burgers were good. Much better than I assumed the ass of a menstruating mule would be. We ate, and found out from Ethel, who was indeed the waitress, where Tom Hoodalay lived.

It was a small house not far off the road near the center of Nesbit. It was down a narrow, cracked, concrete drive, and at the end of the drive was a small, dilapidated house with an old brown pickup in the yard.

Weeds grew waist high on both sides of the house, out to the edge of the drive, and the drive seemed to be fighting a losing battle against the weeds growing up between the cracks in the concrete. Another few months, you could film a Tarzan movie out there. There was a small overhang porch, and there was a long wooden bench on the porch, and on the bench sat a man I took for Tom Hoodalay. He was crouched there like a frog on steroids.

We parked in the drive next to the pickup, got out and walked up to the steps. There were chunks of concrete breaking off in the drive next to the step. Leonard put his foot on a chunk and wobbled it with his boot.

"Who the hell are you?" the man said.

Up close I could tell he was in his sixties, but it was a powerful sixties. He had a head like a soccer ball. It was shaved and smooth as an oiled doorknob and glistened in the sunlight. He had a lot of white teeth and his eyes were both red where they should be white. His pupils, swimming in the middle of all that redness, were chocolate-colored. He had very little neck and was almost as wide as Gardner Moost. I thought the two of them went at it, it might be a close fight.

Nesbit seemed to have a lot of large people.

"We're Avon," Leonard said.

"The hell you are," the man said.

"Naw, just messing with you," Leonard said. "You Tom Hoodalay?"

"What if I am?"

"Might be a prize involved," Leonard said. This had already gone south. Leonard obviously didn't like the guy on sight. I wasn't fond of him either, and all he had said so far was "Who the hell are you?"

"We work for a private detective agency out of La-Borde," I said. "We are looking into the death of a child, James Clifton."

"That worthless little nigger? Shit, he better off dead."

"Why would that be?" Leonard said.

"Ain't got nobody, ain't got no future," Tom Hoodalay said.

"He wrecked a bookmobile that had been missing for fifteen years, one your former wife used to drive," I said.

"Heard about that," he said.

"Any idea where the bookmobile was all these years?" I asked.

"How the fuck would I know? I been asked that already. Years ago."

"Your wife used to drive it," I said. "I thought you might have some clue."

"I ain't got nothing to do with where she went, or where that damn bookmobile went. I ain't got no concern about neither."

"You're saying the kid was better off dead, huh?" Leonard said.

"What I said, ain't it?"

"Cause you wouldn't want James to end up . . . like you?"

"What the fuck you talking about, nigger?"

With that, Tom Hoodalay stood up. He was even bigger than I thought.

"Way we got it figured," Leonard said, "is you used to slap your wife around, because you could. What happened, Tommy? Wife catch you with your dick up a kid's ass?"

Tom actually yelled. More of a bellow really. He turned, and slammed his fist down on the long bench. It shattered, some of the fragments hitting me in the chest.

"Damn," I said.

"You showed that bench," Leonard said.

My man Leonard is never one to use common sense in an excitable moment. He's more akin to the guy that throws gasoline on a fire, then goes to get more.

Tom Hoodalay was coming off the porch. He limped a little, an old injury was my guess. He brought a leg of the bench with him, and he was swinging it about, and he wasn't all the way down the steps yet.

Leonard picked up the chunk of concrete under his foot, cocked it back, said, "Bet you flinch," and threw it.

The sunlight caught the white concrete and made it shine, and then it hit Hoodalay right between the eyes. He staggered, came tripping along and collapsed to his knees. David had just knocked the shit out of Goliath.

Hoodalay loosened his grip on the bench leg. Leonard sprang forward, grabbed the leg, said, "Give me that."

And then Leonard swung the leg, caught Tom Hoodalay right upside the head, causing him to go face down into the driveway.

"There's your prize," Leonard said.

"So much for asking questions," I said.

Leonard tossed the bench leg away and looked down at Tom's unconscious body. "He wasn't gonna tell us anything anyway."

"You hit him pretty hard," I said. "Maybe too hard."

"I just stunned the hippopotamus," Leonard said. "Wakes up, he'll wish he hadn't torn up a perfectly good bench."

"Or got hit between the eyes with a piece of concrete and then battered with a board."

"That too," Leonard said.

TEN

As I was driving us away, Leonard said, "I don't like

that bastard, but I don't think he killed the kids. Call it instinct, and also the fact that though he's big, he gets around like a pig on stilts. Maybe he killed his wife, but a guy like him strangles his wife, then tells the cops it was self-defense. She came at him with a paring knife, or some such. I don't think he's smart enough to plan what to do with the body, and certainly not smart enough to stay quiet about it all these years. He's the kind of dumbass brags about a thing like that."

"Maybe," I said.

I drove us around a bit, nothing really in mind. We tossed out an idea or two, but we arrived at nothing. Anybody we had spoken to could have done it, and none of them could have done it.

I finally convinced Leonard to let me drive back to Tom's place, just to make sure he wasn't collecting vultures.

"He might shoot at us this time," Leonard said.

I drove back there anyway, and as we came up the drive, I could see that he was no longer lying where we left him. Fragments of the bench had been gathered up and stacked by the porch steps.

"All right," I said. "He lives."

We backed out, and I drove us back to LaBorde. There wasn't anything else left for us to do. I dropped Leonard off at his place, and then I called Brett. She was at the office, finishing up some paperwork on a divorce case she had been working. I hated that kind of stuff, but frankly it was the sort of business that kept us in biscuits.

When I arrived at our office and parked in the lot, the

bicycle shop lady downstairs was wearing her shorts, as usual. I noticed, as usual, because I'm biologically driven to do so, then I went upstairs and saw the only woman that really matters to me in that kind of way.

Brett said, "So, find out anything?"

"Found out we don't know anything."

Brett was sitting behind the desk with her hair pulled back into a ponytail. She was working on some papers with a pen. She was dressed in jeans and an oversized tee-shirt, had on slip-on white tennis shoes.

"I got a little bit of paperwork left, then we can get something to eat. Nothing fancy, obviously. I want to stay sloppy."

"LaBorde doesn't have much that's fancy," I said.

"True," she said, and got busy on her paperwork.

I picked up the newspaper on the edge of the desk, started reading. The bookmobile and the murder of James Clifton weren't even on the second page. Third page, at the bottom. The article was thin. James had been driving, he ran off the road, hit a truck (occupants un-named, but unhurt), and there was an investigation into his death and into the mystery of where the bookmobile had been all these years. Some bodies had been found.

By the time I had finished reading the rest of the paper, which didn't take long, Brett was up and we were out. We traveled in my car. After dinner, I would drop her back at the office to pick up hers.

We went to a small joint that served Ecuadorian food. It was off Universal Street, and it was good. After I dropped

Brett back at her car, we met up at the house. It seemed a little empty when we first came in. My daughter Chance had been living with us, along with a rescue mutt we named Buffy. Actually, Leonard had rescued her, but I had ended up with the dog. Now Buffy was with Chance. Until last year, I didn't know I had a daughter. I missed her. I missed Buffy.

We watched a couple TV shows, then we went to bed. I fell asleep quickly. I didn't sleep long. When I awoke it was still solid dark. I had dreamed I was reaching for a butterfly that kept flittering out of the way. I had an uncomfortable feeling that butterfly was representative of me having knowledge I didn't understand. A common problem. Then again, I might have merely been dreaming about butterflies. Thing was, now, I was wide awake.

To keep from tossing and turning, I slipped out of bed, went downstairs and made an early breakfast. After I finished my oatmeal, I sat and sipped coffee, glancing out the kitchen window at the darkness. I tried to collect my thoughts, tried to catch my butterfly. I thought about all of the people we had talked to, thought back on that poor kid's face as the bookmobile barreled down on us. I thought back to finding those oily bodies in the container in the bookmobile. And then I thought, wait a minute.

I called Leonard on my cell. He was none too happy to hear from me.

"It's dark outside," he said.

"All the better for clandestine activity," I said. "Get

dressed. I'm coming to pick you up."

"You don't dare come this way for an hour," he said. "I'm going to eat and shower, but right before that, me and the extra-nice Officer Carroll are going to play rodeo."

Officer Carroll, as we both called him, was Leonard's new love interest. Nice guy and a nice cop, one of Marvin's people.

"Don't get any rope burns," I said. "But an hour is too late. It still needs to be dark when we get where we're going."

"Twenty minutes, then," Leonard said.

"Bring protection."

"We use protection."

"No. Bring it, and I don't mean the kind you're talking about. You show up with a Trojan and I'll beat you to death."

"I use one of those big garbage bags, you know, something that'll hold the meat."

"Yeah, right."

I had another cup of coffee, took a quick shower, wrote Brett a note, dressed and drove over to Leonard's apartment. Officer Carroll was coming out as I arrived. He's constructed like a large artillery shell.

"I hope you boys aren't going to get in trouble," he said.

"Us? Heaven forbid."

"Don't tell me anything. I know it's best I don't know."

After I got Leonard hustling along, a granola bar in one fist, a cup of coffee in the other, I told him what had come to me, and then I drove us back to Nesbit.

ELEVEN

It was still dark, and in East Texas, wandering about near people's homes and places of business during the night is the sort of thing that could get you shot. Growing up I had been able to walk to people's houses if the need came about and ask to borrow their phone, or some such, without expecting to be shot into Swiss cheese by some fearful and angry homeowner. The days of close neighbors had almost passed, and in its place was a cloud of anger and suspicion and a lot of hardware of the killing kind.

Still, we parked to the side of the general store and chanced it, walked between the store and the tire shop, wandered out to the big building at the back of Donnie James's place. There was a night-light in front and back of the building, and we stood out like bugs in a porch light. I took out my handy little lockpick kit, and easily defeated the padlock. Once we pulled the door aside, there was yet another door, and its locks were a little more difficult.

"Hold it," Leonard said. "Alarm system."

Leonard had discovered a little black panel on the inside of the second door fastened to the wall. He took out his pocketknife and popped the cover, used the blade to cut a wire.

"Might as well have been on the honor system," he said.

We got that door slid aside as well, then closed it be-hind us. I took out my penlight and flashed it around. There was a big tractor in the center of the building, some farm equipment attachments, and not much else.

We walked around for a while, but no clues jumped at us.

"Okay," Leonard said. "What are we looking for?"

"I don't know exactly, but I have a strong feeling it's here."

Leonard pulled out his own penlight, and we split up and went around the building looking for whatever might look like a clue.

Reason we were there was I had thought about Donnie James. He had mentioned the boys' and the woman's body in the bookmobile, but then reading the paper, where he said he got his news, I realized that the bodies in the book-mobile had not been mentioned. Marvin had most likely not revealed those things on purpose, to have one up on the killer, so how had Donnie James known about it?

It was possible someone leaked the information, but if they had, I doubted it went all the way to Nesbit and to the owner of a tire shop. Again, possible, but not likely. Marvin ran a tight ship.

We met up by the tractor, turned off our penlights and stood there a moment.

"Nothing," Leonard said.

"Same."

After a brief moment, Leonard turned back on his penlight, said, "Place looks bigger on the outside."

"Yeah."

"Because it is," he said.

I turned on my light again, flashed it around. On the right there were windows in the wall, and on the left there were not. That could have merely been a builder's choice, but something didn't seem right.

I started over to that wall, and Leonard went along with me. When we got there he tapped on it with his fist.

"Okay," he said. "Pretty sure it's hollow."

"No doors. No windows, but a hollow wall means another room."

"Uh-huh. And this aluminum looks fresh, like it's been added lately. Maybe after the kid stole the bus and ran off with it."

That got me excited.

We walked along the length of the wall, and near the front of the building I thought it looked a little odd. I pressed against it. The wall moved a little. There was a separate piece of aluminum that had been used to fill out the wall; it looked all of one piece if you weren't paying attention. I worked with it some more and it slid aside on rollers. It left a gap big enough to walk through, but there was a chain and lock through it and the main wall. We could have slipped under the chain, but I decided to make it easier.

I took out my lockpick kit and snapped the padlock open. Once that was done, we were able to push it wider. We slipped in behind it.

Using my penlight, I found a switch and flipped it. Lights came on along the stretch of hidden chamber. It was a full twelve feet wide, and maybe forty feet long. On the concrete floor was a dark oil stain, and at the far end of the room was a metal chair bolted to the floor. There were leather straps on the arm rest and at the base of the chair. There was a freezer behind the chair, and off to the side a metal box with air holes in it.

It was pretty obvious then. Recently the wall had been put up to hide what had formerly been in the open. Unlikely anyone was ever let in, but after James escaped, paranoia set in, and the wall was built to hide where the bookmobile had been parked, where the kidnapped boys were kept, and obviously tortured. I felt sick to my stomach.

Leonard walked over to the freezer and looked inside.

"Empty," he said. That caused me to let out a sigh of relief.

I went over to the box and lifted the lid. It too was empty. At least there weren't any others.

The bookmobile had been setting here for years, part of Donnie's murderous ritual, that and the oiled bodies that he had eventually put in the tank in the bookmobile, along with Harriet Hoodalay.

"Fits," Leonard said. "Donnie has a bad thing for boys, somehow Harry must have delivered the bookmobile here one night, night she was supposed to drop it off at Will's place, got her wires crossed about where, and in the process of leaving it at the tire shop she must have seen something that got her killed. Donnie hid her body and the bookmobile in here. Must have dug up those early bodies, oiled them all down and put them in the bookmobile with Harry's corpse."

"Sounds right," I said.

"Kept the bookmobile running and in good shape, checked on the bodies from time to time, see how they were marinating."

"Jesus," I said. I could visualize Donnie sitting in the bookmobile, starting it up, listening to the motor hum, feeling the thrill of being in control of the machine that brought children to it; that struck me as something the sick bastard might enjoy thinking about.

Leonard was still piecing it out. "He grabbed James, had him here awhile, but somehow James got loose while they were out, opened the door, stole the bookmobile and got away. Or tried to. Goddamn. Donnie is one sick fuck."

"Not sick, just different," a voice said.

We turned, and there was Donnie standing near the open section of the wall. He had slipped in quietly. He was holding a flat, black automatic.

"I thought I was pretty clever," he said, "way I built this room after the kid escaped. Lucked out he killed himself. If only you two had been killed, that would have ended my problems."

"You almost had me convinced it was Tom," I said.

"What was it, the newspaper?"

"Yep," I said.

"I thought about it later, hoped you wouldn't think about it too hard. You know, I don't mean to do the things I do, but I can't help myself."

"Yeah you can," Leonard said. "You don't want to."

"You could be right," Donnie said.

"There's another alarm, ain't there?" Leonard said.

"Yeah. You killed the obvious one, but there's another. You tamper with one, it sets off the spare. Goes off at the house. Somehow, I figured it was you two. That newspaper slip I made."

Will glided in through the gap in the wall and came up behind Donnie. For a brief moment I thought we had lucked out, but he walked up and stood by his partner.

"Took you long enough," Donnie said to him.

"Came fast as I could," he said.

And then I got the rest of it. Will had worked for Donnie for years, been groomed, and then he became part of the operation. Donnie had created Will in his image. It was the two of them doing the torturing, the killing. I was waiting for the inevitable.

That's when a gun went off. I expected I had been shot, but that's not what happened. I watched as Donnie sagged, slightly. There was another shot, and he went down on one knee and dropped his gun. Blood seeped out of his right shoulder and out of his right leg, splashed onto the floor, looked orange in the harsh light.

Will had darted out of the gap at the sound of the first shot.

I turned. Leonard was holding a little revolver in his

hand, an old-fashioned snub nose twenty-two. I looked back at Donnie. He was trying to pick up his gun.

"Nope, nope, nope," Leonard said, "or the next one gives you a hole in the head. Did you see that, Hap? I didn't miss either shot. Course I was aiming for his head with the first one."

I had forgotten I told Leonard to bring protection, and hadn't noticed the gun tucked beneath his shirt. I was glad that for once, he had listened to me.

"Go get Will," Leonard said. "I got this one."

I raced past Donnie, kicking his gun to the side as I went, then I darted out the gap in the wall, through the front door and into the crisp night air. I could see Will running toward the tire shop. He was almost there. I jogged after him.

When I got to the shop, Will had already opened the door and slipped inside. I eased into the dark building and fetched up behind some tires on racks. There was a shot and a chunk of rubber flew out of one of the tires and hit me in the face, hard. That shot had missed me by inches.

I kept moving behind the rows of tires. The son-of-a-bitch had run in here to get a gun, and I had followed him inside, the way he had wanted. I was a duck in a shooting gallery.

There were three more pops, but all they did was ruin a couple more tires. At least he was a bad shot. I bent down behind the tires and tried to peek between a gap in them. It took a moment for my eyes to adjust, and I could make out his shape on the landing above, framed by the moonlight slipping past a little window up there. He was squatting, the gun pointing in my general direction, waiting for me to stick my head out.

I pushed a tire loose from the top rack. It bounced when it hit the floor, and when it did Will popped off a nervous shot. I was already moving, back along the row of tires, and then under the landing above. I rushed my way along until I was pretty near under him. I glanced at the sagging timber that helped hold the top floor up. I charged it, hit it with my shoulder, heard it crack—the board, not my shoulder, though I was certainly feeling pain. I hit it again, and I could feel it move this time, and then a third time and it came down in an explosion of lumber, tires, dust and unidentified crap. I tried to get out from under it, but I was too slow. I don't know anyone could have been fast enough.

Junk was lying on me. It was heavy. I was trapped. Looking out from under the debris, I saw Will rise up from the floor uninjured. I had only succeeded in making him fall, and pinning myself under the wreckage. He looked about, spotted what he could see of me under the junk and lifted his gun. There was a shot, and Will did a bit of sideways dance, then toppled to the floor.

I heard Leonard say, "Got 'em Boscoe," and then I passed out for a while.

TWELVE

Leonard dragged me outside and propped my back against the tire shop. That's where I was when he slapped me awake.

"Damn, quit that," I said.

"How do you feel?" he said.

"Like a bunch of lumber fell on me and then my brother started slapping my face."

"I enjoyed that a little," Leonard said.

"Did you kill Will?"

"Boy did I."

"Donnie?"

"Yeah. I went ahead and shot him too. He kind of died in a gunfight, but I was the only one shooting. Wasn't like I could tie him up. I knew you needed help. I could hear the gunshots."

"Jesus, Leonard."

"Wasn't like he needed a room with a bunk for the rest of his life, sitting in some cell breathing stale air and making turds. He needed a bullet. You dumbass, you should have took his gun with you."

"I didn't want to kill anyone."

"That's all right," Leonard said. "I did it for the both of us. I'm going to go back down there and fire off his gun a few times to make sure it looked like he put up a fight."

"That's cold, Leonard. He was unarmed when you killed him."

"Yeah. He was."

THIRTEEN

A crowd of people showed up, due to all the shooting. A light was shone in my face. Before their arrival, Leonard had fired off Donnie's gun so he could claim there was a shootout and that he had prevailed. The noise, along with all the other racket we had made, stirred the locals. By the time they arrived, Leonard was leaning against the wall next to me, his gun lying on the ground six feet away. Donnie's gun was back in the formerly secret room, probably firmly placed in his hand by Leonard.

The county was called out. We ended up in the back of a deputy sheriff's car, watching the car hood shimmer in the red and blue from the light bar. In time they brought us in for questioning and locked us up in county for a few days. Leonard at least had a concealed carry license, so illegally carrying a firearm wasn't added to the list.

Brett came to visit. They let her give us food she brought from outside. I don't think they're supposed to do that, but once the county realized what Donnie and Will had been doing, they treated us well. They had discovered photographs of the kids that dated all the way back to the first murder, and the photos had been ugly. The poor kids' dead and rotting bodies had been stacked in seats in the bookmobile and a timer on a camera had snapped away with Will and Donnie posing beside their wrecked remains like hunting trophies, which, in a way, I guess they were. There were all manner of things found on internet files. There were torture devices in Donnie's house. It was a pretty slam-door case. I don't know if they believed Leonard's story about the shootout. But if they didn't, no one said a word. There was also the fact that Donnie and Will had kept records of who the boys were and how long they had kept them, as well as all they had done to them. Their records solved all the murders. The victims, with the exception of Harriet (a relative's DNA proved it was her), were unwanted kids, lost and forgotten, tossed out like used condoms.

I guess Tom Hoodalay still remains an asshole, and Nesbit needs a new owner for the tire and mechanic shop, not to mention some renovation.

We were back home pretty quick, though there was a bit of talk about us getting into trouble for breaking and entering, maybe a fine, a little jail time. That idea got shuffled and forgotten, thank goodness. No one really wanted to punish us for what happened to those two, not even for the lesser charges.

I brooded for a few days over Leonard shooting Donnie in cold blood, stayed home and didn't go visit with him, didn't even take his calls. Then Brett said, "Get over it. Leonard saved your life. And it isn't the first time."

"I know," I said, "but I got to get right in the head. Killing doesn't bother him. Me, I feel different."

"You've killed, Hap, and if you had to, you'd do it again. Quit feeling sorry for yourself. I'm glad Leonard made sure you came home. Stop being a jackass."

She was right. I called Leonard later that day. He answered, said, "You been pouting, haven't you?"

"I have."

"Yeah, well, I knew you'd get over it."

"When it involves you, I always do."

"Yep."

"One question," I said. "After all that, after all the things we've done, the deaths, how do you sleep?"

"Deeply."

"I don't."

"I know."

"But, thanks, Leonard."

"You're welcome. Still sore from all that crap falling on you?"

"A little. Nothing serious. Thanks for pulling that off of me too."

"Welcome again. But you owe me. We working out today?"

"I need another day to feel bad about who I am."

"How about you take this day to know that there won't be anymore kids abused and murdered by those two, and you don't have a hole in your head and about six feet of dirt over you? Want to do that?"

"That's exactly what I'll do," I said.

"Alright, then. And Hap?"

"Yeah."

"Go fuck yourself. Talk tomorrow."

"Good night," I said.

SAD ONIONS

ME AND LEONARD WERE CRUISING BACK from a fishing trip.

We'd been at a cabin Leonard's boyfriend, Pookie, owned on the lake. Pookie couldn't make it, but we had the key, and we spent a partial day and a lot of the night sitting in lawn chairs on the cabin's deck where it overhung the water, sitting with big glasses of iced tea, now and again casting our fishing lines, hiding during the day under the shadows of our wide-brimmed straw hats, pushing them back on our foreheads at night to feel the cool breeze blowing off the lake, rippling the dark water.

We caught four fish and threw them all back. Those fish would have stories to tell. Hope word didn't get back to Aquaman. Things might turn nasty.

Of course, the trip wasn't about fishing, it was about me and Leonard hanging, without distractions, talking. We had been through the mill as of late, and some time off was doing us good, and it probably wasn't hurting my wife's feelings either. She and my daughter were spending a day doing pretty much the same thing Leonard and I were doing, minus the fish.

Now it was over and it was deep night, and I was driving us home. The moon was a silver slice. Shadows hung from the trees on either side of the narrow road like crepe paper at a funeral. We were fifty or sixty miles from home. I was driving Leonard's pickup and he was dozing on the passenger side. There were a lot of curves in the road and the headlights danced around the curves. I wasn't driving real fast, but I wasn't messing around either. I was ready to be home and in my own bed with Brett.

The road straightened out finally, rose up a hill where the trees were thick on my left and thin on my right. As the truck's headlights topped the hill a woman showed up in my lane, waving her hands.

I swerved and crossed into the left lane, wheeled around her, found the right lane again, skidded to a tooth-rattling stop that nearly sent me off the edge of the road, where I would have bumped over a short drop of weeds and rocks, and possibly would have fetched up against a barbed-wire fence. If the fence snapped, they might have found us and the pickup wearing a couple of cows.

Leonard came awake with a shout, looked at me. I didn't say anything. I got out of the truck and rushed back to where the woman stood in the road wringing her hands, crying and yelling, "He's down there."

She was pale of skin, had her blonde hair up in a pile.

Strands of it had slipped loose and had fallen across her face like leaking vanilla. By moonlight, and I assumed by any light, she had a very nice face. She was carrying a white purse. It was draped over her shoulder by a long strap. She was wearing an expensive looking white dress and had on a silver necklace and matching double bracelets on both wrists; they clattered together like the wagging tail of a rattlesnake. She wasn't wearing any shoes.

By that time Leonard was with us. His black skin looked like sweat-wet chocolate in the bright moonlight. It was that kind of weather, even late at night.

I said, "I'm going down for a look."

"I'll get her out of the road," Leonard said. "Come on, lady."

Leonard gently touched her arm, guided her toward his pickup. I watched them go away, him walking slow, her balancing on her naked toes like a ballerina, trying to put as little of her foot on the blacktop as she could manage.

I went down the hill. I could see a white Lincoln at the bottom of it. A ridge of trees stood in front of it, and between the trees I could see the barbed-wire fence that ran behind them. The car was mashed up primarily against a sweetgum tree, though part of an oak had got into the act. White smoke was hissing out from under the hood. The windshield was shattered, but still in place, the front of the Lincoln was as crumpled as an accordion.

I looked through the driver's window. There was an

elderly black man behind the wheel, the side of his head resting against it, a semi-deflated air bag pushed up against him; it made him look like a man hugging an oversized pillow. His face was turned toward me and the front of his bald head was warped so bad it looked like some kind of special effect. His face was coated in blood, his mouth was open and there were teeth missing. One of them had nestled on his blood-covered chin.

I tried to get the door open, but it was locked or jammed up. I went to the other side, and that door came open. I crawled across the seat and touched my fingers to the man's neck. He was as dead as my youth. When I got out of the car, I noticed the lady's high heels were there by her door, where she had left them to better climb the hill.

I climbed up the hill and got my cell out of my pocket, tried to call 911, but there wasn't any service.

I went to the truck and spoke through the open driver's side window.

"Listen," I said to Leonard. "You take her into town, or get to some place where there's service and call. I'll wait here."

"How is Frank?" she said.

"We'll let a doctor decide," I said.

She burst out crying. She sounded like a banshee. Leonard said something soothing, then wheeled them out of there, leaving me beside the road, standing in the moonlight, smelling the heat from the Lincoln's engine as steam rose up the hill in thinning, white plumes.

I went back down the hill, hoping I was wrong about him being dead. Nope. He was so dead there needed to be two of him.

As I walked around the car, I noticed there was a mark on the back end of it, and as I continued around it, I saw the front left tire was blown. On the passenger seat, there was blood. I hadn't noticed any on the woman, so I presumed it was the man's, thrown there by impact and gravity. I noticed too that some of that blood had got on my pants when I crawled across the seat.

By the time I climbed up to the road again, something was itching at the back of my brain.

Leonard came back not long after, but the ambulance and the emergency crew got there first, followed by the law. It was that county's sheriff's department, and we didn't know any of them. We are usually detained or arrested by someone we knew.

The entire hill was lit up by emergency lights. It looked like a night club up there. I answered some questions, gave the deputy, a stout black woman named Celeste Jones, all the information I had. She didn't look down the hill at the car. I guessed she wasn't the one for that. She made it easy for us and let us go.

Going home, Leonard driving, I said, "How was she?"

"Said she was Terri Parker, and she seemed to be rolling with the punches pretty good. She's twenty-seven, and the dead man is her husband, Frank Parker."

"You have that curious tone," I said. "Like the one you get when you realize you have on mismatched socks."

"I'm thinking I got another pair just like them at home. Hell, I don't know, Hap. I got a funny feeling is all."

"You and me both, brother."

When Leonard dropped me off at home, the porch light was on. I used my key, slipped in quietly. My daughter Chance had stayed over. She was sleeping on the couch. It actually folded out, but the thing was far more comfortable if you didn't bother with the foldout bed, which could feel a bit like a torture instrument from the Inquisition.

Her long, dark hair was hanging off the couch, touching the floor. I couldn't see her face. I had only known about her for a short while, never realized I had a daughter until she was an adult. It was pretty wonderful.

I went quietly into the kitchen, got the milk, poured myself a glass, found some animal cookies in one of the shelves, sat down at the kitchen table to snack on them in the dark.

After a while, I crept upstairs to the bedroom, slipped into the bathroom to brush my teeth, pulled on my pajama pants and climbed into bed.

Brett rolled over and put her arm across my chest. I could smell the sweetness of her hair, strawberry shampoo.

"Catch any fish?" she said.

I thought she was asleep and was surprised when she spoke.

"We caught them, looked them over and sent them home. There was something else, though."

She rolled over again and stacked her pillows behind her head, sat up against them. She didn't turn on the light.

"Like what?" she said.

I told her about the woman, the car and the dead man, ended with, "Something didn't seem right."

"You said the passenger seat was bloody?"

"That's right."

"Did she have blood on her dress?"

I thought about that for a long moment, remembered the shimmering whiteness of it. "I don't think so."

"She had her purse, but left the high heels at the bottom of the hill?"

"Yeah."

"Shock can make you do all kinds of funny things, but why didn't she carry the shoes with her is my first thought? Seems staged."

"That's pretty good for not being there," I said.

"I'm amazing. Now I'm sleepy again. Good night."

Brett readjusted her pillows, put her arm across my chest again, and went back to sleep.

I lay there thinking, which can be pretty painful on most occasions, but at that time of night when I should have been sleeping, it was akin to an injury.

I eventually slept.

I didn't go into the office until ten. By that time Brett had already gone to work, and Chance had gone home. Chance left a note.

DADDY. YOU ATE MY ANIMAL CRACKERS.
LOVE YOU. BUY MORE.

When I got to the agency, Brett and Leonard were there. Leonard was having his morning vanilla cookies, dipping them gently in coffee. Brett had her long, red hair clamped back and she was sipping from a mug of coffee about the size of a fish pond.

When I closed the door, Leonard said, "Brett asked me about the blood, and I got to say, like you, I didn't see a drop on her."

"I think she didn't want to sacrifice the dress," Brett said.

"Yeah," I said, "something about this whole thing stinks."

"Did you shower this morning?" Leonard said.

"You know what you can do," I said, and then I told him. It was anatomically impossible, but I told him anyway.

We spent the day tapping pencils against things, looking out the window, wondering what we would have for lunch. No one came in with a job. No one came in to ask our opinion on anything. There was nothing outside the window but a parking lot, and across the street some houses, and in the oak by the lot a squirrel jumped about now and then, but it was more like it was squirrel duty, no real enthusiasm there.

Brett made another pot of coffee and we sat looking at one another some more, saying nothing. Arguing politics wasn't going to cut it. We'd been there before. Leonard was the only black, gay Republican I knew who was a Vietnam war hero and only listened to country music. There are others I didn't know, of course.

Talking religion wouldn't work either. We were all atheist. So, we talked about the night before, kicked that around a bit, and since it was really none of our business, we got right on looking into it.

Leonard drove me and him out to the wreck site, while Brett stayed at the office and looked into the dead man, Frank Parker. Out at the hill, we parked off the road and made our way down to where the car had been.

It had been hauled off, but we could see clearly in the daylight where the tires had made deep marks in the earth as it jetted off the road. My phone may not have had service there, but it took good photographs, and I took a lot of them.

"One thing I realize now is the tree impacted on her side," I said. "But it was Frank who was all messed up. She came out pretty unscathed. And as has been noted, she wasn't covered in blood, even though the seat where she would have been sitting was. It was a hard-enough crash to make the bag pop, but was it enough to kill him? He had quite a lick to the front of his head, where the bag would have protected him."

"It do be curious," Leonard said.

"Let me add something else," I said. "The back bumper, I could see it well enough last night to see it was banged up."

"Like someone had used a car or truck to push it?"

"Could have been a bang from a previous accident, but. . . . And another thing, there are tire marks as the car goes off the road, but no skid marks."

"Yeah," he said. "Add it to the other stuff, it starts to paint a different picture. And you know what else I think?"

"She had help."

"Bingo."

Back at the office Brett said, "Frank Parker founded Sad Onions."

Chance worked with us part-time, and she was there too, her pretty face alight with youth, framed by that lovely hair, dark as the far side of the moon.

She said, "Sad who?"

"It's a chip company," Brett said. "They dry out onions into chips, and the chips are in a kind of . . . I don't know. Droopy shape. Anyway, Frank called them sad onions, because they're droopy. It's stupid, but hey, it caught. Company also makes chips made out of other vegetables. Get this, after the onions, their biggest seller is made from a dried turnip."

"Who eats that crap?" Leonard said.

"I've had them," Brett said, "better than you think. Some of them are salted, some are peppered, and some are straight dehydrated vegetables with no frills. Frank Parker started out an onion grower, over around Noon Day. Soil there is supposed to be great for onions. Makes them sweet. Anyway, he figured out how to dehydrate them and turn them into chips before every other company was doing it, and he got rich. And he got married."

"Terri," Leonard said.

"Yep. He was seventy, and she's twenty-five," Brett said.

"And a hottie," I said.

"Watch it, Buster," Brett said.

Chance snickered. She liked it when I was in trouble.

On the way to the sheriff's department that had investigated the crime, Leonard said, "I don't think that woman was ever in the car, that's what I think. She was down there waiting for someone to come by. Standing down there today, a car went by, and I heard it a long time before it got there, because that's how sound is at the bottom of that hill. She left the shoes there to support the idea she had been in the car, and to climb the hill faster."

"I think you're right."

"That's a first," he said. "Next thing you'll learn to love guns and quit supporting liberal politics."

"I don't think so," I said.

At the sheriff's department, they let us cool our heels in an interrogation room, something we were professionals at. It was a full thirty minutes before Deputy Celeste Jones came in.

"You wanted to see me?" she said, and took a chair at the table across from us.

"We don't think that wreck was just a wreck, and we don't think the lady fair is true and blue," I said.

Celeste turned her head and cracked her neck. I almost expected it to fall off.

"Yeah," she said. "Why are you thinking that?"

We gave her our thoughts on the matter, showed her the photos on my phone. She got out a pad and wrote down some notes, then it was over and all three of us were walking toward the front door.

Celeste said, "Something stinks, gentlemen, but the sheriff thinks it is exactly what it looks like. He's not the sort to disbelieve a pretty, blonde white woman."

"But you are?" Leonard said.

"Sometimes," she said. "But I'll tell the sheriff what you said, how you feel. Up to him to figure out what to do about it."

It was about 9 a.m. the next morning when we heard someone coming up the outside stairway to the office. I went to the window that overlooked the lot and took a gander. There was a sheriff's car from the next county in the lot with a crunched front end. The law showing up is seldom good, even if they're out of their jurisdiction.

There was a gentle knock. I opened the door. There was a young, lean, black man standing there holding his white cowboy hat. He wore a sheriff's outfit and a deputy sheriff's badge. He had hound dog eyes and a soulful look, a smile with enough fine teeth an alligator would have envied him.

I invited him in. He shook hands with all of us, sat in front of the office desk and looked across at Brett, which was a view I envied. I sat in a chair at the corner of the desk, next to Leonard, who had his butt parked on the edge of the desk.

"My name is Journey Clover, and really, that's my name."

I figured that was remarked on a lot, and he wanted to clear up questions right away.

"Okay, Deputy Clover," Brett said.

"I came over to tell you that the whole thing with the wreck, the thing you fellows came across, has been wrapped up."

"You came all the way over here to tell us that?" Leonard said.

"Seemed the polite thing to do, considering you came by yesterday to voice some suspicions. I'm here to tell you we have done a thorough investigation, and it was nothing more than an unfortunate accident."

"That's a quick investigation," Brett said.

"We have good people," he said.

"They must be damn good," Leonard said. "Two days later and it's done?"

"Simple case," he said. "Listen, I don't want to be impolite, and we appreciate your concern, your ideas about this, but people, it's done. It was nothing more than an accident."

"And you'd rather we not poke our nose into it?" Leonard said.

"I suppose that's right. I knew Mr. Parker well, by the way, liked him. I used to be an insurance salesman before I went to work at Sad Onions. Sold him some insurance. He seemed like a really nice guy, did lots of charity work."

"What insurance company did you work for?" Brett asked.

"Regency Mutual," he said. "I wasn't much of a salesman. Sold Parker a policy, liked him, and went to work for him in the office. I have an accounting degree. But it didn't suit me, so I ended up in the sheriff's department."

"That means you knew his wife as well?" Leonard said.

"Not much, a little. On sight, that sort of thing. She came into the office, of course, went to lunch with Parker. But, hey, that's all I got. Celeste wanted to keep you in the loop. She said she had suspicions too, but the investigation closed them out. She feels it's all been answered. Well, got a bit of a drive, so nice to meet you. Just wanted you to know."

After Deputy Clover left, Brett said, "Tell me I'm not the only one that found that odd."

"You're not the only one," Leonard said.

I nodded. "Yeah. Drives all the way over here to tell some civilians how things turned out. Usually you can't get a thing out of the law, even if you're the victim."

"It do be peculiar," Leonard said.

"Yes, it do," Brett said. "Follow the money. Meaning I'm going to talk to some insurance folks I know, then see what I can find out about Mrs. Parker. You and Leonard check up on Clover."

Me and Leonard drove over to Clemency, which was the town where Clover's office was located. Leonard was at the wheel and I was sitting in the passenger seat watching the scenery rush by.

"Front end of Clover's car was smashed in," I said. "Wonder what the story is on that?"

"You're thinking like me. What if Clover gave Parker a little push from behind, sent him down that hill into those trees."

"I was thinking what if Parker was dead before he went over the edge in the car. His head was really bashed in, and it seems to me the airbag would have prevented a wound that bad. I think they killed him and stuffed him in his car and he bled like a stuck hog. Also thinking since Clover knew him and his wife, maybe Clover wanted to be in the clover, decided to help the wife bump the hubby for some insurance money, and she came with it?"

"But why would he leave Sad Onions, become a deputy, if he wanted to be near her?" Leonard said.

"Husband could have got suspicious, so Clover needed to put some space between them."

"Maybe," Leonard said.

We stopped in at a greasy spoon that looked like a railroad boxcar. We had caught it at a time when no one was there but us. We bellied up to the counter, ordered coffee and a burger.

The lady who brought us our food was a middle-aged white lady with a tired face, but a sweet attitude. She wore an old-fashioned waitress cap that was precariously perched on her hairdo, which was intended to be blonde, but looked like an enormous wad of pink cotton candy.

If anyone knows the citizens of a town, it's a café worker, a barber or a bartender. I gave her my most heart-warming smile.

"We're wondering about an old friend of ours, Deputy Clover. You know him?"

"I do," she said, "and if you're such good friends, why are you wondering to me?"

"Touché," I said.

"Thing is," Leonard said, "we're insurance investigators."

"Yeah?" she said. "So not old friends."

"There was an accident outside of town, on that high hill. A man was killed," I said. "We're looking into some possibilities."

"Possibilities?"

We didn't respond to that.

"Cutting to the chase," Leonard said, "you ever see Mrs. Parker come in with Clover?"

"Nope, not once, but she didn't act like much of a wife."

"No?" I said. I tried to say it like the idea of infidelity was something I had never considered or even heard of.

"Way she hung on that woman when she was in here, in the back booth there . . . I just don't get it. Two women?"

"What woman?"

"The black deputy at the sheriff's department."

Click.

Outside in the car I said, "So, what did we learn?"

"We learned that waitress doesn't like two women together, so I have to make sure to bring my Pookie here for lunch someday and rub up against him, see how she likes two men."

"You are such a devil," I said.

"We also learned that Deputy Jones talks a good

game, but by acting concerned about the event, and then clearing it as an accident, it seems she may be throwing suspicion off herself."

"But what about Clover? He's the one that came over to talk with us, and his car has a banged bumper. Might have come from pushing Parker's car off the road."

"You know, we ought to go to the department, thank Deputy Clover and Deputy Jones in person for keeping us in the loop. See how that plays."

We drove over there, didn't find Deputy Jones, but Clover was still around.

In the breakroom at the sheriff's department, Deputy Clover said, "You came all the way over here to thank me for what you already thanked me for? We talked yesterday."

"We're very polite," Leonard said.

"Sounds to me like you're piling up something I might need hip boots to walk through."

"Your cruiser, man, it took quite a lick to the front," I said.

He studied us for a moment. I kept expecting him to pin us and mount us on a board.

"That's Deputy Jones's car. Borrowed it while mine had some general inspection. Just did a favor for her, letting you guys in on things."

"Where is the good deputy," Leonard said, "so we can thank her in person?"

"Her day off. I'm starting to try and figure how I can make things difficult for you boys."

"Boys?" Leonard said. "You call an alligator a lizard?"

"You should go now," Clover said.

When we were in the car, the phone rang. It was Brett. I put the phone on speaker.

"Insurance payout for Parker's death will be plenty," she said. "Enough to live on for the rest of your life."

"Would it be enough for two?" I asked.

"Maybe for four, five, as long as they didn't trade their Maserati in every year."

I told her what we found out.

"Hang on," she said.

I could hear keyboard keys clicking. In a bit she came back said, "I got Celeste Jones's address for you."

Deputy Jones lived in a simple house outside of town, somewhat secluded. There was a cruiser parked in front of the house. There was no garage or carport.

We went up to the door and Leonard knocked. While we waited, I glanced at her cruiser. It was in good shape. Had it already been fixed?

No one answered the door.

"You know, Hap, I'm not feeling good about this."

I walked over to one of the windows, cupped my hands

together, looked inside.

"You're about to feel less good," I said.

Leonard came over for a peek, said, "That's not good."

"No, sir, it isn't."

We could see Deputy Jones sitting on the couch, her head thrown back. She looked very comfortable, not a care in the world, and this was due to the fact that she was as dead as Christmas past.

We hustled around back and used my lockpick to enter through the back door. Deputy Jones hadn't become undead and gone into the kitchen for a soda. She was still in her position on the couch. She had a small bullet hole right between her eyes.

"Up close and personal," Leonard said.

"I think Mrs. Parker may have decided she didn't want to share the money," I said.

"Bingo," said a voice sweet as Georgia honey. It was Terri Parker, of course. She was holding a shiny little revolver, and it was pointed at us. "Sit on the couch."

"By her?" Leonard said.

"Yeah," she said, "by her. She won't bite."

We sat on the couch, away from the blood as best as possible. Terri stood near us, held the gun like someone who knew what they were doing.

I heard a car drive up. From where I sat I could see directly out the window. It was another sheriff's cruiser.

I felt a moment of hope, but when I saw Clover step out of the dented car, I knew we were in a deeper pit than expected.

Terri unlocked the front door and let Clover in. He looked at us and the deputy on the couch.

"Should have left things alone," he said to us.

"I'm thinking kind of the same thing," Leonard said.

"I had to shoot Celeste," Terri said to Clover. "She grew a conscience. Then these two losers came in."

"That's all right," Clover said. "Splits better two ways."

It clicked then. It had really been Terri and Clover all along, and the whole thing with Deputy Jones had been a cold-blooded attempt to make her sympathetic, help clear up the investigation. But Jones got covered in guilt, so she had to go.

And now, so did we.

When night had settled in good, we were walked out to Clover's cruiser, forced into the backseat, along with Deputy Jones's body, which we had to carry. We propped her up between us.

Clover had wrapped Jones's head in towels and then put a black trash bag over it, tightened it around her neck with a bathrobe belt. Leonard and I were both put in handcuffs. I wished for a moment that I had just taken the chance before that was done, been shot out in the open and had it over with.

As Clover drove, Jones's body rocked between us.

"You two have made things kind of messy," Clover said through the wire grating between the seats.

"That's our bad," Leonard said.

"However, there's a nice old abandoned gravel pit full of water where I think Jones and you two will be real comfortable," Clover said.

As Jones wobbled between me and Leonard, I managed the lockpick out of my front pants pocket, and was casually using it to unlock the cuffs. They went easy. When Terri glanced away, I passed Leonard the pick across Jones's body. He sat quietly and looked out the window, but his hands were working.

The car stopped at the end of a narrow road in the depths of the woods. We were near the gravel pit. We were eased out of the car at gunpoint. We could see into the pit, and it was filled with water; it was near big as a lake. The moon was up high and it had grown a little fuller. Its image lay on the dark water like a slice of fresh cantaloupe.

We had the cuffs draped over our wrists and we held our hands close to us. I was shuffled from my side of the car to the other by Terri and her six-shot accessory.

"Drag her out, drop her in the water," Clover said to us, nodding toward Jones's body.

"That's messed up," Leonard said, "us dragging her out and then you shooting us and putting us in the water."

"No," Clover said, "we'll shoot you on the edge of the pit. We won't have to do any carrying."

"Well, you thought that through, didn't you?" Leonard said.

"Get the body," Clover said.

"Sure," Leonard said, moving toward the open back door, "but Hap, first, the elephant of surprise."

That had become a kind of code for us. It meant do something, anything, and do it now.

I wheeled, let the cuffs drop, went low, clipped Terri at the knees, sending her flying over my back. I turned in time to see Leonard fling the cuffs in Clover's face and kick him in the crotch.

Clover staggered, but didn't go down. He fired awkwardly and missed. By that time, me and Leonard were running like gazelles down a wide path and into the woods. The path turned behind a thickness of trees. Several shots were fired at us. They rattled through the leaves like rain, and one of them nipped at my hair.

A moment later, we heard the cruiser fire up, and lights were cutting through the trees. Clover was driving the cruiser back down the path, trying to find us.

The trees were too thick with briars for us to hide in, so we ran down the curving trail until we came to where it ended, the gravel pit, dark water, and the floating moon. It was about twenty feet down to the water and there was a lot of garbage visible. Couches, washing machines, a broken dresser. It had become a dump, and that crap was probably stacked all the way to the bottom. Jumping wasn't going to turn out any better than being shot.

The car came around fast. We were trapped at a dead end. Me and Leonard split up. He went left, and I went right, into the woods on either side where the briars had thinned.

Clover skidded to a stop, got out with his pistol. Terri stayed in the car, slid behind the wheel. The window was down on the passenger side, and I could see her waving her gun through the open window. She couldn't wait to shoot somebody.

"I'm going to make you suffer if you make me hunt you," Clover yelled out, like it was incentive for us to just come on out and be shot.

I looked around, found a piece of pipe that had been tossed in the woods, tried to pick it up, but it was nothing but rust and came apart in my hand. Then I saw an old baseball that had been tossed out. I picked it up. The cover was mostly off, but it was firm enough, and it was all I had.

Clover was moving close to where I was hiding. I couldn't go toward him, because of the gun, and to go through the woods behind me led to the pit. I was between a killer and a wet spot.

I cocked the ball back, stepped between two trees, into the open. Clover saw me. I flung the ball. It was a good throw. There was some real meat behind it.

It sailed beautifully across the moonlit trail, and glided over Clover's shoulder. I felt like an idiot.

Clover looked at me, grinned, raised the pistol.

That's when someone screamed.

Clover wheeled to look, and I dropped back into the woods, out of the line of fire, near the edge of the pit. I saw from my hiding spot the source of the scream was Terri. Leonard had come out of the woods on the driver's side, surprised her, and grabbed her gun arm, which she was hanging conveniently out the window.

Clover stepped to the center of the road, aimed at Leonard and fired. But the shot went wide, punched a neat hole through the windshield. I saw Terri's head fly back, and then, dying, she reflexively stretched out, stomping down hard on the gas.

The car jumped and Clover didn't. It hit him so hard it knocked him flying ten feet in front of it, over the edge of the quarry. The body of Deputy Jones flew forward and hit the wire grating, dropped out of sight.

I watched as Clover's body hurtled down and smashed against a washing machine with a cracking sound like a rotten limb. It bounced over some more junk and slid into where the water was deep.

The car came right after him, shot downward like a bullet, right where Clover had gone under. The car hit with a splash and the moonlight shook on the water. The impact drove Deputy Jones's body back against the rear windshield. Her bagged head hit it hard enough to cause a spider web of cracks, and then she fell toward the front of the car and the car went under.

I walked into the road, stood on the edge of the quarry and looked down. Leonard joined me. The car's taillights creeped beneath the gurgling water, where they glowed momentarily, then went out. The water rippled for a time, finally went still, and it was done.

THE BRIAR PATCH BOOGIE

"Whose idea was this?" Leonard said.

"I think it was yours."

"Yeah, probably."

"You know it was," I said.

"Hap?"

"What?"

"Can I have a drink of water?"

"If you get up and go get it," I said. "There's plenty water in the well. And probably snakes and dirt, and since the outhouse is up the hill, might be some of that in there as well. Who puts an outhouse at the top of a hill so the water might drain in the well? What kind of moron does that?"

"We have bottled water?"

"In the car," I said. "You drank the last bottle we brought in."

"You won't go out and get it?"

"No."

"Why not?"

"I'm not thirsty."

We were lying in cots across from one another in a little fishing cabin out at Caddo Lake. It was not a nice cabin, but it was cheap. It was not near other cabins and there were a lot of woods around it. It was deep East Texas, near Louisiana, and it could pass for either state. The lake had a lot of good fish in it and there were alligators and all along the bank there were big drooping trees that made thick shadows.

We had been there two days. We had caught a few fish and had fried them in butter with corn batter and had eaten them. The fishing had been so-so, and the boat we had rented had a leak in it. There were a couple of large tin cans, and we had no idea why they were in the boat until we were way out in the lake and the water began to ease in. We used the cans to bail it out. When we got back to the bank of the lake, we were so pissed at the guy who rented the boat to us, we pushed it back into the water and sat on the side of the lake and fished and watched the boat float out a ways and slowly take on water and sink.

We cheered when it went down.

"So, you won't go get me a bottled water?

"No."

"I'd do it for you."

"No you wouldn't," I said.

"Would too."

"No you wouldn't."

"I bet I would."

"Okay. Go get me one."

"I asked you first. Look, if you were sick. Say you had a fever, or were dehydrated, and you asked me to go get you a water, I would."

"I'm not sick."

"But if you were, I'd get you a water."

"You're not sick, so why should I get you a water?"

Leonard thought about that for a moment.

"I really don't want to go get it," he said.

"Aha," I said. "Now the truth comes out."

"This seemed like a good idea at the time," he said. "I thought it would be fun. We used to do stuff like this."

"We have been civilized to some extent, Leonard."

"Yeah, I guess so."

"I'm sick of eating fish, and small fish, I might add. We sunk the goddamn boat, and now all we got is bank fishing, and that hasn't been good, and there's not a proper toilet, and there's no running water."

"It's been really hot too."

"It's the summer, Leonard. What did you expect? Seals and polar bears?"

"That would have been nice. I like seals and polar bears."

"You have known neither."

"I've seen them on TV," he said. "You know what would be cool? A goddamn penguin."

"All of them would die of heatstroke."

"Yeah. They would. I'm pretty warm myself. Maybe I have heatstroke."

"I am not going to go out to the car and get you a water. Besides, it would be warm water."

"But it would be water. Hell, it's major hot. Devil's butthole hot."

"We don't need no air conditioning, you said."

"Did I say that?"

"Yep."

"Maybe if there was at least a plug with electricity we could use the fan I brought. That would be okay. One plug. Might be nice too—we didn't have to shit through a hole in the outhouse."

"No electricity and you brought a fan?"

"It's a small one," he said.

"At least it won't work any worse than a big one without electricity."

"See there, Hap. A bright side. Damn. I thought there'd be electricity. The brochure said it was a nice comfortable cabin. I didn't think of it as nice without electricity."

"We used to sleep in tents out in the woods on ground cloths, fish and camp for days," I said. "We didn't have electricity then."

"We were younger then."

"That's true," I said.

"And remember, we had marshmallows on a stick?"

"We did at that."

"I don't guess you brought any marshmallows?"

"Did not," I said.

"That would have been nice."

"Yep," I said. "We could have set this shithole cabin on fire and roasted them in the flames."

"You need a small simple blaze," Leonard said. "That would have been too much. And very warm."

"The marshmallows would have burned," I said.

"That's what I'm trying to tell you," Leonard said. He took a deep breath. "I don't know. Guess it's all right. It's closer to nature."

"Lying under a tree on leaves and dirt with chiggers on our balls would be closer to nature," I said. "I grew up with nature, and I love it. But I like going home to my house and my bed. That has become my true nature. And I miss Brett."

"She and Chance are probably having a good time," Leonard said.

"Don't you know it," I said. "They're watching old science fiction movies and popping popcorn and the dog is on the couch with them. I think Brett said they were going to make hot chocolate too. I don't know for sure, though, because my cell phone doesn't work out here. Oh, wait. I lost my cell phone in the lake."

"Can't blame that on me," Leonard said.

"I can, and I will."

"I don't know," Leonard said. "We used to get along fine without phones. I think it's not having electricity that makes it suck out here."

"That certainly is a factor," I said. "The only electricity nature likes to provide is a lightning bolt."

"How did we get used to a cell phone? How is that? Why is that?"

"I didn't want pussy until I had some, and then I wanted it from then on."

"A cell phone is like pussy?" Leonard said. "No wonder I'm queer."

"I admit that was a bridge too far as a comparison."

"Maybe if we were home and someone ran a bulldozer over this place and sent us a picture it would be all right. We have caught fish, though. You have to admit that."

"Some extremely small fish. Other fish don't even recognize them as fish. You overcooked them too."

"I'm not used to a wood stove cooker."

"I can't even read."

"You should have learned how," he said. "You went to school."

"That's some funny shit, Leonard. Reading by candlelight is hard."

"Lincoln read by lamplight," Leonard said.

"He wasn't used to anything else," I said. "We're spoiled. We're back to the parable of the phone. Besides, you're the one complaining about how bad things are and how it isn't what you expected."

"Yeah," Leonard said, "but you're thinking it. And if you play fair, you have to admit some of what you're saying sounds like complaining too."

"I'm complaining about you. This was your idea."

"It seemed like fun. We haven't gone off and done something like this in a long time."

"Might be a reason for that," I said.

"This can't be the best cabin the guy has to offer."

"Oh, I don't know, this place may be the pick of the litter."

"All the other places in the brochure cost the same."

"Then they're all like this," I said. "Of course, we may be special with the old spoiled well and the extra smoky wood stove."

"The picture looked good."

"They always do," I said.

"Next time I want to do something like this, will you kick my ass?" Leonard said.

"How about I just kick it twice every Tuesday, just in case you're thinking about doing something like this?"

"That seems fair," Leonard said.

We lay there in the dark on our cots for a while. I kept trying to go to sleep, but that wasn't working out. A mosquito about the size of a chicken hawk was buzzing around my head. I imagined I was a ninja master and I could catch it between two chopsticks. Actually, I wasn't having much luck swatting it with my hand. He was a wily bugger.

"Hap," Leonard said.

"What the hell now?" I said.

"Can a mosquito be so big as to have a landing gear?"

And so it went.

Late in the night I fell asleep, and then the rain woke me up, but in a reverse way, it helped me go back to sleep. It rained well into the morning, keeping the sky black.

Being tired from talking a lot of the night, we slept on. It was nearly noon when I woke up and got off the cot.

Leonard was still sleeping. I considered smothering him with a pillow, but went out to the car in the rain and brought in a flat of bottled water and set it on the one table in the room, near the wood stove. The table wobbled under the weight.

I used some tender and got a fire going, put a few slivers of larger wood in the stove, and when that was blazing, I put in a larger, split piece of pine. It caught, and then I added more wood, larger pieces. At least the cabin had come with split wood. Eventually, I had even-burning fire. It made the room hot and sticky. I poured bottled water into the old-fashioned coffee pot, and then dumped in some coffee grounds; that's how old the pot was. It wasn't even an old-time percolator. It was one of those things that Davy Crockett would have had coffee out of. At home Brett had this coffee maker you stuck little pods of coffee into, then you pull down a lever, and that made the perfect cup, and fast. I missed her and I missed the perfect cup. I missed my daughter Chance. I missed our dog Buffy. I missed my books, television set and my pantry with food in it. I even missed our cell phones. Mine was residing at the bottom of the lake and would have to be replaced. Maybe a perch was making a call to Brett right now, trying to find out if she was having fish for dinner. Leonard had let his run out of juice, and now there was no electricity, and he didn't have a car charger.

I wanted to cook with electricity, not wood, and have something to cook besides bad coffee. We didn't even have fish for lunch now. A can of potted meat with a pull tab would have been exciting right then. I missed the refrigerator back home where I kept my pitcher of iced tea and my carton of Sharps non-alcoholic beer. I really had come a long ways from a fellow who lived in the country on the fringe of the woods into who I was now. A guy who wanted to go home.

While the coffee was making, I looked over at Leonard, and could see under his cot a vanilla cookie bag. That bastard had eaten them all and hadn't offered me one. I didn't even know he had any with him, though I should have guessed. He was about those cookies like a druggie is about crack. He may have had them in a sealed bag stuffed up his ass for all I knew. Of course, it was far more likely he had brought them in with his sleeping bag.

When the coffee was ready, I poured a bug out of one of the two cups we had, left two dead flies in the other, and poured that one full of coffee for Leonard. I poured myself a cup and sat on the cot and sipped it. It was god-awful, tasted as if it had been strained through a used jockstrap owned by someone with a rampant venereal disease.

"Leonard," I said. "Rise and shine, easy money. The coffee's ready."

He moved a little, rolled over, smacked his lips and finally swung out of bed.

"Oh, for shit sakes, Leonard. Put on some drawers."

He got up and rummaged in his backpack and came up with a pair of sweat pants and pulled those on.

"I'd known you'd gone to bed naked," I said, "I'd have slept out in the rain. Your coffee's on the table."

He got his cup and sat on his cot and sipped.

"Damn. You shit in this?"

"Not quite," I said. "You know what would make this a lot better? A vanilla cookie. Oh, wait. You ate them all."

"I didn't mean to," he said. "I just got started and couldn't quit. You know, woke up hungry."

"You meant to."

He drank his coffee, then spit one of the flies on the floor.

"You knew that sucker was in my cup," he said.

"I wouldn't do that to you, Leonard."

"You might," he said.

"Okay. I might. Watch out for the other one."

We went outside. It was still raining. It was a misty rain, and we wore our slickers with hoods and our good boots that laced up high and tight and were oiled to help shed water.

From where we stood we could see the lake and we could see the water sloshing against the shoreline.

"If we had a boat we could have better fishing," Leonard said.

"Like the one we let sink out in the lake?"

"That one precisely," he said.

"We can walk in the woods, there, fish close to all those tree roots growing out in the water."

"Tangle our lines."

"Might. But I bet there's some catfish there we could tie to a boat and have them pull us across the lake."

"If we had a boat."

"Yeah, if we had a boat."

"A boat like the one we sunk," Leonard said.

"That would be the one, yes."

We wandered into the woods. It grew dark with the shade from the trees and the clouds from the rain. The mist was nice, as it kept mosquitoes off a little and it made the air taste like greenery and dirt, but it lay on our faces like damp cobwebs. It made me think of when I was a kid growing up, and I'd go out in the mist and the rain until my mother caught me and called me in for fear of lightning.

We walked on, and a few hours later we found a place where the land rose up and was sprinkled with trees and tangled undergrowth. Near our feet a water moccasin crawled out from under a wad of dead leaves and slithered toward the water. As it plopped into the lake, Leonard said, "Won't be any fish there for a while."

"And I won't be anywhere near there for a while myself," I said.

As we topped the peak of the hill, a sound struck us.

Someone was moaning.

———————

We left our fishing gear up on the rise and found her at the bottom of the hill lying in the leaves with her head on a rotting log. She was a young woman with long blonde hair, in her thirties I figured. She might have been pretty before, but the way she had been beat, it was hard to tell. She wasn't wearing much, a formerly white blouse now mostly the color of the leaves and dirt. She wasn't wearing pants or underwear. Her head was swollen and she was bruised on the arms and legs, and her bare feet were a bloody mess. She was lying in an ant bed and was covered with ant bites.

All of that she could get over in time, but the wound in her side wasn't something that merely required bed rest and a couple of aspirin. Something was sticking out of her. I looked. It was an arrow with plastic feathers on the end of the shaft.

I brushed the ants off of her, and we picked her up, Leonard at her head, me at her feet. We carried her to a pile of leaves that was better than the ant bed.

Her eyes were slits. She had taken such a beating she couldn't quite open them, at least not completely. She looked up at me and cried.

Leonard said to her, "We'll get an ambulance."

"They're out there," she said, and when she opened her mouth I could see her front teeth were chipped.

"Who's out there?" I said.

166

"Those men."

"How many?" I said.

"Two men and two women. They rented me. Like a carnival ride."

"You saying you're a working girl?" Leonard said.

She nodded.

"They're after me. They're hunting me."

"Who's after you?" I said.

"Them." By then she hardly had the breath to speak.

I took my canteen off my belt, slipped my hand under her head, lifted her up and gave her a drink of water. She gulped greedily. I only let her have a small amount to keep from making her sick, then I laid her head down gently on the leaves.

"They took me off a Houston street," she said. "I do it for my daughter."

"No judgment from us," Leonard said.

"They spent days raping and beating me, and then they took me out here, drove out onto a trail, made me walk deep in the woods. They raped me again and set me loose, said I had an hour. They caught up with me and shot me with an arrow, but I got away. I don't know how I did it, but I got away. But they're coming. They'll find me."

"Take it easy," Leonard said. "When did you last see them?"

"I don't know. It was night. That's what helped me. Oh, Jesus, my head is swimming."

"It's all right," I said.

She quit talking and lay still.

"We got to get her back to the car, drive her to a hospital," Leonard said.

My thought was she wouldn't make it that long. That wound in her side was bad and she had lost a lot of blood.

"Hap," Leonard said.

She had stopped moving. One moment she had been talking and now she wasn't saying anything or making any sounds, no moaning, no breathing. Her face was slack and her lips were turning blue.

I put my head to her chest. No heartbeat. I touched her throat to feel a pulse. Nada.

"She checked out," I said.

"Damn. . . . Do you believe her story?"

"There's an arrow sticking out of her. She was either telling the truth or Robin Hood missed a shot at a deer."

That's when we heard a noise, someone coming, being loud, purposely. My guess was they wanted her to hear them coming and cause fear.

Two men began to call out.

"Come on out, whore. We have a few points to make with you."

"Yeah," said another voice. "You might as well give it up, cause these points really hurt."

The voices were coming from out in the deeper woods.

"Come on," Leonard said. "She's gone, and she said they had weapons."

We rushed up the hill, and no sooner had we laid flat amongst the brush and were spying downward, two men came into the clearing beneath us. The two women she had mentioned did not appear.

The men were dressed in camo, carrying modern bows and quivers of arrows strapped to their backs. One of them had arrows fastened to his bow in such a way he could pop them loose and load them up quickly. They had machetes strapped to their sides in scabbards. They had canteens of water on their belts. One of them was wearing a backpack with his quiver of arrows strapped to that. Both wore high-top, waterproof boots. One of them was stocky, but solid, and had on a green baseball cap. The other an Aussie-style hat with one side pinned up.

Making their way down the hill they came to the body and stared at it.

"The arrow is ruined," I heard the one in the cap say.

"Yeah," said the other. He was taller. He took off his Aussie hat and ran his hand through his hair and put it back on. "Shaft's bent, but it made a hell of a hole. Forget the arrow. It was a good shot, one of your best."

"Bitch," said the stocky man wearing the baseball cap. He laid his bow on the ground carefully, pulled his machete out of its scabbard and went to chopping on the woman with it, hacking at her legs and privates and chest. She was still fresh enough to bleed, and she bled a lot.

Leonard started to rise up, but I grabbed him. He looked at me. I shook my head and spoke to him by forming words but not saying them. "Not yet."

Leonard tried to relax and lay still. He managed, but

just barely. Leonard is the kind of guy that will attack a rhino barehanded and expect to come home with its horn. Sometimes you have to remind him he's just a man.

Baseball Cap hacked on the poor woman some more. It was all I could do not to stand up and scream at him and run down the hill with my hunting knife. But the other guy was holding his bow, and from the way they carried themselves I knew they were trained woodsmen and hunters. There was a good chance me or Leonard would look like a porcupine by the time we got down there. A good bowman can thread several arrows and fire far more quickly than you can imagine.

When Baseball Cap grew tired of hacking, he wiped his face with his forearm, took a deep breath and then hacked one more time, cutting off the woman's head. I heard Leonard let his breath out, or so I thought, and then I realized it was me. Still, I hadn't been too loud. We were still safe and hidden.

There were strands of flesh still attached to the neck and the head. The man chopped again until the head was free. Aussie Hat brought out a bag, and Baseball Cap put the head in the bag, leaned down and rubbed the machete across her shirt to clean the blade, and then he put it away. Aussie Hat fastened the bag to the back of his pack, which for a moment he had removed, and then re-slung it.

"I forgot the camp shovel," said Baseball Cap. "Shit. We can push her off in the water, I guess. Gators, fish and the heat will take care of her in a few days."

"Hell with that," said Aussie Hat. "Who the hell comes all the way back in here? There are thousands of acres. She'll rot quick, and then there's the ants and animals, all this fresh blood. No guarantee a gator will find her, but something will."

"That's right," said Baseball Cap.

"Sure it is," said the other.

They started walking back the way they had come, and when they disappeared into the trees, I said, "We got to call some law. Bring them back here."

"By the time we get to the car and find a phone, they'll be long gone," Leonard said. "There won't be any justice for that poor woman. Those guys might never be found. They hunted her like a deer. And you can bet they've done it before, and will do it again. We got to track after them. Keep them in sight."

"You mean more than that, don't you?"

"Maybe."

"I've seen enough killing in my time," I said.

"Listen. You go back, drive and find a phone. I'll stay after them."

"She said there were four, remember? Where are the other two? Hell. I'll come with you. I can't let you go up against four. You might hurt them."

"There you go," Leonard said.

We went down to her body for a look. It was sickening.

"Can you believe that shit?" Leonard said. "Chopping off her head."

"Have to," I said. "Saw it."

"We ain't got time for a burial, Hap. I know that's what you were thinking."

That was exactly what I was thinking.

"Yeah," I said. "I know. And we got nothing to dig a hole."

We went after them.

The rain had blown out, but with the heat of the day rising there were ribbons of fog in the low land, and it wrapped around us like damp serpents. The trees seemed to come out of the fog and then go back into it. It didn't take long before we lost them.

We paused to examine the ground and find tracks, but the fog was too thick and too close to the earth for us to see well. We stopped beneath a tree as it warmed up, waiting for the fog to lift, hoping we could follow their tracks as we were once able to do, back when we were younger and had grown up near nature.

We drank water from our canteens and split a granola bar. Until then we hadn't had anything for breakfast or lunch but bad coffee and some sips of water. The sun melted the fog like cotton candy. Now we could see their tracks, and the limbs they had bent while moving through the brush. They might as well have left us a map.

Looking where they had gone, we saw that there were a lot of ancient cedar stumps in the middle of a long patch of brackish water. It went on for some distance. There were only a few grown trees; most of the others were scrubs. It was patched like that for a long distance, and in the distance we could see those two moving along at no particular pace, seeming to take their time about it, not worried in the least. I figured, why worry when you thought no one had any idea what you had done and where you were.

And then I thought: Well, you sons-of-bitches, we know, and if you knew us, you'd start worrying.

They got well ahead of us, and we let them. We tried to stay near the larger stumps and the clumps of greenery as we went. There were long leaves that grew out of the water, looked like blades, and they were sharp too. We hid behind those when we thought we ought to, and when we had to truck across large expanses of water, we made our way so as not to make the water splash too loudly, in case our prey might look back and see us. We were too far from them to do anything, but with their arrows, they weren't too far from us.

They had planned all this well, let the woman off in the thick of the swamp and hunted her down. Now they had time to walk out and be a great distance away from her body. The question was, where were they going now, and why were they carrying her head in a bag?

Snakes swam all around us, and once we saw an alligator hustle along between two stumps in our direction, but it turned, went out where the marsh was deep, and with a flick of its tail it was gone. Let me tell you that took my breath away.

In time the woods swelled up again and the swamp water thinned. Before long we were in tall grass, and then the grass gave way to even more woods, a lot of thin trees growing close together. The sun had begun to crawl up high. A bit of water had seeped into my so-called weatherproof boots.

Far away we saw a split in the woods and we could see water beyond the split, not brown, but blue. We were coming out of the low-level muck, and to the bank of the larger and cleaner-looking Lake Caddo, the only natural lake in Texas.

I added that because I learned it in school. I wouldn't want you to think I wasted my education.

There was a line of willow and cypress trees along the water, and we could see the men walk out of the green growth, and keep walking onto the water, which for a moment gave me pause until we came up a little higher on the rise, ducked down behind some swamp grass and saw they had stepped onto a large barge. It was like a great, high-setting raft and there was an enormous cabin in the center of it with a band of large windows that went around as far as we could see. Inside the cabin was where the wheelhouse and living quarters would be. The part of the wheelhouse we couldn't see would have to be glass as well, and it would give a good view of the water ahead.

As they stepped onto the barge, two women came out of the cabin and each grabbed a man in turn and they hugged, and then the man with the head in the bag took it out and showed it to them.

You would have thought it was Christmas and their birthdays all rolled into one. The women giggled with glee. They were long, sun-browned women, one with her dark hair tied back, the other with short blonde hair cropped close to her head. They looked good in tight tee-shirts and shorts and flip-flops, and it was obvious both were braless and could make that work. They didn't look like monsters.

Leonard turned and looked at me, his forehead scrunched.

I shrugged. I didn't get it either.

The man with the woman's head, which he was holding by the hair, put the head in the bag, and the women went inside the barge.

We eased back behind the rise.

"What kind of people are these?" Leonard said.

"They're not people," I said.

Easing through the weeds, crawling on our bellies, we made our way down to the trees along the bank near the barge. I took up behind a cypress, and Leonard eased into a clutch of small willows.

Aussie Hat picked up a pole lying in a groove on the barge and pushed at the bank with it. Baseball Cap had already unhooked a line tied to a large root sticking out from the shoreline. He picked up a pole and helped Aussie Hat push off. The motor began to hum, and then the barge began to move. One of the women was motoring them away.

"Damn," Leonard said.

"Wait," I said.

They glided along on the water, not going far from

shore. We watched as the barge chugged around a bend in the lake.

"They seem to be staying close to land," I said. "Maybe they're not going far."

"All we can do is follow around the edge of the lake and hope," Leonard said.

We got up and trucked along the way they were going. It was hard work. The trees were thick and there were a lot of mosquitoes now and they moved in little black swarms like living clouds. The sun was dipping and the sky was already dark from clouds filled with rain.

It was a slow slog, and finally it began to rain. It was a soft but steady rain. We stayed close to the curve of the lake and only went away from the shoreline for any distance when we had no choice; when the bushes and trees and vines grew thick enough to make a fence. We went wide then, but we always made it back close to shore. We could see the barge had lights on inside the cabin. It was still close to the bank. Finally it came to a place far up from us and drifted over for a moment, then chugged back out into the lake.

"What was that about?" Leonard said.

"Maybe they thought they'd camp there, decided not to."

"Doesn't matter," Leonard said.

We took a breath and drank some water and split another granola bar, which was good. I was so hungry my stomach was starting to gnaw at my insides.

After a few minutes we got our wind back and started onward. A surprised nesting of birds startled by our presence flew up in a burst, causing me to nearly pass a turd.

Before long the barge pulled over again and stopped and the man in the baseball cap came out and secured a line to shore. He went back inside. It was growing darker, and the lights in the barge looked warm and inviting, even if the people inside were as cold-blooded as a snake. Rain had begun to come down like bullets.

I pulled the hood on my slicker close around my face and we eased closer to shore. We could see through the windows, and we could see people in the light. There was hard rock music coming from the barge and Baseball Cap was dancing with the women. The dark-haired woman was holding up the decapitated woman's head as she danced. I glanced at Leonard.

Leonard pulled his knife from its scabbard. "I say we surprise them and kill their asses."

"The women too?"

"I don't see any difference," Leonard said. "You and your chivalry are going to get you killed some day. I don't make one whit of difference in them."

"We could still go for help."

"They'd be gone by the time we come back, and they'll never get what they deserve."

"I'm kind of worried we might get what we don't deserve," I said.

"Here's what I will do," I said. "We make a citizen's arrest."

"What?" Leonard said.

"I'm not going to kill these people, go back to the cabin and go fishing. When I said I'd had enough of death, I meant it."

"I thought we'd kill them, go back to the cabin, get the car and go home. We might stop somewhere for a burger."

"No."

"So, we going to go in and say 'Citizen's Arrest,' hang out with them and a decapitated head hoping some cops show up?"

"I thought we'd surprise them, tie them up, use the barge itself to make our way back to where our cabin is. We can put them inside the cabin, one of us can watch them, and the other can drive out and get the law and bring them back."

"How about this?" Leonard said. "We make a citizen's arrest unless we have to kill them."

"You're opening a door I don't want to open," I said.

"And they might just kick that door open in our faces, brother. Say we do our best not to hurt anyone, outside of kicking their ass a little and tying them up? But if things get a little wonky, I'm going Attila the Hun on them and I expect you to bring the horses."

I thought about that. Leonard was right. They'd motor away and escape. It might not even be their barge. It could be stolen. They could do this again. And they would.

"All right," I said. "We go for the compromise."

"Good," Leonard said.

Behind us we heard a slight crack of someone or something stepping on a branch. We whirled about. A light came on. The light was a little thing fastened to the top of a pistol, and there was a man behind it, and in that instant I realized something obvious. We had only seen one man in the cabin with the women. I guess we logically thought the other was in the shitter or pausing in a back room to consider the nature of the universe, but now I knew we were a couple of dumbasses and our logic had been full of holes.

"Howdy boys," said a voice. That would be Aussie Hat.

I knew then that when the barge pulled over it was because they knew we were after them, had spotted us. Aussie Hat got off at that stop to sneak up on us. And he had done it well. Until that stick cracked, he could have come up behind me, combed my hair and wiped my ass, and I wouldn't have known he was there. He was that good.

Aussie Hat and his pistol pointed us forward and he trailed behind. He led us to the barge and said for us to step on board. Then he called out, "Open up."

Shadows tumbled through the windows and moved along the wooden deck, and the music went away. Baseball Cap opened the door and the light came with him.

He and the women stepped out on the barge deck. We all stood in the rain.

"Well, well," said Baseball Cap. "What have we here? Heckle and Jeckle?"

"Told you I saw someone," Aussie Hat said.

"Hey, we're just fishing," I said. "We don't want any trouble."

"Where's your fishing gear?" said Aussie Hat.

It was back on the hill where we had left it when we started following them, but I said, "We ditched it after we got lost. We been trying to find our way out."

"Have you now?" said Aussie Hat.

"Yeah," I said. "We don't mean you guys any harm."

"You know," said Aussie Hat, "I doubt that."

The short-haired blonde said, "Fresh meat."

"Get their knives and canteens, the belt packs," Aussie Hat said.

Baseball Cap took them away from us and gave them to the blonde woman, who took them inside somewhere.

Aussie Hat beckoned us into the cabin. It was tight in there. There was a fold-down table attached to the wall and there was a gap in the wall where it folded up. There were snack foods on it. Beneath the windows were benches. There were a couple of folding chairs on hooks on the wall. There was a door off the little cabin. It was closed. I assumed it would be the bedroom and off of that would be the wheelhouse. The woman's head was on a silver platter on the table next to a bowl of pretzels.

Baseball Cap removed the platter and head, placed it

on the bench, then he put the food away inside the other room, came back and folded the table into the wall, fastened it there with clamps.

"You boys sit down on the other side," he said.

We sat on the bench there. I couldn't take my eyes off of that poor woman's head.

Aussie Hat nodded toward the head and the platter. "If you didn't know what we were all about and are just lost fishermen, well, now you know something about us."

"Is that real?" I said.

"Oh come on," said Aussie Hat. "That was lame."

"You guys shooting a movie?" I was still working it.

"It may end up starring you guys," Baseball Cap said.

The blonde woman giggled. Her hair was wet and plastered to her head, and though she was pretty, something about the way she looked at us reminded me of a ferret. The dark-haired woman's hair looked like a damp helmet.

"Let's take them outside and shoot them in the head," said the short-haired blonde. "I want the black one. I want to shoot him."

Aussie Hat turned off the light attached to the pistol. He sat by the head and let the gun rest on his thigh. I was watching for my moment. I knew if I went after one of them, Leonard would be on the other like a duck on a june bug. But they were watching us intently. Aussie Hat was probably hoping we'd make that move. He looked like he was itching to shoot that pistol.

The barge bobbed in the water and we could hear the

wind picking up and the rain was brutal now. Aussie Hat took off his hat and shook the rain off of it and put it back on. He hadn't let go of the pistol in his other hand.

"Good thing you're inside," Aussie Hat said. "You won't get as wet, and you aren't lost anymore. Isn't that good?"

"It's a fucking treat," Leonard said. "If I had some clout, I'd get you guys some kind of Samaritan medal. . . . You better hope the first shot kills me."

"Oh, it will," said Aussie Hat. "And the second will kill him. I'm a good shot."

"He is," said the dark-haired woman. Then to Aussie Hat, "You're not going to let them ruin our fun, are you?"

"Nah," said Aussie Hat. "We got fun coming out of the ass."

"Let's just do them and toss them overboard," Baseball Cap said.

"Can't we have their heads?" said the short-haired blonde. She was watching me carefully, licking her lips. "For target practice. Like the others."

Aussie Hat said to the short-haired blonde, "I don't like the way you're looking at him."

"What do you mean?" she said.

"You look like you want to fuck him."

"I want to fuck him over," she said. "Not fuck him."

Aussie Hat looked at me. "You want to fuck her? I think she wants to fuck you. That's what I'm getting here."

"Actually, that was the farthest thing from my mind, and I'm sure from hers. But I was wondering if maybe you had a cup of coffee, some of those little chocolate doughnuts, and then maybe later, I'd settle for a hand job from any one of you. Provided you're gentle, of course. And just for the record, I like it dry."

"You're not getting coffee or doughnuts," said Baseball Cap.

"So I could still get that hand job?"

"Just shoot him," said Baseball Cap.

"We don't have any doughnuts," said the dark-haired girl. "But we got coffee."

We all looked at her.

"Not that I'd give them any doughnuts if we had them," she said. "Or coffee."

"You hunt humans," Leonard said. "And like most hunters, it's not sport at all. There's nothing fair about it. You catch defenseless women, run them through the woods and shoot them with arrows. That's some sport. That's some brave business. That's shit. That's what that is."

"We give them plenty of a head start," said Aussie Hat.

"Yeah," Leonard said. "But they got nothing."

"They got a chance, and that's more than they deserve," said Aussie Hat.

"Some chance," Leonard said.

"They're whores," said the man with the pistol.

"Unlike these two upstanding young ladies," Leonard said.

Aussie Hat lifted the pistol in our direction. I flinched. Leonard didn't even blink.

"The whores we kill," said Baseball Cap, "they're just

a waste on society. Spreading disease. They could do better if they wanted. They are at the bottom of the food chain by choice, by laziness."

"You think so?" Leonard said.

"I think so," said Aussie Hat. "We pick ones that are on the downhill slope, ones that never darken the doorway of a church."

"You are one choice dumbass," Leonard said. "Jesus always said, you don't go to church, you get hunted in the woods with a bow and arrow. I think you can find that in the scripture marked Assholio, first chapter, first verse. What do you do, mount their heads like deer?"

"Of course not," Aussie Hat said. "We're not crazy."

Aussie Hat stood up, pointed the gun, said, "We got to tie you up."

"No," Leonard said. "I don't think so."

"You think you get to choose?" said Baseball Cap.

"You got to get me tied up first, and that will be one hell of a fight."

"Then we got to shoot you," said Aussie Hat.

Leonard shrugged. "What's the difference? Shot tied up, or shot untied. I'm not going to make it easy for you. You're not tying me up, at least not without working for it or killing me."

"What about you?" Aussie Hat said to me.

"Me? Oh, I'm with him. I'm not going to let you tie

me up. Shoot or fight, that's what you get from me."

"You can fight now," Aussie Hat said.

"Well," I said. "I'd rather not get shot, as I have plans next week, and I don't mind being cooperative to keep from being shot. But not that cooperative."

"Difference is you two might get a chance to live," said Baseball Cap.

"You don't seem like a couple of fair and square boys to me," said Leonard. "Suddenly when you want to tie us up, you're talking chances?"

I thought: Leonard do not antagonize them too much. Do not poke the dragon too hard. But that was like politely asking a starving dog not to eat a greasy pork chop.

"You let me and him go, you'll never catch us in these woods," Leonard said. "You haven't got any chance unless it's with someone doesn't have the strength to run, or experience in the woods. Your idea of sport is breaking a deer's leg, giving it five minutes' head start with a sack over its head. Me and him, we can give you a run for your arrows, we get loose. We'll give you some real sport."

"Just take them out on the deck and shoot them," Baseball Cap said.

"You shoot us," Leonard said, "it'll probably be right here. I don't have to do a goddamn thing you say. I'd rather get shot right here than make it easier for you to clean up the blood out there on the deck."

"You know," said Aussie Hat. "I think he means it."

"Shoot them," said Baseball Cap, "and then we'll clean up the mess."

"Oh, sure," said the blonde. "You know who ends up cleaning up the mess? It won't be you two. It'll be us. Women's work. Think the black one's right. I think you boys don't want to give someone a fair shake. We don't get to hunt. We get the shit jobs and you two have all the fun."

"Life is just full of little disappointments," said Aussie Hat, as he turned and looked at the blonde woman. His voice was so raw I could feel paint peeling off the wall behind me.

The blonde shut up, looked at the floor and tried to grow small. It was as if she realized for the first time she wasn't the one wielding power. Sex could only take you so far. Step on a man's pride, he can be silly. Step on a psycho's pride, and he can go crazy. A man steps on it, that's bad, but a woman steps on it, that's terrible.

"I'm sorry," said the blonde. "I'm just tired."

Aussie Hat kept staring at her, eventually eased his gaze back to us.

"You're not going to shoot them here, I say we take them ashore," said Baseball Cap. "I say we let them run. Won't be any different than any other time. We'll catch them, cut off their heads like all the others. I say we take their balls too, bat them around a bit."

"Hope you got a tow sack on board," Leonard said. "You'll need it for my balls. And maybe some kind of special knot to keep them hemmed up inside. Kind of got a mind of their own."

The dark-haired woman looked at Leonard and smiled. It wasn't a smile that made you want to start skipping through the tulips. It was a bit more the way a cat looks at a mouse it's cornered against a wall. I think she liked thinking about Leonard's balls in a sack.

"I don't know," Aussie Hat said. "Let me think."

For the next few hours I felt sick to my stomach and scared, but I didn't let them see it. I had dealt with bad people before, and some as bad as this, and the thing is, you got to not let them see how frightened you are. It feeds their passion.

After a while, liquor came out and everyone got drunk, except the man with the pistol. And us, of course. Aussie Hat didn't drink, didn't lose focus. Finally, the women went into the back room with Baseball Cap and closed the door. We could hear them in there, going at it. The barge rocked.

Leonard said, "What's the matter with you? Can't get it up? That gun about as much as a dick as you got?"

"You are asking for it, aren't you?" said Aussie Hat.

"They're in there slamming together like hogs in heat, and here you sit."

"You want a bullet in the teeth," Aussie Hat said.

Leonard was trying to pull the ole Uncle Remus Brer Rabbit trick. The one where Brer Fox catches Brer Rabbit, and the rabbit tells him to go on and do whatever he wants, kill him, whatever, but please don't throw him in the briar patch.

Brer Fox hears this, thinks, so, that's the worst thing can be done to that ole rabbit, so I'm going to do it. Brer Fox throws Brer Rabbit into the briar patch, and Brer Rabbit calls out, "Born and raised in the briar patch, Brer Fox. Born and raised." And away went Brer Rabbit, doing the briar patch boogie.

If they were to throw us into the woods and come hunting us, they'd be throwing us into our briar patch. Born and raised in the woods, we were. Born and raised.

Okay. It wasn't exactly like that. We were offering to head into the briar patch and show our skills there, but in a way, it was the same kind of challenge. Don't shoot us, Bad Guys, as that's too easy. Make it hard for us, and show us what sportsmen you are. Throw us in the briar patch and see what we got.

"Listen to that meat slapping in there," Leonard said.

"Don't worry about my love life," said Aussie Hat. "I get plenty. We all share."

"For the record," Leonard said, "I have not for one iota worried about your pathetic love life."

Aussie Hat lifted the pistol and pointed it right at Leonard. Leonard didn't flinch. After a long moment where my heart quit beating, he lowered the gun.

"Just shut up," said Aussie Hat.

The night crawled along, and after what felt like about three thousand years and a long afternoon, the morning light came through the barge windows and spread over the floor and lay on the woman's head on the platter. There was blood leakage in the platter, and the blood had the look of congealed strawberry jam. There was a faint odor of decay from the head, like a refrigerator that had been unplugged for a few days with a ham roast in it. Aussie Hat sat beside the head on the bench and placed his left hand on top of it and held the pistol in his right, resting it against his thigh, his unblinking, lizard eyes focused on us.

"Good morning, assholes," he said, stood up, touched a switch on the wall and turned off the cabin lights.

It was still raining and you could hear the drops falling into the water like plums falling off trees. The man who had spent the night with the women came out looking the way you might think a man would look who had spent the night banging two women. Then the women came out behind him. It was still slightly dark outside.

The man had his baseball cap in his hand and he put it on his head and then went to adjusting his belt. The four of them spent a few moments watching us, like we were monkeys in the zoo. Like a monkey, I wanted to throw shit on them.

"Move us to the spot," Aussie Hat said to Baseball Cap, then to the blonde: "Make us some coffee."

The blonde knew she had pushed a little too hard the night before. She tried to sound sweet. "Sure. Them, too?"

"No. Not them, too. What's with you two cunts and the coffee?"

"I'd like some coffee," Leonard said. "We both take it black, though Hap here, now and again, likes some artificial sweetener, though he's picky on which kind."

"Cream's all right if you got it," I said.

"Fuck you," said Aussie Hat.

"Oh, that's a wish you won't fulfill," Leonard said.

"Depends on the definition," Aussie Hat said.

Baseball Cap unfastened the mooring line, came back inside, trudged into the bedroom and on through to the wheelhouse. I knew that because we heard a door open on the far end, and shortly thereafter he started the engine. The barge eased away from the shore, chopping at the water, chugging like a large lawn mower.

Through the row of windows across from me I could see the night had lifted and the rain had stopped. An early morning fog was hovering over the water, twisting in amongst the shoreline trees. Within moments the fog that had so quickly arrived started to lift and fade. Big, white birds dipped into the water looking for a fish breakfast. Blue morning shadows formed by the shapes of trees along the lake made patterns on the water. Squirts of apple-red morning poked between thick limbs. The sunlight fled over the water and made it look brightly dyed, and then the red water gradually became yellow as polished gold, and the sunlight rose higher, and all the woods began to glow, the evergreens shiny with rain, sighing in the wind, their bare limbs shedding sun-sparkled drops of water like tears.

I wanted to feel and see and smell it all. If this was going to be my last time in the woods and on the water, I wanted it to be as much on my terms as I could manage; I wanted to go out with the world I loved nestled in my head.

Throw us in the briar patch, assholes. Throw us in the briar patch and let us run.

The barge chugged along for a while, and then around a bend in the river. The trees cleared considerably there. There was a great patch of darkened land where lightning had struck and trees had burned.

The barge churned toward that spot, and we came up against the shore slightly, bouncing the barge back a bit. The blonde woman, trying to get in Aussie Hat's good graces and be as helpful as possible, jumped ashore with the docking line and tied it off. The barge motor coughed a little, there was another bump, and then we were as still as a craft can be on water.

"Get the whore's head?" Aussie Hat said to the dark-haired woman, and motioned us ahead of him and out the door. I thought as soon as we were on the deck of the barge, where the blood would be easy to clean, he might shoot us in the head.

I considered making a leap for it, hit the bank and keep on running, but I didn't. I gambled there were greater opportunities for us, but I've never been a good gambler. Besides, I wasn't going to leave Leonard behind. We ran together, or we went down together.

Aussie Hat waved us on shore with the pistol, and we went. The others came after, except for Baseball Cap. The dark-haired woman carried the head and sat it on a low, charred stump some distance away, then went back to the edge of the water.

Baseball Cap came out carrying two bows and two quivers of arrows. He gave one bow and a quiver to Aussie Hat, handed the blonde the pistol. She held it on us while he swung the quiver into place, threaded several arrows onto the rack on the bow after stringing it.

He turned then and an arrow flew from the bow almost without effort. It hit the dead woman's head and tore so cleanly through it, it didn't even knock it off the stump. They all cheered like a touchdown had been made.

Baseball Cap fired his bow, and the arrow went into one of the eyes, lodged there, deep in her skull. I thought, you don't get much worse than these assholes, and if you do, it would be so bad as to be otherworldly.

Aussie Hat took his pistol back, and handed the dark-haired woman the bow. She notched an arrow and shot at the head. The arrow stuck in the stump just below where the head was mounted.

"That's why we do the hunting," Aussie Hat said.

"Let me," said the blonde. She took the bow from the dark-haired woman and took a shot. She hit the head in the cheek and the head tumbled off the stump and rolled across the damp, blackened ground.

"That was alright," said Aussie Hat. "But you shoot it right, arrow hits so hard it'll go right through it, might not even knock it off, it can be such a clean shot. You got the edge of her face. But it was good. It was good."

"You think so?" she said.

"Sure," he said. "It was really good. Hey, give me the pistol."

Baseball Cap gave the pistol to Aussie Hat. I thought, well, this is it for us. Aussie Hat held the bow in his left hand, held the pistol in his right hand. He said, "Lois."

The blonde looked at him and he shot her square between the eyes, spraying blood on Baseball Cap. She hit the ground so fast it was as if her legs dissolved.

"What the hell?" said Baseball Cap, his face was covered in the blonde's blood.

"She talked back to me last night," Aussie Hat said. "I couldn't let it go."

"Jesus, Cameron," Baseball Cap said. "Jesus."

"Churchgoing pussy is a dime a dozen, same as the whores we kill."

Okay. Convictions of any kind were out the window. Jesus had been tossed overboard. I could feel my nerves tightening inside my body like the strings on a well-tuned harp.

The dark-haired woman stood extremely still, as if she might be able to disappear if she didn't move.

Aussie Hat laughed. "You can relax, Mavis. You're all right. Nothing's going to happen to you."

"I can't believe you did that, man," Baseball Cap said. "Lois was all right. Damn, I liked her."

"She had a mouth on her," Aussie Hat said, and gave Baseball Cap a long study.

"All right," said Baseball Cap. "You're right. She talked too much about the wrong things."

"Woman ought to keep her mouth full of dick to keep from talking, way I see it," Aussie Hat said. "You agree with that Mavis?"

Mavis nodded.

"Good, cause your mouth is going to be full of my dick a long time tonight."

Baseball Cap said, "What about them?"

"It's going to go bad for them. I was thinking we could cut Lois's head off and put it on the stump, do the same to these boys, have a few hours of target practice, but you know what? I think we let them go, see what kind of sport they are. But I'm not giving them an hour. I'm giving them fifteen minutes because they're such smart-mouth boys. I don't like smart-mouths. Ask Lois. Well, never mind on that."

I was hoping Leonard wouldn't say anything at just that moment, wired as Aussie Hat was, and thankfully he didn't.

Aussie Hat held one of the arrows up. "See that point," he said. "That's real fine steel. That point, I've shot it through old refrigerator doors. Went right through it and ripped the feathers off the shaft."

"Yeah, but we ain't no refrigerators," Leonard said.

"No, you are not," said Aussie Hat.

"Giving us less time, why not make it a little more sporting?" Leonard said. "Give us our knives and canteens back."

"You're not going to live long enough to need a drink," Aussie Hat said. "Shit, give them their knives, not that it'll matter. No canteens."

Mavis, wanting to make an impression, hurried to get them.

No one said anything until Mavis came back with the knives. She handed them to us, and then looked at Lois's body on the ground. A fly had lit on one of Lois's blue eyeballs. Mavis trembled ever so slightly.

"I knew her for years," Mavis said. It was something that just slipped out.

"Well, you won't be knowing her next year," Aussie Hat said. "You got any complaints you want to lodge, baby?"

Mavis shook her head.

"So, you got no problem with holding down the barge and not going hunting? Am I right?"

Mavis nodded.

"Am I right?" Aussie Hat said again.

"Yes," Mavis said. "You're right."

"Thought I was. All right, then. Fifteen minutes for our Daniel Boones here, and then we pincushion their asses. See that path there? You are clear to begin there, and you get a fifteen-minute start. After that, hell's coming."

"So far we're still standing here without a countdown," Leonard said, "and I can smell your rotten breath from over here. I'd like to move on, if you mean it."

I saw Aussie Hat's eye twitch.

Leonard could do that to a person.

"Go now," Aussie Hat said. "Or I'm going to kill you both right here. Mavis, mark the time."

Mavis grabbed Baseball Cap's wrist, lifted his hand and looked at his watch. Baseball Cap let her. His face looked as if it were full of Novocain. I believe he was still thinking about Lois. Even he had been surprised at that.

"Starting . . . now," she said, and dropped his arm.

We started running across the burnt clearing and into the woods where there was a wide deer trail. It went straight for a while and we went straight with it. When the trail bent around behind some trees and we were concealed by them, we darted into the first slightly clear spot we saw in the underbrush, hunkering low, crawling through gaps in the greenery, raising up when we could, running hard when we were able to.

The sun was full up now, and we wanted to go in the direction from which it had risen—East. That led back across the water, back to our crummy rental cabin and to our ride. We could drive out of the deep woods then, down the red-clay road that led to the highway.

We came to a small run of water that wetted down our boots and jumped on the other side of it and ran along the edge of it. It was down below the main trail bordered by brush and trees and wads of vines.

The assholes had actually waited fifteen minutes, or so I estimated, because we could hear them running along the main trail. They hadn't figured out we had gone off the path, thinking maybe we were complete rubes. Soon they would realize our footprints weren't showing up, and they'd backtrack and find where we had dodged into the thicket.

On the other side of the thin run of water was another hill, but we didn't go up that. If they were to come through the brush fast as we had, along the path we had made, they would see us up on that hill, and with their weapons they wouldn't have to be close to get a bead on us. We continued along the edge of the little creek, leaving tracks, but too much in a hurry to worry about it. Finally the hill sloped off sharply, and there was a rent in the trees to the left of the creek. That's the way we went, along another animal trail, this one much smaller than the first.

We eventually halted long enough to see if we could hear them coming. We couldn't. They could have been sneaking, but I didn't think so. They were confident and had been charging about like bulldozers. Not being able to hear them meant they had gone the wrong way, or had paused and were trying to figure which way we had taken. If they had any hunting skills at all, that wouldn't take long.

"We ought to fix ourselves up," I said.

"You got an idea?"

I found a small tree and bent it over until it snapped. Where the little tree had broken off there was a somewhat sharp point. I edged this keener and shaper with my knife, trimmed the small limbs off until I had a spear of about seven feet long and about half as thick as my wrist.

Leonard did the same with another young, thin tree. When we had spears made, we started moving again. I was beginning to feel thirsty, and I might have been hungry as well. I couldn't tell if the gnawing in my stomach was a need for food and water, or the churning acid of fear.

They found the way we went, because we could hear them back there. Pretty soon they would cross the creek and be on the path we were running along, and they could come quickly too, and they could shoot at us with the arrows or the pistol, and they could do it from a distance.

Without really talking about it, we found a path between two great oaks, and we took that. It didn't go far before the trees were entwining and it was hard to go that way, but by then there was no going back. We kept at it and fought our way through. After that we came to the swamp we had crossed before and started wading into it. It wasn't deep, but as before, it was a slow slog. Snakes were everywhere, though I only saw one moccasin; the rest of them were water snakes of one sort or another. The water was a scummy-silver in the sunlight.

Through the trees to our right was a slope, and down the slope were weeping willows, and between them you could see the lake. The slope actually rose up like a rim at first, and then where the water was high it flowed over a little in a shiny waterfall, more of a trickle really.

About halfway across the swamp, with thicker woods in sight, an arrow passed over my shoulder with a sound like someone sucking in their breath real hard. It missed me by less than an inch.

I glanced back, and there they were, stringing arrows and sending them at us. One clipped the top of Leonard's ear, shooting up a little streak of blood. Leonard veered right and yelled for me to follow. To stay where it was swampy was suicide. They could stand where they were for a long time and have us in range as we mucked along.

Toward the slope we went. Another arrow slipped between us, close enough had I been an inch thicker I'd have been wearing it. We jumped down the slope, still holding our spears, slipping and sliding on our asses, coming to the willows below. We both laid on our backs and let the wet slope of wild grass coast us down. I went right through a split in willow trees and was jettisoned off into the lake with a splash as loud as if an anvil had been dropped from an airplane. I tried to cling to the spear, but lost it. Leonard was hung up between willows by his spear, the ends of it sticking out on either side of his body. He turned it so it was straight, pushed off, and was sailed out into the water near me.

By this time I realized the water along the bank was shallow because of sand deposits, and I had recovered my spear. When I looked up, the two of them were at the top of the slope. I could see them through the trees.

Aussie Hat was stringing his bow, and about that time Baseball Cap, who was standing too close to the edge, slipped, and down the slope he went on his belly, losing his bow and the arrow. I watched as he sailed perfectly between the trees I had gone through, and then he shot up and out, like he was doing an impression of Superman.

I stuck the butt of my homemade spear in the sand, buried it deep, and lined that point up with him, the way a Masai warrior might do on dry land with a leaping lion.

He came down on top of the spear point with a hard impact. I could hear the thud of the spear, then a ripping sound. Baseball Cap screamed and the force of his hit rocked the spear backwards and I lost my grip and he went sailing over my shoulder, speared on my crude lance.

Leonard had managed his way back to shore, where he picked up the bow Baseball Cap had dropped. The bow had three arrows in the special rack on the side of the bow. Leonard pulled one into position as an arrow whizzed past him, lifted it and shot. His aim was terrible. He might as well have been trying to hit a gnat on the other side of the swamp.

"Hap," he said, and gave me a look of frustration.

I half-walked and half-swam to him and took the bow and pulled another arrow in place, just as Aussie Hat, who had now dropped to one knee on the edge of the swampy slope, was aiming down at us. I don't know how to explain it, but I have an unerring aim with most weapons, rifles, shotguns, handguns, and from past experience, I knew I wasn't any slouch with a bow and arrow either. I pulled the arrow back, the bow cord groaning as I did, and let it go. The arrow flew straight with a whistling sound. Aussie Hat moved to one side, so it didn't hit him in the throat like I had hoped. Still, he took the shot in the shoulder, grunted, dropped his bow and fell back out of sight. His bow tumbled down the hill and caught up amidst the willows. We waited to see if he would show with the pistol, but he didn't. A few minutes later his hat came floating down on the water slide and hung up in some brush growing out of the side of the slope.

Edging my way along the bank, I found a place where I could get behind some trees. I strung another arrow from the bow rack, crouched, peeked between the trees and waited, but Aussie Hat didn't poke his head over the slope.

I looked back in the water. Leonard had gotten the spear I had stuck in Baseball Cap, and he was using it to guide the body to shore. Except Baseball Cap wasn't dead. He was stuck like a fly on a display pin. He groaned slightly and blood ran out of his mouth. His cap floated between his legs.

Leonard got hold of his head, pushed him under water and held him there. After a glance up the slope, assuring myself Aussie Hat wasn't in sight, I slipped back down and into the lake, and partly swam and partly walked over to them.

"Leonard," I said. "Let him go."

"He's going to die anyway."

"Let him die then. Let him go."

"You're no fun."

Leonard let him go and dragged him up so that his head and shoulders were on the bank. He stuck his arms through roots growing out from the bank, and they held him in place. The back end of the spear stood straight up out of his chest.

Baseball Cap, minus the cap, coughed blood and water. I eased over to him. He looked up at me.

"You're the only ones ever got away," he said.

"Told you we would," Leonard said.

"Goddamn it," he said. "Lois. She was all right."

He gulped big and was still, his eyes open and unmoving.

"One down," Leonard said.

Leonard and I went wide of each other, made our way up the slope. It was a hard go, but we made it by using the willows and wet roots sticking out of the grass on the incline. I had taken the quiver from Baseball Cap's body. It was one of those things where the arrows are well-fastened in them and are not easily able to fall out. They had survived his slide and his dunking in the water, not to mention a spear through him where the point came out of his back and moved the quiver to one side. I gave Leonard three arrows, and I took three. Leonard found Aussie Hat's bow, and he took that. Now we were both armed. Leonard couldn't have hit an elephant in the ass with one of those arrows, if he was standing twenty feet away, but it was something.

When I got to the top of the slope, Aussie Hat wasn't there, nor did he seem to be lying in hiding. He didn't take a shot at us from concealment.

It made sense to us that he would try and go back

toward the barge. He was wounded now and it seemed smarter of him to try and escape than to stay with the hunt. But a guy like that, you couldn't be sure.

Wet to the bone, and sliming with the swamp and the lake, we stayed apart, but within eyeshot, and made our way back the way we had come. When we got out of the swamp water, we found blood in the brush and against trees. Aussie Hat was making his way back the way we had come. When we came to the last true trail we were on, we found him lying in the center of it with his back against a tree and the pistol clutched in his hand, his hand on his right thigh. The arrow I had shot was sticking out of his shoulder.

It was obvious he was dead.

"Bleed out," Leonard said.

I took the pistol. We decided we'd go back to the barge and get Mavis, and use the barge to make our way around to the part of the lake where our cabin was, but when we got to where the barge had been, it was gone. Lois's body was gone. The head of the poor murdered woman was still there.

Without any recourse, we started back through the woods, past Aussie Hat's body and on through the swamp. Eventually we passed the woman's headless body. It took some time, but finally we came to the cabin and our car. We didn't get anything out of the cabin. Leonard had the keys with him. I put the pistol on the seat between us, and Leonard, without a word, drove us out of there.

Not a whole lot to tell after that, but I will say this. We were jailed for three days. They wouldn't let us go and show them where the bodies were, and they didn't believe our story. It was obvious they thought if anyone was dead out there, it was because we killed them. They were partly right.

Finally they let Leonard call Marvin, our cop friend in LaBorde, and some words were exchanged between the chief there and Marvin. We spent another night in the cell, Leonard on one cot, me in the other across the way.

Silver lining was they gave us plenty of water to drink, and they were serving macaroni and cheese again for the third time in a row. For lunches we had been having peanut butter sandwiches with water, but it wasn't perfect. What kind of heathen serves a peanut butter sandwich without a glass of milk?

Marvin came, and at first that didn't help much, but finally he talked them into letting us lead them to the bodies. We showed them the woman's body first, and in that short time it had already started to decompose in the heat and as the two men had predicted, animals had been at it. It had been pulled about ten yards from where we had seen it last, and it was ripped up good. Ants and maggots had done their work as well. We took them on a guided tour that ended up with the bodies of the men, Baseball Cap still floating partially in the lake, and Aussie Hat still holding down his spot on the animal trail. The barge and Mavis, and Lois's body, were still gone, of course.

We described Lois and Mavis to the cops. Three days later, they found Lois's body on the barge, which had been abandoned, tied to the shore in a narrow cove off the lake, about a mile from where it had been the last time we saw it.

They found the skulls of other women at the spot where the barge had been parked. All the skulls had arrow or bullet holes in them. They finally took our detailed statement and let us go home.

To shorten it up, the two men's bodies were identified. Both had been in prison, and though there had been suspicions about them before for other crimes, none of those suspicions had anything to do with missing women. Nothing had been proved, but much had been considered.

Lois was discovered to have been a hard worker in the medical profession, a party girl who liked to run with a rough crowd, or so her co-workers said. No one really claimed to be her friend, but her penchant for men on the bad side was well known. And though the cops were certain once they found Lois it would lead to them finding Mavis, none of the people Lois worked with had heard of anyone named Mavis. In spite of her party girl persona, no one could believe Lois would be involved in what she was involved in. Mavis went unfound.

I checked six months ago and they still hadn't found her. I hope they do, but I have this odd and unfounded feeling they may not. I figure soon as those two men traveled down that trail, she had dragged Lois out of there as a sign of respect, and then sailed away, severing ties with the men because she had realized that she, same as Lois, was expendable, nothing more than a warm body to pass the time with.

Yet, she wasn't one of life's innocents. She may have taken Lois's body away from there, but I had seen her dance with a dead woman's skull, and didn't have one ounce of sympathy for her. I hoped she was somewhere in a dark room hanging from a rope with a turned-over chair at her feet.

Me and Leonard got lectures from the cops, but in the end we got a nice write-up as heroes in a few newspapers. Our involvement in the whole mess was ruled as two citizens trying to find out who the killers of the young woman were, and it was more importantly decided those two who had died at our hands were killed in self-defense, which was true enough.

The woman we had come upon, the dying lady, had been named Sally Ernst. She had a daughter. I wondered how the kid was doing.

So far, neither me nor Leonard have talked about going fishing again.

COLD COTTON

ONE

"You know I'll love you, no matter what," Brett said, "but I think maybe you ought to get something."

"Something?" I said.

We were lying in bed. I had just made an attempt to make love to my wife and had failed. It was starting to be a regular thing. I had the urge, and just looking at her always warmed me up, but now my mind warmed, but the tool for the job didn't.

"You aren't a spring chicken anymore," Brett said.

"But we aren't that old, either," I said.

"I know I'm not," Brett said, "but we're talking about you."

"Oh, that's nice."

"Okay, here's the thing. You can't get the sock to fill up, you can always do other things."

"I'm all for that," I said, "and we already do other things, but what's the end game for me?"

"Yeah, I guess it ought to be good for you too."

"Ha, ha."

"All I'm asking is you go see your doctor, ask him about it."

"Don't think I need pills."

"You can be sure with a checkup."

"What's he going to ask me do, get a hard-on in his office, jack me off? I don't think so. It's all guesswork."

"Right now, it's not any kind of work."

I turned on my side and looked at her. She showed me a Bugs Bunny grin.

"Love you," she said.

Who would have thought me worrying about my erection problem was going to lead to murder?

TWO

"I think I'm okay, just tired," I said.

I was in the doctor's office and he had me sitting on the end of one of those tables they have, a paper cover stretched over it. I was only wearing my shorts and socks, as he'd given me an overall exam. I noticed one of my socks had a hole where the big toe goes.

"You're okay, but you can't get it up?" Doctor Sylvan asked.

"I haven't been able to get it up lately. It's a phase."

"How long is lately?"

"I don't know, couple months."

"You are older, but you know, we can fix that."

"You can make me young again?"

"Very funny. All the king's horses, and all the king's men, they couldn't put your ass together again."

"You mean Viagra?"

"Perhaps. You know, Hap, been your doctor a long time, and we're close. I can't tell you how many times I've had my finger up your ass feeling your prostate—"

"Always my favorite part of an exam," I said.

"And mine. You are about as affable as anyone I know, a little smart-mouthed, but considering I have that disease, I let that go. Thing is, though, there's rumors all over town about you and Leonard."

"About our clandestine sexual encounters in the men's restroom at the bus station?"

"No. About how maybe you two have done some things that are, shall we say, on the dark side."

"Rumors. Said it yourself."

"Lot of rumors, and some from good sources, and listen here, any of what I've heard is true, you're doing what a lot of us would like to do."

"Really?"

"I too would love to fuck sheep, but, you know, I have to be careful, being a doctor."

"Oh, fuck you."

"Look. Not kidding. I know you and Leonard have

had your moments with miscreants. I tend to believe those stories. Some of the scars you got, I didn't sew those up, and some of the work looks like it might have been done by a veterinarian."

"Their work looks different?"

"Not so much, but I can spot a different kind of stitch, also, some of those scars you got, they look to me to have been from knives, and gunshots."

"I've been in the hospital for being stabbed, Doc. You know that. You were there."

"Uh-huh, but a lot of those wounds, don't remember those."

"I was out of town. I live a clumsy life."

"Here's what I'm getting at, Hap. I'm all for giving you a pill that will turn your pecker into a Zeppelin, but I'm not eager to give out things like that if I think there might be another reason."

"You're buying that whole thing about me being tired?"

"Nope. You look pretty perky to me, and you're in good health for someone your age."

"I think Mickey Mantle said if he knew he was going to live this long he'd taken better care of himself."

"What I'm going to suggest is you see a therapist."

"A therapist? What the hell for?"

"If, and I say if, you have done what I think you've done, you might ought to talk to someone. Things like I think you might have done, and we'll say it in code, killing a lot of fucking people, might build on your conscience. This tough guy thing, I don't buy it."

"I'm not really trying to sell that image. And by the way, that wasn't code."

"No?"

"No."

"Gonna give you a name. See her a couple times, and there doesn't seem to be something under the surface, we'll talk about Viagra. Thing is, though, if it is something other than needing lead in your pencil, and this other stuff is causing it, it's probably affecting you in other ways as well."

He leaned over and tapped my head with his finger.

"Might be a lot of stuff in there you're dealing with and you just don't know it. Little therapy might help you do more than get a stiff one back."

"I don't know Doc."

"I'll go get her card."

THREE

The name on the card was Carol Cotton.

I sat out in the car in front of the doctor's office for a few minutes and looked at the card and thought about things. I could go see her, spend money I didn't want to spend, and really, what could she tell me that I didn't actually already know?

I had killed a lot of people.

I'm mixed on the whole idea of therapy. I think it's

more of an art than a science, and I felt like I would be a kind of art project. Still, I knew of people therapists had helped, but I wasn't sure I was one of those it would do much for. As for those people who went to see them because they had been named after a successful father, and just couldn't live up to the name, or some such problem, fuck it. Get over yourself.

I had some real shit in my lunch pail.

I had done my killing in self-defense, and in some cases for justice. Saying that was the way I made myself feel better about it, but all of it haunted me from time to time, though I had learned as of late to deal with it better. It didn't quite settle the reptilian stirrings and the dark red memories at the back of my brain.

Recently, I had died and come back, gone way down there in the big deep dark, and had resurfaced, seeming whole, and feeling whole for quite some time. Then the deep dark rose up again.

That was the problem. I knew that as I sat there in my car in front of the doctor's office and wondered how I could explain that to anyone who had not been there. Leonard had been there, and talking to him helped. Both of us had been close to death a number of times, but the thing about Leonard was when something was over with, it was over for him. Oh, I can't say I know what all went on deep down in his brain, what memories he carried from being in a war, and what memories he carried since we had been friends, but whatever they were, he could tote that water better than me.

How do you tell those things to a shrink, let them in on your innermost thoughts? Tell them you have killed and nearly been killed, and that things would be fine for long periods of time, and then one day you can't get it up because you are riding the nightmares while solid awake. How do you do that?

I decided I couldn't.

I drove home.

FOUR

Me and Brett had finished up a light dinner of salad and iced tea, and were about to sit on the couch and snuggle and watch television with bowls of popcorn, when my cell phone rang.

I picked it up and went into the living room and sat on the couch.

It was my doctor.

"Did you call her?" he asked.

"Who?"

"Don't play games with me, Hap. You know who. Carol Cotton."

"Are you minding my business after your business hours?"

"I am. I contacted her, didn't tell her a damn thing about what your problem might be, didn't mention the rumors, but told her you might call and set up an appointment."

"That is nosey of you," I said.

"I told her you're a smartass."

"So are you."

"Yeah, but I wasn't recommending me, I was recommending you."

"I thought about it, but I didn't call her."

"You should. She's good. I had a time or two when I talked with her."

"Yeah?"

"Yeah. I got a few war memories."

"It helped?"

"It did. It's not like a headache, you go in and take one session like you take an aspirin and the headache quits. But it helps."

I listened to the microwave humming in the kitchen as Brett popped corn. I turned my head and watched her move about, filling our tea glasses up while the popcorn popped.

"You still there, Hap?"

"Yeah. Thinking. I hear you. I'm not miserable, but I'm not good either," I said.

"Call her."

Brett came into the living room as I clicked off the phone. She was carrying two bags of popped microwave corn. She gave me one, sat the other on the coffee table. She went back into the kitchen and came back with two glasses of iced tea. She placed them on the coffee table, sat down and tore open her bag of corn. The aroma of it filled the air, and the memory of trips to the theater in

Marvel Creek filled my head, then faded away.

"Anything important?" Brett asked.

"The doctor. He gave me a card today. A shrink."

"Oh. How do you feel about that?"

"I don't know. I mean, do I tell a stranger about what I've done, what we've all done, and let her ride around with the guilt of being my doctor and not being able to say a thing about it to the law, and then me worry she might anyway? I don't know."

"Draw a line."

"What?"

"Decide you will tell only so much, and don't tell the stuff like that. Hint at it maybe. I don't know, but don't tell it all."

"Wouldn't that go against what I'd be trying to accomplish?"

"It could. Hell, Hap. I don't know. But I can tell you're aren't quite yourself, and I'm not just talking about sex. Doctor says you seem fine physically, then it might be in your head. You might need to get it out, or learn to find some place comfortable inside your head to put it, some way of dealing with it."

"I'll think it over," I said.

We watched an old silent film on a movie classics channel, *The General* with Buster Keaton.

I laughed a lot. Maybe a little too loudly.

FIVE

I didn't call Carol Cotton after all, but she called me two days later.

I was sitting at the kitchen table, sipping coffee, reading the *New York Times* headlines on my cell phone, when it buzzed and I answered.

After she introduced herself, I said, "I thought I was supposed to call you? I wasn't sure I was going to."

"Understand," she said. She had a nice voice, and I couldn't help but imagine that she was lying in bed as she called, nude, nice-looking. For all I knew, she was seventy-five years old, sitting on the toilet working out a big one, and that gave her the throaty sound, but I liked the other idea better. Of course, even if my gal let me date, I probably couldn't get it up with a rope and a pulley.

"I'm not sure I need a doctor," I said.

"That's up to you, and frankly, it's not why I called."

"What else could you be calling for?"

"You're a private investigator, right?"

"I work for an agency and I'm private, and I investigate with my boss, Brett Sawyer, and my brother, Leonard Pine, so I guess I am."

It was still hard for me to think of myself as a private eye. In my mind, real private eyes, they actually knew something about investigation. All I knew was persistence. Also, unlike private eyes in stories, I didn't drink or smoke cigarettes or chase women. I had the woman I wanted. I looked at the supplies and fantasized about it now and again, but I wasn't shopping.

"That's why I'm calling. I need your services. Maybe we could find a way to trade our expertise. If not, I can just pay you. But I need someone."

"To do what?"

"To make sure I don't get killed."

SIX

"Who's trying to kill her?" Leonard asked.

Me and Leonard and Brett were at the office. They were seated. I was standing at the big glass window that looked out at the parking lot, two stories down.

"She doesn't know," I said.

"But someone is?" Leonard said.

"That's what she wants us to find out," Brett said.

I had already told Brett about the call, and what Carol Cotton had told me.

"We go over there around eleven, have an early lunch at her house, and she's going to give us the whole nine yards and a fat retainer," I said. "She has had threats and she doesn't know who it is. She said she had a whole roster of patients, some of which might want her dead, simply because they are disturbed, or have somehow latched onto her in an unhealthy way."

"Disturbed means crazy motherfuckers, right?" Leonard said.

"It just might," I said. "But she doesn't know it's a patient. That's merely a possibility. She may just want a bodyguard for a while. It could be nothing. I mean, the threats might be real, but then they might be idle. She thinks that's possible too, but reasonably, she wants that sorted out. She said someone killed her cat."

"That's low," Leonard said.

"Could be it merely died, she said, but she thinks it was poisoned. She admitted that because the cat is dead and the threats are real, she decided they were connected, but they might not be."

Brett glanced at the clock on the wall.

"We better saddle up," she said. "Hope she's serving something good. I'm hungry."

SEVEN

Carol Cotton's therapy business looked to be booming. Had to be. She lived behind a high wall with an electronic gate. When I leaned out of my open window and told the speaker who it was, the gate snapped open instantly, and I drove us inside.

First thing we saw was a very nice three-story house only a little smaller than Buckingham Palace, but maybe with a better lawn.

We drove up the winding drive that curled around to the back of the house and parked next to a tennis court. On the other side of the court there was a pool house about the size of the house where Brett and I lived, and there was a large heart-shaped pool near the tennis court full of bright blue water. Between the pool house and the pool there was a gazebo with a table and chairs inside, a curtain of netting around the gazebo to keep out flies and mosquitoes.

Inside the netting a woman sat at a table. She had on a white pool robe and as we parked and got out of the car, she stood up, came through the netting and started walking around the pool to meet us.

As she walked toward us, the robe swung open and I saw she was wearing a two-piece bathing suit, and both of those pieces were having quite the workout. The bottoms were light on material and hid only the main goodie. The top barely contained her breasts the way a thimble contains a cantaloupe. Her hair was short and black and shaped her face beautifully. She had tanned skin and long legs. Perhaps there is a god after all.

"That can't be her," Brett said. "She looks to be in her twenties."

"Maybe she is real smart and got through college quick-like," I said.

"Has she cured your problem already?" Brett said.

"Very funny, dear."

As she got closer, she pulled the robe together and tied it with the cloth belt. Woman like that could make a eunuch grow balls.

"Pardon me for the informality," the woman said, extending her hand to Brett. "I let the time get away from me."

She and Brett exchanged names, and she was in fact Dr. Carol Cotton. She shook hands with me and Leonard. She had long fingers, warm to the touch, that wrapped around my hand like a sweet little spider.

"If you would like, you can wait under the gazebo and I'll dress and be right back out." I will say this, she didn't have that nice throaty voice I had heard on the phone, but it wasn't bad.

We agreed it was fine that we would wait for her. She sashayed to the main house and we trucked on out to the gazebo.

Inside the netting, Brett said, "She let the time get away from her? Shit. I think she just wanted to show off the merchandise."

"It is nice merchandise," I said.

"You think you aren't getting any now," Brett said, "keep at it."

Leonard said, "How about them Mets?"

"She isn't what I expected," Brett said. "I've decided you don't need therapy. Not with her, anyway. I had in mind someone like Doctor Ruth."

"She's dead," I said.

"No. It just seems that way."

Leonard said, "Aren't we here about something else other than Hap's pecker? Threats?"

"She doesn't look all that scared to me," Brett said.

"Sitting out here in her underwear."

"That's a high-priced bathing suit," I said.

"How would she have felt had I worn mine to this meeting," Brett said.

"Jealous," I said.

"Oh, you are winning back some points," Brett said.

It was then that Dr. Cotton came out of the main house and headed toward us. She had put on jeans and a white tee-shirt and was still wearing the pool shoes.

When she pushed aside the netting and stepped into the gazebo, she wore a big smile but no bra; she bounced under the shirt. This was either a woman comfortable in her own skin, or something of an exhibitionist.

"Thanks for coming," she said. "Linda is bringing out lunch."

Linda was a short, stocky Mexican lady whose birth name was probably not Linda. She came out with a younger woman who looked like a younger version of her, minus the stocky. She was cute and had a nervous smile, and like Linda, she had a tray with food on it. She said her name was Mindy.

The two women looked at Dr. Cotton, both with expressions that were hard to read, except to say they were uncomfortable.

"Thanks so much, ladies," Dr. Cotton said.

The women put the trays on the table and we thanked them and they smiled.

"They are so sweet," Dr. Cotton said.

The sweet ladies stepped off quickly and went into

the house while Dr. Cotton told us about how much she liked tennis and swimming, and then from the house a woman dressed in jeans and a loose, blue top, blonde hair swinging around her shoulders, was walking fast toward us.

Leonard had just picked up a finger sandwich when the woman came through the netting carrying a tote bag. She looked at Dr. Cotton, and said, "Katherine. Sugar Muffin. You know better than this."

Dr. Cotton, a.k.a. Katherine, giggled, got up and nodded at us, walked by and touched my face with the back of her hand, and then she was through the netting and heading toward the house.

The blonde lady, who was a fine-looking woman herself, probably in her forties, said, "So sorry. You might say that's one of my patients. I'm Dr. Cotton."

EIGHT

"Does this mean we're still having brunch," Leonard said. "I'm damn sure hungry."

The real Dr. Cotton laughed, and sat down. "Of course. That woman is my niece as well as a patient. It's a long story. She was supposed to be in her room. She isn't really sick, she just has . . . well, a need to be noticed."

"Don't we all?" Brett said.

"Not like her. She has to be the constant center of

attention. I probably shouldn't tell you much about her condition, but, since she's my niece, and not really an official patient, I can say it. She's sexually dysfunctional, or what they used to call an exhibitionist with nymphomaniac tendencies."

"Is that a bad thing?" I said. "I mean, it sounds functional."

Brett slapped me on the shoulder with the back of her hand.

"Don't mind him," Brett said. "I rescued him from a wolf den, where he was raised."

The doctor laughed, and she had an even throatier voice than on the phone; it seemed to come from someplace dark but sweetly nasty. "I'm really more of a caretaker, and I am her therapist as well, but not in an official way. It's personal, and I'm aware that I have limitations when I'm dealing with my own family. She has an official therapist for that."

"Is it helping?" Brett asked.

"Sometimes you don't know until you do know," Doctor Cotton said. "I know that sounds vague, but that's how it works."

Leonard was eating another sandwich when Carol said, "Go ahead. Dig in."

We ate and drank iced tea for a bit, and then I said, "Doctor. Seems to me you're playing it pretty loose here if you're being threatened."

"The wall around the house is reasonably high, and there are cameras and alarms. So, I don't know there's much more I can do as far as normal security. That's why I want to hire your agency."

She said that like we were part of some big network of investigators.

"Tell us about the threats," Leonard said. He had moved onto the cookies by this time. He ate one delicately, nibbling around the edges. Had it been a vanilla cookie, especially a vanilla wafer, he'd have been all over it like a termite on rotten wood.

"I have my office here, and I've decided to put my practice on hold for the time being—briefly, I hope. I have inherited money, so that's not the problem, but wanting to get back to my patients is, but right now I'm scared to let anyone in that isn't vouched for. Doctor Sylvan was your voucher. But frankly, I'm just being cautious. I don't think it has anything to do with my patients. I don't have any with violent tendencies, nor have I ever felt any of them pose a threat. What happened was I began to receive things in the mail. . . . A dead rat in box. A letter with a photo of my face attached to a nude foldout from some men's magazine. And then it got worse. Notes made from letters cut from magazines or newspapers, very crude notes saying what they wanted to do to me."

"You have them?" Brett said.

Doctor Cotton picked up the tote bag and rummaged through it and came out with a fist full of letters. She handed them to Brett. They were all copies.

"Where are the originals?" Brett asked.

"Police. I went to them first."

"Wise idea," Brett said, and she began splitting up the notes, handing me and Leonard a few. "They didn't find prints, anything like that?"

"Nothing," Doctor Cotton said.

I looked at the notes. They were all vulgar and said things about what they'd like to do with her, and maybe they were sexual, and maybe they were just mean, and maybe they were lots of things I couldn't figure, but one thing was certain, they were indeed threating. Some had photos taken of Doctor Cotton in public, and they had arrows drawn through her body, and one spelled out how the note maker would like to cut Doctor Cotton's head off and shove it up her ass, and how there was a way to do that if the ass was cut open wide enough. It was more than a prank, that was sure. Were they meant merely to unsettle Doctor Cotton? Maybe, but she was wise to take them seriously.

"When did you get the last one?" Brett said.

"Yesterday," she said.

Doctor Cotton leaned over her bag and came out with one last note, as if it were the saved pièce de résistance, and handed it to Brett. "I copied it, and had it sent to the police as well."

It was a note like the others, only it had a photo stapled to it. It wasn't a very good photo, but it was of the area where we now were. It had been taken at night, and as I said, not a good photo, but clear enough to recognize the location. Someone had been inside the walls.

"Damn, girl," Brett said. "And what did the police say about this one?"

"They came in, took a look, and they have a patrol car drive by, but that's it. Something to do with their budget."

"Yeah, chief before Marvin Hanson, who's there now, spent all their money on riot gear, as if that's our big problem here in LaBorde," I said. "They even have a military assault vehicle. I think it did get used once to take everyone at the cop shop to Dairy Queen for ice cream. All that money was eaten up for stuff like that, you know, but not real police work."

"All I know," Doctor Cotton said, "is I'm scared. I have a gun in this bag. I carry it in my purse when I go out, and frankly, I rarely go out. I have it on me at all times. And I hate guns. I've become paranoid."

"Being paranoid don't mean they ain't out to get you," Leonard said.

"Popular therapy joke, actually," she said. "What I figured is maybe you could find out who this is, and in the meantime, give me some protection. I can pay whatever you require."

"You know," Leonard said, "I don't want to be a jackass about this, but did you consider maybe your niece?"

"I knew that might be your thought. Police had the same one. But she's harmless. I love her, and she loves me. I take care of her since my sister couldn't. She became very ill, and then died."

"All right," Leonard said, but like me, I knew he was thinking just because you don't think a person is dangerous or incapable of a thing, didn't mean they weren't dangerous and capable. But, on the other hand, the doctor struck me as someone who knew her business.

"What we can do," Brett said, "is start by giving you a bodyguard, and in the meantime, we can see if we can figure out what's what."

"I still don't know why the police couldn't do it," Doctor Cotton said. "Budget or no budget."

"Because they have a number of crimes to attend to, bureaucracy, and we don't," Brett said. "We can devote pretty much full time to it."

"Thing I figure," Leonard said, "is I'll stick around first, as a bodyguard, and I'll need to look through the house, get the lay of the land, that sort of thing."

"Of course," Doctor Cotton said.

"I will need a couple boxes of vanilla wafers."

"We'll provide those," I said.

"You know, I think I have a box, for banana pudding," Doctor Cotton said.

"If I wasn't gay," Leonard said, "you'd be the woman of my dreams."

NINE

Leonard stayed behind with a pistol of mine he took from the glove box, and me and Brett drove over to the police station, caught Chief Marvin Hanson in.

"Hey," he said after we were buzzed into his office, "one of my favorite people, Brett Sawyer, and one of my least favorite, Hap Collins."

"It never grows old," I said.

We were in his office and we all took chairs, and Brett told him we were taking the job with Doctor Cotton.

"Ah. Well, I hate we couldn't do more. I tried to have a cop put there for a week, but the money folk didn't like that idea. They agreed to having a car drive by a couple times a day. I send it a little more than that, a lot more than that, but it depends on someone trying to do something bad while they're driving by, and being visible while they're doing it. She's got a good rock fence and all, but frankly, someone wanted to get over it and inside, it's not that hard. Course, she's got the alarm and the cameras, but that wouldn't stop someone determined and didn't care if they were seen, and from the nature of those notes, I'm thinking it's a nut. It could be someone merely trying to scare her, get her goat, but I recommended you guys to her."

"As did Doctor Sylvan," I said. "Well, indirectly."

"We were wondering if you had any ideas," Brett said. "Thought we'd start with you, and also so you can let your drive by know we'll be around. We don't want to get shot doing our job, cops thinking we're someone else."

"I'll do that the minute you leave," he said. "As for anything else, we had the original notes dusted for fingerprints, but they only had Doctor Cotton's on them, her niece, who is a piece of work, and her servants. The niece ended up opening a couple of the letters herself. Doctor Cotton says she does that. She invades privacy, among other things. I'm afraid that's all I got. Other than saying it all feels screwy. Since your main man isn't with you, I assume you left him at the doctor's place."

"Good assumption," I said.

"Well, that's a good choice," he said.

"Did you consider the kooky niece could be behind this?" I said.

"Did, but nothing led there. Then again, as you know, we were sort of in and out."

"That's what she said," Brett said.

"Really, Brett," Hanson said.

"Yeah. I know. Been around Hap too long."

"Five minutes around him or Leonard is too long," he said.

"All right," Brett said. "Good enough. We're out of here."

TEN

So, we got it going, the three of us taking turns for the first few days, and then we got Leonard's boyfriend, Officer Curt Carroll, known to us as Pookie, to come in now and again on his day off.

Me and Leonard and Brett had the one pistol between us, as we felt that was sufficient fire power. We traded out each time we had the changing of the guard. Pookie, he had his own gun and always brought snacks, even though anything he could have wanted was provided by Doctor Cotton.

After a couple weeks, we hadn't seen a thing, and Doctor Cotton hadn't received another message. Each time it was my turn, I spent at least an hour a day fighting off Katherine, a.k.a. Sugar Muffin, who would have screwed a doorknob and called it sweet baby.

Brett said she even tried it on her, but Brett said she told her, "I'm on duty, and the only thing you're going to get off me is a black eye for taking my mind off the job."

Brett also assured her that she was batting for a standard team.

Harsh, but effective. Sweet Baby decided she was through bothering Brett.

Leonard said she tried it on him, but he was on a different team too. He said, "Hey, I only suck dicks," and it was over for him. He said Pookie had a similar experience, and he had to explain his position being similar to Leonard's, though I suspect his comments were kindlier. Pookie is a nice person.

That left me. She knew my affiliation.

It was a big house, and when on duty we wandered throughout, not really expecting anybody, but it was part of the job, checking the place for ninja assassins in the sock drawer or the shower stall.

What I figured, due to the nature of the threats, was whoever was doing this would hope to scare his target for a while, then maybe come in by means of subterfuge, claiming to be someone they weren't, or catching Doctor Cotton out doing errands. We put an end to the errands, took them over for her.

One late morning, Sweet Muffin made the usual play for my Johnson. We were both sitting on the couch. Suddenly she was sitting very close. I could smell her perfume and something more primal drifting off of her.

She put her hand on my thigh.

I turned and looked at her. Her eyelids were heavy and her lips seemed fat and desirable. I like to think it wasn't just my erection problem that cause me to make the choice I did.

I gently lifted her hand off my leg and placed it on the couch, said, "My gal doesn't let me date."

"She wouldn't need to know."

"But I'd know."

Katherine turned to pout mode and moved away from me and sat on the far end of the couch. She said, "I'm not being threatened. I should be able to go out."

"They might use you to get to your aunt," I said. "Sorry, we got to wait until they make a play or the threat seems to be gone."

"Haven't heard from them in a week," she said.

"That's not very long."

"It is when you're horny."

"Don't you have any toys?"

"Plenty, but I've never found it to be the same."

"We can agree on that," I said. "But really, Katherine,

you have to go somewhere else and play."

"I don't think I like you, Hap."

"There's a club you can join," I said.

She got huffy then and left the room.

Doctor Cotton was entering the room as Katherine was going out.

"I heard her," she said, "and I'm sorry."

"Not a problem. I figure she's doing the best she can about the whole business. I think she's tired of being cooped up in here."

"I know I am," she said, "and I'm sure you are."

I shrugged. "It's the job. Beats working at the chicken plant."

"I'm about to make myself lunch. Would you like a sandwich?"

"I would," I said.

We went into the kitchen and I sat on one of the stools at the long bar there.

Doctor Cotton opened the refrigerator and pulled out some cheese and lunch meat, slices of tomato, mustard and mayonnaise, a few odds and ends, put those on the bar. Then she got bread from the shelf by the refrigerator and put that with the other goods, grabbed us both Diet Cokes.

We had done this routine before with me and her.

She placed silverware on the table with plates, and we made ourselves sandwiches.

"Katherine really can't help it. It's the same as if she were an alcoholic."

"I understand," I said.

"But you played it right. I'm sure that's not the first time you've had to with her."

"We've all had to," I said. "But it's fine."

"So, Leonard and Curt?"

"She's hit on both of them, even though they're gay."

"I think she likes the challenge, Hap. And she can't help herself. So, Leonard and Curt, they are a serious item?"

"We call Curt Pookie. And yes. They are an item. Pookie really seems to make Leonard happy."

"And you and Leonard are good friends?"

"We are closer than good friends. We're like brothers."

"Yeah. Well, it's obvious Leonard is crazy about Curt. Sometimes he stays a second shift when Pookie is here."

"It won't keep them from doing their job," I said.

"Oh, I know that. I didn't mean that. I like it. It's sweet."

"This is a red-letter day. Someone has called Leonard sweet."

"I was wondering, why no more messages? They came like clockwork before."

"I was wondering the same thing. Whoever has been threatening you knows we're here, and they haven't bothered. I think whoever is doing it needs to scare you, and with us here, I don't think you getting a note or some such is going to be the same to them. They know you have us to fall back on. They want you on your own and afraid."

"Do you think it's one of the servants? I can't imagine

that, they're so nice, and I like to think well paid and appreciated, but I won't lie. I wondered."

"That was considered, of course, and Brett looked into it. Nothing seemed to point in that direction. They appear to be hardworking people, end of story. No. This is someone who knows you, or knows of you, and they want you scared, distracted."

"You're still thinking Katherine?"

"I don't really know what I'm thinking," I said. "But there's something screwy about the whole thing. Who could be that mad at you, and why?"

"I don't know. I really don't. I've been taking care of Katherine ever since my sister died. She had her problems, but I have a hard time believing it has to do with her. Still, the notes and threats have stopped since you've been here, and she's been under closer surveillance, not allowed to leave."

"We really can't tell her she can't leave, but we don't mind giving her that impression. Maybe . . . well, let's say we consider her. Why would she do such a thing?"

Doctor Cotton shook her head.

"Could she be mad at you for monitoring her sex life? Mad at you because she's obviously immature for her age and doesn't like being told no? Another thing is there's no one on your cameras from past events, no recordings of anyone that shouldn't be there, I mean. Whoever is doing this knows how to avoid the cameras. Have to so they can put notes in your mailbox."

"Meaning my niece again."

"She has to be considered."

Doctor Cotton nodded. "I suppose so."

We ate lunch and went on about our day, and things continued like that for another two weeks, and no note.

But the next week, on Wednesday, a note was found in the drive when Leonard drove in to trade places with Brett. I got a call, and joined them.

The message was not sealed, but was inside a loose-flapped manila envelope. Leonard gave it to Brett and Brett looked at what was inside. Then I showed up where they were waiting for me in the driveway outside the gate. Brett showed me and Leonard what was inside the envelope. It was certainly a surprise. I got back in my car and drove inside and parked near their cars.

We went and got Doctor Cotton, who was dressed in a white tennis outfit, and we all went out to the gazebo. Brett placed the envelope on the table.

"Would you check your cameras from last night until now before you look at the envelope?" Brett said.

Doctor Cotton got up and went inside to look at her monitors.

We sat there a while and I tried to tell a joke, but neither Leonard nor Brett would listen. After quite a while, Doctor Cotton came back.

"The cameras were turned off last night," she said.

"Do they switch off inside or outside, or more than one place?" Brett asked.

"No."

"Okay," Brett said, and tapped the envelope.

Doctor Cotton pulled the envelope to her and opened it, looked at what was inside. The tan drained out of her face, her lips trembled and she let out a little gasp, one hand going to her chest as if to hold her heart in place.

"Oh, my god," she said.

ELEVEN

It happened kind of quick. Doctor Cotton was on her feet, stomping across the concrete, and then the grass, toward her house. After a moment, Brett said, "I think Sugar Muffin is about to get the shit stomped out of her."

"We better stop it," I said.

"Let's give her a moment."

When we heard the screeching inside the house, we sauntered over, went through the sliding back doors. Katherine was in the living room and Doctor Cotton had her by the hair and had pulled her head to the side, and with her other hand she was knocking knots on Sugar Muffin's head faster than a cobra can strike.

Brett went over and caught Doctor Cotton's arm with her own, and then she twisted and threw Doctor Cotton over the back of the couch and onto it. The good doctor rolled off the couch and onto the floor.

Sugar Muffin went for Brett, as if to claw her. Brett stuck a finger in Sugar Muffin's jugular notch, causing her to gag and go to one knee.

"Uh-uh, sister," Brett said. "You might find yourself in need of a nose job and a wig."

Katherine sat on the floor and started crying. By this time, Doctor Cotton had gotten up, brushed herself off, straightened her tennis dress and fluffed her hair. She was once again a professional.

"I apologize for that," Doctor Cotton said.

"Nah, that's all right," Leonard said. "Brett can handle herself, and Sugar Muffin had it coming."

TWELVE

I suppose you could call it puppy love, sweet, sweet, puppy love, but not exactly the kind you might be thinking. They were photos of a woman, obviously, photos of Doctor Cotton in her teens, nude, lying partly across a bed with a Rottweiler mounting her. I shit you not.

There were several shots that showed Doctor Cotton's good angles, and the Rottweiler's as well. I think the dog looked best from the left side. He looked happy in his work. His tongue was hanging out.

There was also a note inside the envelope requesting five hundred thousand dollars or the photos would hit the internet with explanations of who was in them. Something like that could be devastating. At least the dog wasn't around for the humiliation, though my guess is he could have gotten over it.

Within minutes the lady servants appeared, drawn by the racket. Linda and her daughter stood close enough together they were almost Siamese twins.

Doctor Cotton looked at them and smiled. "It's quite all right," she said. "A bit of a misunderstanding."

"Yes, ma'am," Linda said, took her daughter's elbow and walked her out of the room.

Doctor Cotton didn't look directly at us when she said, "I can't tell you how embarrassed I am. About those old photos, and doing what I did."

"Like I said," Leonard said. "She had it coming."

Doctor Cotton went out of the house and we followed her to the gazebo. We all sat in chairs. She picked up the envelope, said, "I was young and stoned, and my boyfriend had a dog. Katherine is not the only one who had problems with exhibition and what you might call kinky sex. I was pleasing someone important to me, doing what I thought I was supposed to do. He took some of the photos. The rest were taken by my sister, Katherine's mother. She did it for the same someone. My god, a Rottweiler."

I wondered if she would have felt better had it been a German shepherd. Somehow, I couldn't imagine a chihuahua that could do the work without a footstool.

"I didn't know those pictures still existed. They must have been in my sister's stuff. After she died. She died of a drug overdose. I had her stuff brought here. Her personal items. Katherine has been looking through those. I encouraged her do that. To get in touch with her mother that way, to deal with her death. But those photos, I thought I had destroyed all the copies. They were taken before the internet was the big thing and there were only a few copies, or so I thought, and I was sure I had destroyed them."

"Could it be the person who you made these photos for?" Brett said.

"No. It can't be him. He died years ago. Car wreck."

"Why would your sister keep them?" Brett said.

"To hold them over my head at some point. She was always jealous of me, my becoming a doctor, changing my life. Taking control of my sexual problems. It had a lot to do with how we were raised. Part of a commune that lasted up into the nineties. Way past the expiration date. It was started in the early seventies by a preacher, a hippie preacher. Only he was more of a pervert. Cult leader. He thought all the females were his, like we were cows and he was the bull. I was very young when he started having sex with me. Eleven. My sister was a year older. It messed us up, and in turn, my sister messed up Katherine. It's complex, but those are the roots, an explanation in a peanut hull."

"The preacher was for the dog business?" Leonard said.

"Yes," she said. "He took some of the photographs."

"Bless the beasts and the children," Leonard said.

I elbowed him.

"One thing, though," Brett said. "It looks as if it's been your niece all along."

"It does," Doctor Cotton said. "She could only have gotten those photos out of my sister's things. What an idiot. Like I wouldn't know where they came from, wouldn't figure she was behind all this. Oh, hell, sure she knew I'd know. Goddamnit. She wanted me to know. She constantly torments me. I don't know why I put up with her. I should put her out. I really should, but I don't know where she'd go, what she'd do. She's pretty helpless, really. I'm all she's got."

"That's one way of looking at it," Leonard said.

"What do you mean?" Doctor Cotton said.

"I think she's an ungrateful shit," he said. "She gets out there and has to asshole and elbow it a bit, she might get over a lot of things."

"It's not that simple, Leonard," Doctor Cotton said. "It's like telling you to stop being gay."

"No," Leonard said. "It ain't a damn thing like that."

Doctor Cotton sat with her head hung. I think she was beyond argument now, beyond believing she knew shit from wild honey or piss from lemonade.

After a while, she picked up the envelope from the table and put it in her lap. "I suppose I won't be needing your services anymore."

"Listen," Brett said. "I know it seems obvious your niece has been behind this, but maybe she isn't."

"No one else would have the photos," Doctor Cotton said. "They had to be in my sister's stuff. It's her."

"Still, there might be more to it."

"No. It's Katherine. My sister reaching out through her beyond the grave. I would like to ask that you never mention this. I'm going to destroy the photos, look through my sister's stuff, see if there's anything else of this sort. I hate to admit it, but there might be. This gets out, my career is over. Not to mention my life. I won't be needing you anymore. Please leave, and send me your final bill."

"All right," Brett said. "But if you think there's more to it, need us back, you have our number."

"I do," Doctor Cotton said. "But I won't be calling."

THIRTEEN

We thought it was over.

It wasn't.

We'll come back to that.

That night Brett and I lay in bed in the dark. She lay with her hand across my chest. She said, "Why would you fuck a dog? Is that some kind of neurosis? You didn't get a puppy when you were little? Dog was the only one that seemed to love you? What is that all about?"

"Like I'd know. I think it has to be about pleasing whoever asked her to do that, the preacher. Probably did as she was told, thought it was god's will because it was coming from a man of the cloth. Hell, she had been groomed to be a plaything, like her sister. Others I presume."

"I can see nymphomania being a mental or emotional condition, but dog fucking. How do you get there?"

"Again, not about the dog," I said.

"When you're getting off, you look a little like that dog," Brett said.

"Do I?"

"Oh yeah."

"Grrrrrrr."

"Down, Rex, or I'll get the rolled-up newspaper."

"The problem is I haven't been able to get it up, let alone off."

"I thought the growl was a sign of things to come, so to speak."

"Dogs growl to fool people into thinking they are fierce. And you know what else, I lost my therapist to be. So now I don't get to find out why losing my teddy bear at three is keeping me from laying pipe."

"Poor baby."

"Don't worry. We'll get there. The other day when you bent over at the stove, I thought I felt it rustle in my jeans."

"This is where I say things are looking up."

"It's not you that's the problem," I said. "Wanted you to know that."

"Hell, I know that," Brett said.

FOURTEEN

The next day was the day of the discovery of the mass murder. Murders happen in LaBorde and on its outskirts with greater frequency than would be expected. But nothing like this.

We had just made it to the office. I was standing at the window looking out at the parking lot. Leonard had parked outside and was walking toward the stairs. I watched him saunter. Today he had on his fedora. That and cowboy hats were what he rocked best.

By the time I heard him coming up the stairs, the office phone rang. I turned and watched Brett pick it up.

The moment Leonard came in the door, Brett said, "Oh hell. Yeah. We'll be there."

Chief Marvin Hanson wanted us there due to our association with the victims. Pookie was there too. He wasn't in uniform. Marvin had us all meet at the curb in front of Doctor Cotton's house.

We could see the cop cars parked directly in front of the house, but not in the drive leading to the gate. Pookie was standing with Marvin on the short lawn that divided the curb and the big house. From a distance, they looked like a salt and pepper shaker.

We parked down the street some distance from the house and walked over.

"So, what exactly?" Brett said, after we had all nodded at one another.

"You saw them last yesterday?" Hanson asked.

Brett nodded, started answering Hanson's questions. They're the things you expect a cop to ask. None of us believed he thought we did it, but certain questions had to be asked.

"Can your people tell when this happened?" I asked.

"Not yet," Hanson said, "but since everyone was in night clothes, they think last night."

"Doctor Cotton and a young white woman?" I said.

"And another woman," he said. "Mexican. Cuban. Whatever."

"Hispanic," Pookie said.

"There you go," Hanson said.

"The Hispanic lady?" I asked. "Older, younger?"

"Middle aged, I guess. Certainly not getting any older."

"Probably Linda," Pookie said. Like us, he hadn't seen inside, and because he had been helping us part time, he was not at this point allowed to be part of the case, lest there was some great conspiracy between him and us.

"I'm going to need you folks to put on some footies and a paper suit and come with me," Marvin said. "Since you knew them a little, I need some identification."

FIFTEEN

The paper suit was blue, which brought out Pookie's eyes. The suits rustled when we moved, and the footies made crunchy sounds as we walked.

We went through the open gate and just inside the gap was a large pile of cut flowers heaped on the driveway, wilting in the heat. They were all manner of colors.

There were enough flowers there for an Easter Parade float. A cop was there filming the flowers and moving the camera around to take in other things.

"What's the flowers about?" Brett said.

"No idea," Marvin said.

We were led by Marvin to the pool.

He stopped and stood at the edge and we joined him, looked down. In the pool, strapped with duct tape to a chair, was Doctor Cotton's nude body. The chair sat on the bottom of the pool and there was blood in the water, and though there was a lot of blood, there was more water. The blood gave the water a thin, crimson sheen you could see through. Doctor Cotton's hair floated up like seaweed above her head. The blood was spreading slowly. Pieces of flesh had been peeled back from her face and breasts but were still attached; the pieces drifted in the water.

Taped to another chair, this one turned over, was Linda, fully clothed. Through the thin haze of blood, I could see her eyes. They were open and the whites appeared red. She hadn't been cut up from what I could tell, maybe a closer look would reveal otherwise.

"It didn't happen here," Brett said. "Not enough blood."

"You been reading again, haven't you?" Hanson said.

"I've seen a thing or two," she said.

"Come on," Hanson said.

We went in the house, on back to one of the bedrooms. It was neat, even Katherine's corpse was neat. It lay on the bed with her hands crossed over her chest. She almost looked peaceable, except for the bullet hole in the center of her forehead. Where the bullet had exited the back of her head, the blood had soaked into the pillow, into the sheets and the mattress. There was a lot of it. You could smell it in the air, a kind of coppery smell.

"Now here's a surprise I saved," Hanson said.

He walked us around to the other side of the bed. A young Hispanic male lay on the floor, face down. He didn't look as tidy. His leg was bent and his arms were spread. His head was turned to one side and we got a good look at his face. What was left of it. He had been shot with a larger caliber in the back of the head, and the entry had scooped some skull, but the exit wound had knocked a hole in the front of his face about the size of two fists pressed together.

"Who is this?" Hanson said.

"Ain't anyone we know," Leonard said. "Or if we knew him from somewhere else, we don't recognize him now 'cause he hasn't got much of a face. Right gang?"

Brett, Pookie and I nodded.

"This," Hanson said, "is what we in police work call a goddamn mystery."

"Do you?" I asked.

"No," Hanson said. "I just thought it sounded cool. We already ran his fingerprints. His name is Jaime Cabalas. Ring any bells?"

"Nope," I said.

Pookie raised his hand. "My bell rang. We arrested him and his brother, separate times. The brother for breaking and entering, the younger brother, the fellow you see napping before you, on shoplifting cold medicine. He had a face then. Nice-looking kid."

"So, his dear old mother had a cold," Leonard said.

"Probably not," Pookie said. "He stole a case of it out of the back of the store's warehouse. The case meaning several boxes taped into one container setting on a forklift. He also stole the forklift. Might have got away with it had he driven the forklift into the back of an enclosed truck, but no, he drove the forklift down the road. It being a forklift, and it being about three in the morning, he was thought suspicious right off. The only thing missing was a pirate flag waving off the back of the forklift."

"That happened when?" I asked.

"Some time back," Pookie said. "Spent some time in jail, but he paid off the theft, and got out pretty quick, all things considered. He was going to sell the cold medicine to some tweekers to make meth. I guess the forklift was going to be his around town ride. He's been a good boy since then."

"He's a really good boy now," Leonard said.

"Going to show you another little something," Hanson said. "I shouldn't, but hey, if you're going to get the tour, why not the whole tour. And, you knew Doctor Cotton, and maybe you'll shake an idea loose if I show you around."

"Didn't know her that well," I said.

"Knowing her at all is more than I know," Hanson said.

In another room, we saw a large painting had been removed from the wall and leaned against a dresser. There was a place in the wall with a large safe stuffed in it. The huge painting had obviously hidden it. The door to the safe was wide open.

"There was money in it at one point, is going to be my guess," Hanson said. "I think they tortured the folks here to find the safe, to get inside. It hasn't been blown, so I think it had to be cracked, or more than likely Doctor Cotton or Katherine gave it up and they took what they wanted, what they had been blackmailing her about."

I told Hanson about all that, about the dog picture.

"Ah, a nice family portrait," Hanson said.

"Thing I got to wonder about," Leonard said, "what's the Mexican boy doing here, and how did he end up dead?"

"He ended up dead because someone shot him in the face," Hanson said.

"Ah," Leonard said. "Part of the mystery solved."

"Someday I think I'll get tired of you jokesters," Hanson said.

"Our personalities remain fresh," I said.

"And I have good legs," Brett said. "And I'm smart."

"Yeah," Hanson said, "but that don't explain the other two guys or why you hang around with them."

"Hap has nice legs," she said.

As we came out of the house, I said, "Linda's daughter works here too. Didn't see her. I'd find out if she's home and okay."

"I'll do that," Pookie said. "I'll do it now."

"You're not on duty," Hanson said.

"I can be, though," Pookie said.

"Cameras?" I said. "Anything there?"

"Another sweet thing, the cameras and the alarms were turned off. So, nada. Come on, let's stroll."

We left the house, and as we neared the front gate, one of the uniforms came over and said to Hanson, "We got a little treat for you, Chief."

He walked us over to where the shrubbery was thick and up close to the fence. Between the fence and the shrubbery, off the ground due to being caught up in the shrubbery, was a dead man. Or he was very good at being still and looking dead.

A closer look.

Nope. Dead.

He had a large hole in his chest and his mouth was twisted into what could have passed as an ironic smile.

"Seems to have been trying to climb over the fence, and someone popped him, fell back here," said the uniform. "My guess is the shooter, and maybe some compatriots, hoofed it out pretty quick after this, as I don't think this was a silenced weapon. Lady down the road said she heard some loud pops about four a.m. last night."

Hanson said, "Okay, does anyone know him?"

"Yep," Pookie said, "That, sir, is Vincent Cabalas, the young faceless Cabalas's older brother."

"I can see the family resemblance," Hanson said. "They both have a hole in them."

SIXTEEN

That night I dreamed the world was full of marching people, marching around the globe in circles, and I was with them, and we marched over the oceans because they were covered in concrete.

We were in rows, all of us marchers, but we were no more than an elbow length apart. We were marching and we couldn't stop marching. Space kept getting smaller, filling up, and there were people with whips. Fat people with meat-greasy lips and protruding eyes, very froglike, very satisfied looking, and the rest of us were part of this marching system, and I realized our marching was turning the world, and all of us were making it happen, the world turning for the fat frogs who I guess owned everything, and as we marched, our clothes were rotting off some of us, and there were some men and women marching who were completely nude, and the flesh was falling off many of them, as if their skin was the same as the rotting rags. As I marched, I began to wish for a plague to kill the fat frogs, maybe kill us all, and then I came awake.

I got up and went to the bathroom and washed my face and sat on the commode with the lid down, sat there and gathered myself. I felt as if I were trying to figure my place in the new world, one where everything that was good seemed to be going backward, and everything that was bad was moving forward at a high rate of speed, and all the poor people, all those who might have been considered well off some time back, were now not so well off, and were marching for the big, fat frogs. Keeping the machine working. I couldn't shake the dream, silly as it was, and silly as it was, it made me sad and scared and disappointed, and not sure of what it was I was dreaming about.

The kind of greed that destroys everything, maybe. The kind of greed that drives people to kill other people, the kind of greed that allows someone to lock themselves behind a wall and think they're safe, removed from the daily grind, avoiding brushing up against the unwashed masses, and there were those among the unwashed who wanted to be less unwashed, wanted what the big frogs had, and they were willing to do whatever it took to have a piece of that, even murder.

As I sat there, my legs felt as if they were hurting from all that walking.

SEVENTEEN

Hanson stopped by mine and Brett's place the next morning about nine. I invited him in and fixed him some buttered toast and a cup of coffee.

Brett, who had been showering for a late entry into our office, came out of the bathroom dressed in jeans and a loose shirt, barefoot with her damp hair mounded up under a towel.

She came over to Hanson's chair and gave him a hug, then she joined us at the table.

Hanson sipped coffee, said, "I didn't want to take Linda's daughter in, on account of she might be illegal, and with things insane like they are now, I fear she'll be on a bus to Mexico, compliments of Immigration. You know, she's been here so long, she doesn't even speak Spanish. Don't get me wrong, she had something to do with the crime, I'll put her behind bars so fast the door will lock before I close it. Otherwise, I might have a witness, or a suspect being shipped across the border, and might not can get them back."

"And you've come to us why?" I said.

"I need you and Brett, Leonard if he wants, to go over there and talk to her, obviously not in a police capacity. She knows y'all a little, and she might be more comfortable talking to you. Way her mother, everyone at the house was murdered, Mindy thinks she might be next. She's scared to death. That's about all I could get out of her, really."

"Maybe she's scared with good reason," Brett said. "Seems Doctor Cotton and us thinking the niece was behind it were wrong."

"You did warn her to not drop us right away," I said.

"Whole thing looks like an inside job, and she's the only survivor. Got to consider her for it, at least a little. Maybe she had help. Might have been responsible for the threats, building up to blackmail, scaring Cotton, and then she found those pictures, and figured it was time to go for the whole enchilada. Another thing, she might have seen how this would make Katherine look, and that meant Doctor Cotton would decide it was her niece and she didn't need you guys for protection. That would damn sure make it easy for her and accomplices to get inside and do what they did."

"But her own mother?" Brett said.

"I've seen enough to think people are capable of anything," Hanson said.

"They seemed close," Brett said.

"Still, I got to think scenarios. Find out what you can for me, and that'll take care of some of the favors you guys owe me."

"Fair enough," Brett said.

"Here's another little tidbit. Photo of Doctor Cotton and the canine. It's on the internet this morning. Dead or not, someone still went after her. Maybe someone posted the photo out of spite. If Doctor Cotton were alive, she'd been selling up and packing out, maybe looking for a job in dog porn. Tell you another thing, whoever tortured Doctor Cotton the way they did, they didn't do it for money. They did it for fun. First time they cut her face she'd have told them where the safe was, gave them the combination and helped them carry the goods to the car. No one is that tough, not when they're having their skin ripped off. People did this, I think they got the combination, and after checking it out, taking what was inside, they decided to finish what they started. Maybe Cotton gave them the combo without them laying a hand on her. Could be they just decided to do it because they're mean. Think that's why they went ahead and posted the photo. It can't hurt Cotton now, but it shits on any reputation she might have had. Whoever did this is into slash and burn."

"You got Mindy's address," Brett said, "soon as we can get out of here, we'll go over and talk with her."

EIGHTEEN

We decided to fill Leonard in later, tell him what we found out. We thought it might seem less overbearing for two people to show up instead of three.

When we got there, we saw that Pookie was parked down from the house in his own car. He saw us and gave a little wave but didn't get out. We waved back and went on up to the house.

Mindy answered. She looked as if someone had run over her with a truck. She seemed barely able to stand.

She grabbed Brett and hugged her. "Oh god," she said, "it is so horrible, horrible."

"I know," Brett said. "And we're so sorry."

Mindy began to bellow and bawl. It was tough to listen to. It made me sad and sick.

Brett eased her back into the house and I shut the door and followed them into a modest living room with cheap paintings of Jesus and biblical scenes on the wall. A large cross hung above a small screen TV, and another had been placed above the portal of the doorway we came through.

After we were in the living room, Mindy sat on the couch, which was covered over with a plastic protection sheet, and Brett sat by her. I sat in a stuffed armchair across the way. The air smelled clean and sharp with disinfectant and a sheen of lemon deodorizer.

A few minutes passed with Mindy clutching Brett, and Brett holding her back, saying soothing things to her. Eventually Mindy got control of herself.

After I let a few more moment pass, I said, "I know it's horrible to discuss, but why weren't you there last night, when this happened?"

"Mom asked me to stay home. She said things were tense at the house, and Doctor Cotton was feeling private. My mom had worked for her so long, the doctor felt comfortable with her. Me, I had just started working there. I was still a bit of an outsider."

"Did you know of Katherine having a boyfriend?" I asked.

"She had plenty, but she had a main one," Mindy said. "I knew that much."

"Katherine seemed a little too, shall we say, *free-spirited* for a boyfriend," I said.

"I heard her tell Doctor Cotton her boyfriend didn't mind what she did with other men, that he liked the idea. That they belonged to some group, sliders or some such."

"Swingers?" Brett said.

"That's it. Katherine, she was always talking about things like that, to embarrass me, and she even tried to get me to go to bed with her once, but I hit her. I thought I was fired. I busted her lip. But she put her finger to the blood and looked at it and laughed at me. She was very strange."

"This boyfriend, he come around?" I said. "Ever see him?"

She nodded.

"What did he look like?"

"Not so tall, kind of thin, and good-looking. Mexican, illegal like me."

The general description fit the body by the bed, except I couldn't say about the handsome part. He didn't have a face.

"Do you know anything about the boyfriend, where he worked, anything?"

"Katherine said he was going to be a painter. His brother was a painter."

"When you say the boyfriend wanted to be a painter," Brett said. "Do you mean an artist?"

"A house painter. He was trying to start his own business with his brother, but he didn't have the money for it. I heard Katherine say that. He came to the house once, no twice, which is how I know what he looks like. Doctor Cotton didn't like him. She wouldn't let him come back."

"Do you know why she didn't like him?" I asked.

"She said because she thought he was no account, but I think it was because he was Mexican, same as me. We were all right, me and my mom, because we worked for her. Had he been the yard or pool boy, he'd have been fine. She used to have men who worked there daily, doing the yard and the pool, but Katherine wouldn't leave them alone, so she let them go. Got a service to come in and take care of things. They did their work and left."

"Did you ever meet the boyfriend's brother?" Brett asked.

"No."

I said, "I'm getting a vibe here that you think Doctor Cotton wasn't really as open-minded as she seemed?"

"I got that feeling," she said. "I don't know. Maybe with all what's going on, way people talk about us, way I got to worry about being picked up and sent to Mexico, I might not be thinking straight. . . . You aren't going to send me back, are you?"

"We don't do that," I said. "We're private. You know that."

"Yes, but. . . ."

"We're white?" I said.

She nodded and looked slightly embarrassed.

"Far as we're concerned, you're fine. Listen, any idea where we can get in touch with the boyfriend's relatives?"

"Like we all know one another," she said.

"No," Brett said, "like maybe you heard something through Katherine."

"I'm sorry," Mindy said. "I'm feeling sensitive."

"No problem," Brett said. "You have that right."

"I think he worked for a painter in town, but I don't

know the name, but I think he did. Like I said, he wanted his own shop."

"I know the police didn't tell you all that happened, merely that your mother, Doctor Cotton and Katherine were dead," I said. "But, Katherine's boyfriend, or who we think is her boyfriend, and the boyfriend's brother are dead as well."

"I don't understand," Mindy said.

"That's all right, no one does," I said.

Mindy sat quietly for a moment, her hands folded in her lap.

"You know, I think they said something about Smatterly Paint or some such," she said. "You know, I'm not sure. But something like that."

"Let me ask something else," I said. "The safe. Who knew where it was? Did you?"

She nodded. "We all did. It wasn't a secret. I knew it was there and so did everyone in the house, and we all knew Doctor Cotton had expensive jewels in it, as well as money."

"Who knew the combination?" Brett asked.

"I don't know. I didn't know it. Mother didn't."

"What about Katherine?" I said.

She shook her head. "I don't know. But I got the impression that Doctor Cotton was the only one."

NINETEEN

We couldn't locate a business by the name Mindy gave us, but we did find one called Smallette's Painting. We thought that might be close enough to be the right one. Me and Brett drove over there.

It was on the loop well outside of town, and it was a large building with a larger fenced-in area off to the side and attached to the main building. Signs said they painted houses, cars, and there was a sign that read: IF IT ISN'T MOVING, WE CAN PAINT IT.

Behind the desk, toward the back, was a middle-aged woman with her hair combed straight back and tied with an orange scrunchie. She didn't wear makeup and had on coveralls. She was a little plump and was leaned back in her chair doing damage to what looked like a leaky meatball sandwich.

Me and Brett walked up to the desk. The lady reluctantly stopped eating, stood up and walked over. She was tall and broad-shouldered.

She looked at Brett. "Damn, aren't you the pretty thing?"

"You ought to see me on Tuesdays," Brett said.

"We're looking for the owner," I said.

"No, you're not," she said, "you're looking at her."

"Ms. Smallette?"

"Small. My mother and father called me Smallette as a joke, 'cause I was the youngest and the only girl, only I turned out bigger than they expected. My dad never could quite get over that. I think he wanted a girly-girly who didn't like girly-girls, but that isn't how things shook out. He stopped calling me Smallette when I reached my twenties. Everyone else kept calling me that, though. When Dad died, I took over the business because both my two older brothers, and my mother, are in prison for fraud. I decided to call the business Smallette's instead of Small's."

"That's really interesting," I said, but really, I didn't give a shit.

"What you need painted?" she said.

"Nothing," I said.

"You're looking for the taxidermist, that's down the loop a little."

"No," Brett said. "We're looking for you."

"Oh, that's nice. I hope you're especially the one looking."

"We're married," I said.

"So are a lot of people," Smallette said.

No way to contradict that.

"The Cabalas brothers worked for you?" Brett asked.

"Still do, but after today they may not. Didn't show for work last couple of days. Course the day is young enough. I'm flexible 'cause good painters are hard to find, but they may be asking me to be too flexible."

"You know," I said, "you might want to put a want ad in the paper for a painter."

Smallette studied me for a moment.

"Something happen?"

"They got dead," I said.

TWENTY

Smallette brought us behind the desk and into a small office with a struggling air conditioner. She sat behind a desk that took up too much room, and Brett sat in the only other chair while I leaned against the wall and listened to the air conditioner try not to die.

From where I stood, I could see she had a pistol on a stool next to the desk. If you were sitting where Brett was sitting you wouldn't be able to see it. It looked like a .22 revolver from where I stood.

Painting business must be a tough gig. Then again, in Texas, every asshole walks around with a gun and thinks they're Wyatt Earp. I tell you straight, it doesn't make me feel safer. Even preachers have guns.

"Man, that's some shit," Smallette said after we explained what happened to them, told her about Doctor Cotton, her niece and maid. She didn't seem all that torn up about it actually. We could have told her they were having a two-for-one sale on socks at Walmart, and it might have got more of a reaction. "Any idea why?"

"We got some thoughts," Brett said, and we did. We had discussed them in the car on the way over. I thought I'd give Smallette a taste of our idea, see if that elicited anything. I gave her a general rundown on what had happened, that the doctor was murdered, very general stuff, then laid out some things that were more specific.

"Way we're thinking," I said, "is the brothers, along with the murdered doctor's niece, were trying out intimidation, which was a plan to have Doctor Cotton real scared before they tried out blackmail. They finally got there, but that didn't play out the way they wanted. We're thinking the brothers wanted their own paint business, and we're thinking they had partners to help them get it, but those partners wanted the jewels and fewer partners."

"So, they were going to leave my ass," Smallette said.

"We're here to see if you got anything you can give us that will help us figure out who the brothers were in with," I said.

"Not an idea one," she said. "Thought you said this doctor laid you off."

"She did," Brett said, "but you might say we feel unfulfilled."

"That so. Well, they were good painters and will be missed, but you know Mexicans wanting work are a dime a dozen. They hadn't been in some kind of bad business, they wouldn't be dead."

"You have an address for them?" I asked.

"Yeah, I think so. I got cell phone numbers, but I bet no one answers," she grinned when she said that. "Hey, they were going to fuck me over, leave me high and dry, start their own paint business. Oh, hell, bless the goddamn dead and their family, of course, but one thing I don't need is more competition."

Charming.

I got a card out of my wallet. It was a little dog-eared. I gave it to her. It had the name of the agency on it and two numbers, the office landline and my cell. Each of us had the same cards, except our personal cards had our individual cell numbers on them. Brett had a set of cards with all our numbers on it, written on the back. On the front was BRETT SAWYER INVESTIGATIONS, and under her name was the silhouette of a bloodhound.

"Think of something, anything might help, give a call," I said.

"Sure," she said. "Shame the way they were done. Tortured and murdered, the safe robbed, and that being a walled home in a good neighborhood. You can't be too careful these days, no matter where you live."

"This is true," Brett said, and we walked out.

TWENTY-ONE

Outside the paint business, I said, "She didn't seem particularly curious."

"No, she didn't," Brett said, "First thing I want to do, we leave here, is buy today's paper."

"And I know why," I said.

We passed the fenced-in section. Through the fence, we could see three men air-blasting a travel home. Well, one was doing the blasting. The other two were standing around, as if holding the concrete flooring in place.

I found the gate and opened it and we stepped inside.

As we got nearer to them, one of the men who was watching one of the others use the air blaster noticed us. Or rather he noticed Brett. You can always tell when they notice Brett.

Brett showed them all her teeth, including the caps she had on a couple of back teeth, and said, "How are you boys?"

The boys all looked pretty much alike, except one of them was very tall, six-seven, if I had to guess. They all wore gray coveralls and gray caps and work boots, had long, ragged beards that rested on their chests, had faces that looked like the seats of a well-worn saddles. They had small noses, noticeable small, as if genetics was all out of the good noses the day they were born, so they had to take the emergency back-up children's variety.

"Damn, ZZ Top," I said. "As I live and breathe."

"Well, we do have a band," said the one switching off the blaster, turning to give Brett the once-over. "We ain't any good, though. We was going to be rock stars once, twenty years ago. Turned out we can barely carry a tune in a bucket with a lid on it."

The third man, the smaller of the three, was standing by the travel trailer. He looked at Brett and actually licked his lips. Not something I enjoyed seeing, but Brett was a big girl, and no doubt luscious looking, so I decided not to kill him.

"You work for Ms. Smallette, of course," Brett said.

"We got a piece of the pie here," said the man with the blaster.

I held out my hand. "Hap Collins."

The air blaster man put the blaster on the concrete and shook my hand.

"Wilson Small. That goober by the trailer, that's Rat, least that's what we call him, and this fellow by me is Too Tall. We're brothers."

No surprise there.

"Smallette is your sister," I said.

"Yeah. She kind of runs the business."

"No offense," Brett said, "but Ms. Smallette said her brothers and mother were in prison."

"That's right, but we're the other brothers."

"Oh," Brett said.

"Yeah, there's a bunch of us," Too Tall said. "Us three are fancy-free and looking for love."

He showed Brett a big smile when he said that.

"I'm sure you're going to be a fine catch for some nice woman," Brett said.

"Hell," Rat said. "We don't want them nice."

The brothers laughed together, ended up making snorting sounds. Ain't genetics wonderful?

We told them the same thing we told Ms. Smallette, and they said that was too bad about the brothers, but Rat added, "Them spic brothers wasn't good workers anyway. Jaime, he could paint, but he was slow as Christmas on a crutch. Always had to get everything just right, like people can tell two coats of paint from one."

How picky of him, I thought.

We gave them our cards and went away.

TWENTY-TWO

We drove over to the newspaper office. They have machines out front, and they have papers in them. We bought one and went back to the car and sat there. Brett read about the murders on the front page.

"Here it is," she said. "I was thinking Marvin wouldn't have told reporters all the details. There's nothing about torture or a safe, so even if Smallette read the papers this morning, how would she know that?"

"Maybe she's psychic," I said.

"I'm thinking it might have something to do with her being in on that shit," Brett said. "That's what I'm thinking."

"Me," I said, "I'm sticking to psychic."

"Sure, you are," she said. "I think Smallette not only was in on it, but so were those bearded, moronic brothers of hers."

"Do we tell Hanson?"

"No, we caught this one and we dropped the ball, so we got to pick it up."

"Doctor Cotton dropped the ball," I said.

"Still, I feel we have to pick it up. I think we start by

checking florists, see if anyone bought a hell of a big load of flowers this morning. Something they took from the florist to deliver themselves. My guess is that's how they got through the gate."

She didn't start the car up though.

"Little turns of fate can sure mess a person up," she said.

"Fucking a dog on camera is bound to lead to bad things," I said.

"That was years ago. She had changed her life, was trying to do good for people."

"You were less on her side when we talked about this before."

"I've had time to think. Doctor Cotton didn't start this, the niece did. The ungrateful bitch was going to rob her. She knew her aunt knew her boyfriend. Which means to me, she might have planned to kill her aunt and the maids right from the start. She was bad as the Smalls. Then she got snookered. There's some cold irony in that."

"I'm thinking the boyfriend shot Katherine," I said. "I like to think they forced him to. She was the only one that was killed in a, pardon the term, comfortable way. Lying in bed with her eyes shut. They let him do that, and then he thought he was still going out with the money and jewels. But he wasn't. They killed him. The brother made a break for it, and Smalls nailed him too."

"There's a reason those other Smalls are in prison," Brett said. "They're a family of vipers."

"Now, now, don't insult vipers."

TWENTY-THREE

Brett took me to my car and caught up with Leonard and filled him in with what me and my lady were thinking.

"I was thinking that too," he said.

"So now you're going to pull that," I said. "Me and Brett do all the work, and all the thinking, and you're going to claim you were all over it."

"I was."

"No, you weren't."

"I kind of was."

"You are priceless, Leonard."

"I have my fedora on."

"Yes, you do. And I'm sure glad you explained that, and here I sit looking at it on your head. That's something," I said, "but it wouldn't surprise me if you had your underwear turned around backwards."

"You want to check, don't you?"

"I do not."

"I think you're thinking about it."

"Don't change the subject," I said. "You didn't know shit."

"Where's Brett?"

"You're changing the subject."

"Am not."

"Am too. . . . She's checking out florists," I said.

"What are we doing?"

"Lunch," I said. "Brett wanted to do the florists by herself. She likes flowers. I'm also supposed to tell you not to tell Pookie what we think we know. We're keeping the law outside of this. Brett wants to get even with the sonofabitches did this, let it be us that proves what they did and turn them in."

"Brett knows what the fuck is up," Leonard said.

We went to the El Salvadorian restaurant we like and had a light lunch, and then to a coffee shop on North Street. I had hot chocolate, Leonard had coffee, and a couple sitting at a booth against the wall almost had sex. I think they were getting the better deal.

"Let's change seats," Leonard said.

We took our drinks upstairs and went out on the veranda that overlooked the parking lot.

"You know, one of the cops at the scene might have blabbed to someone about what was found and seen at Doctor Cotton's, and this Small lady picked it up from somebody who heard it from somebody."

"Maybe, but then again, let's see what Brett says about the florist."

"By the way, how's the old pecker?"

"The pecker is fine, just a little limp lately."

"Man, Hap Collins with a limp pecker. Who'd have thought it. Listen, my man. It happens. Even my very well-trained anaconda has days. I get up, fix breakfast, my oatmeal is lumpy, I get backed up and can't shit, lose my keys, spill my lunch, you know, a bad day, and when

I have one like that, well, the snake can go to sleep."

"No matter how bad my day is, I don't normally have that problem. Getting the tool to work usually makes a bad day better."

"Now, though, I'm thinking you might want to go into the priesthood."

"Shit, they get more nookie than I do these days. Sometimes what they get they shouldn't get."

"Yeah, they use priests to scare children now," Leonard said. "You better be good, or the priest is going to molest you."

"Watch out for the politicians too," I said.

"Yep, they fuck you then pass a bill that makes you the rapist."

The phone rang.

It was Brett.

She'd found the florist.

TWENTY-FOUR

We stayed where we were and Brett drove over to join us. She came upstairs with a coffee and sat with us on the veranda. We were the only ones out there. The air was beginning to become sticky, and out to the west we could see a bit of darkness as rain clouds drifted in our direction. It would be drizzling by nightfall, if not sooner.

"The florist said a lady paid in cash for the flowers,

didn't give her name, but had them loaded into a large van. That's where Small messed up. The van had Smallette Painting written on the side. A name like that the florist remembered."

"So, Smallette did, in fact, set this all up," I said.

"Yeah," Brett said.

"Wow," I said. "We did some detective work and it worked."

"And I think the robbery, the whole thing, went down pretty much like we were thinking it did," Brett said. "I looked into the Small family, the ones in prison. They were in there for fraud all right, but they were also in there for jewel robbery. Pretty big heist in Houston."

"No shit," Leonard said.

"And the rest of the family was under suspicion for the same thing," Brett said. "Wasn't enough proof. I'm thinking if Smallette and the Small brothers have the kind of jewels I think they got from Doctor Cotton, they haven't moved those yet. They'd be the kind of things you wouldn't deal out to a crooked pawnshop dealer. You'd need professional fences, and to do that, to get top dollar, they'd have to wait for the theft to cool."

"Look at you," Leonard said, "all robbery expert and such."

"I know where this is leading," I said. "You think they stashed the jewels."

"Yeah," Brett said. "And my guess is somewhere at their place of business. They aren't suspected by the cops, so that's safe enough. Stuff can cool down there, and the whole family is around, so no one has to depend on anyone else to watch the goods. They may have already spent the money from the safe, or they've split that. May never find that, but we just might discover the jewels. We do, their gooses are cooked."

"That means we got to go take a peek," I said.

Brett sipped her coffee, said, "That's about the size of it."

TWENTY-FIVE

I'm a feminist, but that only goes so far. I insisted that when we arrived, Brett should stay in the car. She had done things that showed she was tough, but still, me and Leonard were way more used to the rough and tumble stuff, and besides, if she heard gunfire, she could call the cops. Sue me. I didn't want my woman hurt.

My hope was they wouldn't be around, and Smallette would have packed up the jewels in a nice tote bag and left them on her desk with a note that read: HERE THEY ARE.

We veered off the loop and parked off the main road not far from the Smallette Paint business, among some trees, and unless you were looking for our car, you couldn't see it from the road, not the way the shadows clung.

It was starting to mist a bit, and now and again I could

hear a rumble of thunder. I got my automatic out of the glove box, and Leonard left his fedora in back and took my sawed-off club from under the seat, stuck it in his pants, beneath his windbreaker, and away we went, two soldiers in the mist.

Well, Leonard was a soldier. I was just some guy with an automatic pistol and a dick problem. But we did have matching black windbreakers. Brett insisted. They had deep pockets for lockpicks, our flashlights, and my pistol.

Still, the windbreakers were heavy for the sticky weather. I was sweating like a goat at a barbecue who had just realized he was the guest of honor.

As we came up on the paint shop, we avoided the lights that were out front of the place, the ones out back as well. We took to the side fence where it was dark, and stopped at the gate. Leonard went to work on it with his lockpick. Bolt cutters would have been better. Enough time passed with him working that lock I almost walked back to the car to see if Brett could drive me into town to pick up some coffee.

Finally, there was a faint clicking and the lock snapped open and we cracked the fence gate and slipped inside. There was the obvious smell of drying paint in the air, chemicals I couldn't identify. The travel trailer was still in its place. Off to the side were black, metal barrels containing who knew what. No junkyard dogs reported for duty.

We crossed the fenced-in lot and came to a back door. It was locked, of course.

Leonard went to work again with his lockpick.

This one was much harder than the first, but with diligence and a lot of soft cursing, the lock finally opened and we slid inside. We were damp from the mist in the air and sweaty from the windbreakers, and inside it was as stuffy as having a wool sock forced over your head.

We took out our flashlights and turned them on and poked them around. On tiptoe we went along, hoping not to trip any burglar alarms, but there didn't seem to be any.

It was easy.

TWENTY-SIX

Easy up until it wasn't.

Let me tell you. I been to a bunch of county fairs, a dozen goat ropings, and once saw a fat tourist woman in Mexico so drunk her ancestors were drunk get up on a bar, drop her drawers and pick up a cigarette lighter with her snatch, and that didn't surprise me as much as the sudden coming on of the lights in the paint shop.

I felt as if Leonard and I were on stage under a spotlight and that we should break into song. We had actually done that once, but that hadn't worked out too well. This looked to work out worse.

When my eyes adjusted, I saw Smallette and the ZZ Top imitators standing in a kind of horseshoe shape no more than twenty feet in front of us. Too Tall had a shot-gun pointed at us, the opening of which looked about the size of Carlsbad Caverns. The others looked as content as if they'd just had a wet dream.

"You've brought a little friend, huh," Smallette said. "Bad choice for a playdate, but I'm glad you're here. I was afraid you'd go to the police, on account I realized I slipped up. No one knew about the torture but us."

"Let's just go on and blow their heads off," Wilson said. "I got to get home and set the DVR."

"I like to gloat," Smallette said, and then to us: "My cousin works at the florist shop, told me that redheaded smoothie talked to her manager. Overheard her. Ain't that some shit for you?"

"Ain't it," Leonard said.

"So, she tells me we was asked about, and I think about the ego that redhead has got, how the only real proof would be the jewels, maybe the flowers, but I'll figure out a lie around the flowers eventually. But if you were to get your hands on the jewels, well, that could cook our gooses. That redhead, I figured she'd want to solve this herself, or send someone to do it for her. And here you two are. By the way, where is she?"

"Bali," I said. "Took a vacation."

"I don't think so. I think we got to find and kill her too, and I tell you, I hate that. I could lick that redhead's ass until her crack grew flowers."

"Eeeeeewwww," Wilson said.

"Just 'cause you don't never get any," Smallette said,

"ain't no reason to wish it on others."

Now she gave us her full attention. "Come on, ass-holes. We got a room with a drain in it. Easier to clean."

"What the fuck, sis?" Too Tall said. "You a James Bond villain? Let's get this over with. Come on prune balls, march."

"She's talking to you," Leonard said.

I started moving slowly, and Too Tall stepped to the side to let me get in front of him. Me and Leonard know each other's moves as well as a trapeze act, so when he sort of shuffled a step, looking like he was moving forward but wasn't, I yelled out, "The Elephant of Surprise."

That was code for the element of surprise, and that's when Leonard moved, hit the shotgun up and it went off. Leonard twisted the weapon from Too Tall's hands, but he couldn't hang onto it. It sailed away, went clattering into cans of paint, tipping them.

Smallette produced a pistol from inside her coveralls, that little dear of a weapon I had seen on a chair in her office. A bullet whizzed by my head as I gave Rat a left and a right so fast it was almost subliminal. He went down.

Leonard kneed Too Tall in the balls. Too Tall staggered. A bullet from Smallette's revolver nipped the air, but didn't hit anyone. Too Tall was bent over, grunting in pain. He managed to say, "Goddamn, sis. You near shot me."

Me and Leonard dodged behind some racks of paint cans as another bullet punched a hole in one and paint shot out like a geyser, splashing my shoulder with a very attractive blue color. We hustled down behind another row of paint cans, and then veered off, heading toward the door through which we entered. We pushed a rack of paint over as a distraction, then bolted toward the door. The space between there and freedom seemed the length of a football field.

As I pulled the door open, a bullet smacked into it. Glancing back, I saw Smallette and Wilson running at us. Too Tall was in the background, still bent, spinning around and around like a top, clutching his balls.

We went through the door and I jerked it closed. As we hustled toward the gate, I saw that Rat had got his shit together and had made his way through the main building, out to the gate, into the misty rain, and what was now a high wind. That little fucker was quick and, like a real rat, had good recovery skills. I saw too that he had produced a pistol from somewhere.

"We got you now," he said, and it certainly appeared that way. I heard Smallette and her brother coming through the door behind us.

"Trailer," Leonard said, and we darted toward it.

TWENTY-SEVEN

We jerked open the trailer door, thankfully unlocked, and jumped inside. Rat's bullets smacked the door and the side of the trailer. Fortunately, the Smalls were all terrible shots; they couldn't have committed suicide with a shotgun under their chin.

I locked the door and pulled my pistol out.

"Now you draw it," Leonard said. "That's like closing the toilet lid before you shit."

"Is it?" I said. "Is it really?"

I lifted my head and peeked through the window, yelled, "Duck."

A shotgun blast took out the window, raining glass down on top of us.

"Guess who's up and running?" I said.

"That would be Too Tall," Leonard said.

I yelled out to them, "You're going to have to repaint, I think."

"Come on out and get yours," Too Tall said.

"Nice invitation, but no," I said.

Leonard had pulled the club out from under his windbreaker. Considering the situation, he might as well have pulled a toothpick out.

I heard something rolling then, but I was afraid to look out the window again; I figured they were focused on it. I moved to the rear of the trailer. There was a kind of bunk bed, and near the top bunk was a small, round window. I climbed up on the top bunk, eased my head up and looked out the window, saw what was rolling.

It was a big black barrel, and it was being rolled on its side toward the trailer by Wilson. He stopped it about six feet from the trailer, grabbed a crowbar off the floor, jammed it into the edge of the lid and popped it.

A clear liquid chugged out and fled toward the trailer.

Even inside, I could smell what was in the barrel. Paint cleaner.

Smallette moved out of the shadows and into view, walked over to the barrel, pulled a cigarette lighter from her highly practical and well-pocketed coveralls, and flipped it open. A little flame popped up, guttered savagely in the wind, so much so that Smallette cupped the flame with a palm.

"Ah, shit," I said. "We're about to get lit up."

With a shit-eating grin, Smallette flipped the lighter into the paint thinner.

Let me tell you how it rose, the fire I mean.

It jumped, baby, and I mean jumped.

There was a roar and a flash of light, and I guess the shifting wind was the bulk of the intensity, though that paint thinner had an intensity of its own. But the wind, like the proverbial worm, had turned, and it wasn't blowing in our direction. The gust caught the flames and carried them to Smallette.

Once, when I was a kid, my friend, Richard, stuck a feather in the ground and doused it with gasoline and lit a match to it. Having some fear of gasoline, I stood back a few paces, and when the feather lit, it went up in a rocket of flame and the flames licked high above the peak of the feather.

That's how it was with Smallette. That flame grabbed her and wrapped her up as it blew off the gurgling paint thinner. Almost simultaneously the can, which still had the bulk of the thinner in it, exploded. Shrapnel rattled through the air. Some hit the trailer, but most of it blew over Smallette and her family in a wave of fire. One moment she was standing, and in the next she was a blackened shape within a wad of flame. She crumpled to the ground and ash wafted up from her and spun away on the wind.

The fire kept whipping, and I could see shapes moving in and behind the flames. I heard shots, and then I heard screams, and then I could see the far fence through the flames, and I could see police cruiser lights flickering on the other side of it.

It was like an arsonist's Christmas.

TWENTY-EIGHT

We got heated up pretty good inside that trailer, and then the heat wave passed, and it was merely warm.

Leonard was looking out the window below the bunk, now. He said, "I think Smallette is well done, and them other motherfuckers are kind of medium rare."

I slipped off the bunk and came down for a look. The flames had spread and the building to the right had caught on fire. I guess all those paint products weren't helping. Cans were popping, flames were leaping up here and there, but there was a gap in front of the trailer and to the side where the fence ran.

We didn't even consult one another. We headed out the door and went to the left. We climbed over the fencing. The fence was warm, but not too hot to climb. We went over it like squirrels. That fire was a great motivation. Barrels exploded behind us, nearly knocked us off the wire.

Dropping to the other side, we looked back as the flames hopped and crept across the lot.

Hanson and Brett and Pookie came around on our side, hustling toward us.

"You dumb motherfuckers," Hanson said.

"Hey, how's it hanging?" Leonard said.

"Goddamn you, Leonard," Pookie said, grabbed him and kissed him like it was the end of World War II.

Brett came over and grabbed me. I held her, and we walked around to the front of the place. We stood for a moment in front of my car, which Brett had driven up, and watched the flames. Wilson had not only been burned, but shot by the police. He was lying on the ground next to a cruiser, his hands handcuffed behind is back. He was dark as inside of a hog, smoking like an overheated hot dog. I thought the handcuffs were probably not needed. He was done.

Rat was handcuffed and smoky, but alive. He was leaning against a cruiser. His beard and hair were cooked off, his face blackened in spots, raw pink in others. He looked stunned.

We could see what was left of Too Tall cooking inside the flames. The fire had jumped him too quick for him to escape, and police bullets hadn't helped.

Smallette was little more than a bent crisp of meat, though I could make out her hands, clutching inward like talons.

Hanson said, "Good thing Brett called. We're going to need the fire department."

"Yeah," I said, "my guess is what they stole is inside the shop, so you might want them to try and save that first. Whoops. There goes the travel trailer."

It had caught fire now with a re-shifting of the damp wind. It cracked and wrinkled and began to collapse.

"Damn, that's quick," Pookie said. "If you had been inside, Leonard."

"I wasn't. But if I was going to go I had good company."

I reached out and patted his arm. "Thanks, Leonard."

"I was talking about the Smalls."

"Fuck you, Leonard."

TWENTY-NINE

We didn't know about it for a couple of days, but the fire department got there in time to save the shop, and they did find what was stolen. Some of it was jewels, some of it was money, and there were some odds and ends from the house in there. Expensive crystal, that sort of thing. It was all worth close to a million dollars fenced, which split four ways beat splitting seven ways.

"Well," Brett said, after Hanson phoned and told us all the skinny, "our client is dead, robbed, and the bad guys are burned up, and you can say with confidence we lost money on this deal. We may not get in too bad trouble for breaking and entering and trespassing, but Hanson said a fine might be in order."

"And I never did get that therapy."

THIRTY

That night I showered and readied myself for bed, because I realized that the whole excitement of what we had done, some of it successful, some of it not, had cleared my head a little. I felt good about myself. Maybe Leonard was right. We were doing our best and we were doing it for good, and that was all you could ask.

If I thought too long, I would start defining good, and then splitting hairs, and trying to make a chart in my mind, positive on one side, negative on the other, but tonight, I didn't want to go there.

Brett had been in the bathroom a long time, and I had been reading a bit of Lewis Shiner's novel, *Black and White*. I had just laid it aside when Brett said from the bathroom, "Turn out the light."

I did.

The bathroom door opened and there was light in there, but it was a blue light, and then there was a click of machinery in there, followed by music, Frankie Lymon and the Teenagers singing "Little Bitty Pretty One."

I knew the song from the first moment it began.

That humming is magnificent.

Brett's long, naked leg appeared, gently kicking the air, a red high heel on her foot, and when Frankie got to the lyrics, Brett shook out of the bathroom, dancing, wearing as little as one could wear without being naked, and somehow, it was sexier than if she were nude, a red bra, red panties, and high heels, a blue light behind her, and a shimmy vigorous enough to make the statue of David have an erection and cause California to slide into the Pacific.

When she turned, and worked her butt left and right, up and down, I can assure you any feelings of needing a therapist went south, and I knew I was back because I had reconciled things with myself, at least for now. I was for the moment off the trek around the world, across the concrete ocean, turning the earth with a crowd. I was free.

Brett moved toward me, and as she did, she worked her red bra loose and dropped it. She swung it over her head and all about, snapped it off and over the bed and out of sight. She stopped dancing as the song neared the end, brought her legs together, pushed at her panties, let them drop. There was a bright red nest in the fork of her tree, and I wanted to live there.

And then the song was over and she was in bed with me and I was holding her. She touched me in the right place and said, "I see Little Hap is back in the game."

"He's been on vacation."

She took hold of me, "Welcome back, honey," she said.

I rolled her over and kissed her and she kissed me back. She said, "Had that song had one more lyric, I would have fainted, and let me tell you, try doing that in high heels."

"I'll leave that to you," I said.

She wrapped her legs around me and clicked those heels together behind my back, reached between us and pushed down my pajama bottoms.

"How about an expedition to the cave?" she said.

"Packed and ready," I said, and indeed I was.

ABOUT THE AUTHOR

The author of more than fifty novels and short-story collections, **Joe R. Lansdale**'s prodigious output also includes work for comics, television, film, newspapers, and magazines. He has won multiple awards in crime, western, fantasy, horror, and science fiction. The crime thriller *Cold in July*, the cult classic *Bubba Ho-Tep*, and Sundance Channel's hit show *Hap and Leonard* number among his many stories to be filmed. Founder of the martial arts system Shen Chuan, Lansdale was inducted into the International Martial Arts Hall of Fame. He lives in Nacogdoches, Texas, with his wife, Karen, and their pit bull, Nicky.